D0065683

LAUREN MYRACLE

AMULET BOOKS
NEW YORK

shine

Cataloging-in-Publication Data has been applied for and may be obtained from the Library of Congress.
ISBN 978-0-8109-8417-2

Text copyright © 2011 Lauren Myracle
Book design by Maria T. Middleton

Printed and bound in U.S.A.
10 9 8 7 6 5 4 3 2 1

Amulet Books are available at special discount when purchased in quantity for premiums and promotions as well as fundraising or educational use. Special editions can also be created to specification. For details, contact specialmarkets@abramsbooks.com or the address below.

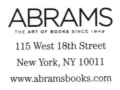

THE ART OF BOOKS SINCE 1949
115 West 18th Street
New York, NY 10011
www.abramsbooks.com

To *Sarah Mlynowski* and *Emily Lockhart:*
Your love is so bright, I have to wear shades.

"You are the light of the world."

—Matthew 5:14

Bloody Sunday
Teen Brutally Attacked

Stunned residents of Black Creek, North Carolina, pray for seventeen-year-old Patrick Truman, beaten and left for dead outside the convenience store where he works.

"There was blood in his hair, blood on his face . . . blood everywhere," says Dave Tuttle, the motorist who discovered the unconscious teen early Sunday morning. Tuttle was driving from Atlanta to his mountain house in Tuckaway, North Carolina, when he pulled off the single-lane highway to refuel.

"Stopping at the Come 'n' Go has become a tradition," a shaken Tuttle told The Pulse. "They sell boiled peanuts and homemade jams. Sometimes fresh cobblers. It's a reminder of simpler times."

Simpler times which, apparently, aren't so simple after all.

Truman, who worked the closing shift the previous night, was scheduled to open the store at seven a.m. on Sunday morning. When Tuttle pulled up to the store's single pump at seven thirty, he found Truman slumped on the pavement, bound to the guardrail of the fuel dispenser. The gasoline nozzle protruded from his mouth, held in place with duct tape. Across the teen's bare chest, scrawled in blood, were the words *Suck this, faggot.*

FIGHT FOR LIFE

Since the tiny town of Black Creek boasts neither a hospital nor an urgent care facility, the teen was transported twenty miles by the local EMS unit to the Transylvania Regional Hospital in Toomsboro, where he was treated by Dr. James Granville.

According to Granville's report, Truman suffers from a fractured skull, multiple facial contusions, and four cracked ribs. The depression in Truman's skull indicates a violent blow from behind, possibly inflicted by a pipe or a baseball bat. While epidural bleeding is the most probable cause of Truman's comatose state, the inhalation of gas fumes could also play a role.

As for how soon—or if—the teen will recover, it's simply too early to predict. "I'll tell you one thing," Dr. Granville told The Pulse. "He's durn lucky that driver came along when he did."

HATE CRIME?

The slur written on Truman's chest, coupled with the placement of the gasoline nozzle in the victim's mouth, suggests that Truman's attack was motivated by antigay sentiments.

Tommy Lawson, who attended high school with the victim, doesn't discount the possibility. "He never did hide what he was, if that's what you're asking," says Lawson, son of Ronald Lawson, who owns the Come 'n' Go as well as a chain of discount stores. "He doesn't swish around or nothing, but it's no secret what team he plays for."

Verleen Cox, organist at the Holiness Church of God, offers a different perspective. "Patrick's a good Christian boy who knows right from wrong," she avows. While she acknowledges that the teen struggled in the past with "sexual brokenness," she informed The Pulse that ". . . he faced his demons and escaped their bondage with the help of the Lord Jesus Christ."

Orphaned at age three, Truman was raised by his grandmother, a woman described by members of her church as "a saint if there ever was one." Still, church deacon Steven Raab laments the teen's lack of a male role model during his formative years. "A boy needs his daddy," the deacon asserts.

Last winter, Truman faced further hardship when his grandmother passed away, leaving him to fend for himself at his grandmother's small but tidy house. The North Carolina Department of Social Services could not be reached for comment.

A TOWN FORGOTTEN

For upper- and middle-class Americans, the story of Truman's hardscrabble life could well read as fiction. But for those who endure it, the gritty truth of poverty is far too real. As in many poor rural towns, the residents of Black Creek—population 743—struggle to survive in an environment where all odds are stacked against them.

"What with the new Walmart in Asheville, almost all the stores in town went on and closed," says Misty Treanor, who worked at a nearby paper mill until it went out of operation last August. "Do I wish things were different? Heck yeah. But they ain't."

Despite such difficult circumstances, young Patrick Truman tried to keep his spirits up. "He's one of the special ones," says Verleen Cox. "Hasn't dropped outta school, doesn't do drugs, got hisself a good job. He's always ready with a smile."

For now, Truman has nothing to smile about—and neither do Transylvania County law enforcers, who have no leads in their search for Truman's assailant(s). Yet Sheriff Doyle assures The Pulse that he and his colleagues "will do everything in [their] power to make sure justice is served."

The question is: Will it be enough?

sunday

ONE WEEK AFTER

1

PATRICK'S HOUSE WAS A GHOST. DUST COATED
the windows, the petunias in the flower boxes bowed their
heads, and spiderwebs clotted the eaves of the porch. Once
I might have marveled at the webs—how delicate they were,
how intricate—but today I saw ghastly silk ropes. Nooses for
sawflies and katydids and anything guileless enough to be
ensnared.

Movement drew my attention to the upper corner of the
porch, where a large web swayed as if it were alive. I stepped
closer, and a sour taste rose in my throat. A mourning cloak
was trapped within a mass of threads. One wing was pinned
to its body, but the other wing, dark brown rimmed with gold,
fluttered feebly.

That golden wing made me think of Mama Sweetie, Patrick's grandma. It made me think of her Bible, in particular. Its gilt-edged pages were as thin as tissue, and when I ruffled them, the gold shimmered. For Christmas one year, Patrick made Mama Sweetie a wooden stand for her Bible, and I knew if I pressed my face to one of the dirty windows, I'd see both the Bible and the bookstand displayed proudly in the front room.

Well, no, I *didn't* know that, for the simple reason that just because things used to be a certain way didn't mean they'd stay that way forever. Patrick could have stuck the Bible in a drawer, or given it away, or burned it. I couldn't imagine him doing any of those things, but my thoughts on the matter meant nothing.

Sometimes I felt like my entire existence meant nothing.

I went through the motions, however. I showered and generally kept myself clean. I ate at mealtimes, I slept at night, and when it wasn't summer, I went to school and read a lot of books. When it was summer, I still read a lot of books. But mainly, I moved through the world feeling invisible—and maybe I was. Maybe God was a giant eyeball in the hazy June sky, only there was a burn mark on His pupil in the exact spot of Black Creek, North Carolina, and that was why He didn't see me.

If He didn't see me, that meant He didn't see Patrick, either. Was not seeing us better than seeing and not caring?

I backed away from the porch, my head buzzing. I felt blurry around my edges, like smoke, or the soft *sssss* of a snuffed candle, and I couldn't for the life of me remember why I'd come to Patrick's house in the first place. Church started in half an hour, and it would take me almost as long to bike there. What had I been thinking?

The sun pressed down on me, making me sweat. Back when we were kids, Patrick and I escaped the summer heat by worming into the crawl space beneath his house, which was cool and private and, best of all, *ours*. It was our secret hideaway, and we spent countless hours down there with no one to keep tabs on us but blind and sluggish bugs. The sort of bugs that would eat us one day, we used to say for the shiver of it. Coffin bugs.

The entrance to the crawl space was a small access door made from a scrap of plywood painted yellow to match the siding. It was all of two feet tall and two feet wide, and it blended in with the house almost perfectly. The only thing that gave it away was the rusty hook-and-eye latch that kept it shut.

Patrick didn't much like the dark, so we snuck down candles and matches, which would have given Mama Sweetie a fit if she'd found out. We spread a tarp on the moist soil, and we set up a milk crate for a table. On any given day, we'd toss snacks through the crawl space hole and then wiggle in after them, and once we were settled, we'd just gab away. That was the magic of it, that Patrick and I could just talk and talk.

The crawl space beneath Patrick's house held happy memories for me, so that's where I went when I left the front porch with its spiderwebs and dying butterflies. I walked around the house and found the access door, and the sight of it sent my blood pulsing.

I sat on the overgrown lawn beside the plywood door. Aunt Tildy would kill me if I got grass stains on my church clothes, but I didn't care. I drew up my legs, tucked my skirt between my thighs, and hugged my shins. Tiny no-see-ums nipped at my ankles. Humidity pasted my hair to my neck.

The last time I was here at the house was three years ago. I was thirteen, and I was so happy I glowed. That's what Mama Sweetie told me, anyway. She said I was lit from within, and I believed her, because I felt it and knew it to be true.

I haven't known that feeling for a long time.

But that last day sure was a good one. Patrick and I had biked here after school, our feet kicking up dust when we hopped off in his dirt driveway. Mama Sweetie met us on the porch and hugged first Patrick and then me, saying, "Well, hey there, Cat. Ain't you as pretty as a picture." Fresh-squeezed lemonade waited on the small outside table. No garden spiders or mummy-wrapped bugs that day, because though Mama Sweetie wouldn't kill a spider, she did use her broom to clear their webs away.

I dropped into one of the sagging fold-out chairs and accepted the glass she held out to me. It had a decal of the Tasmanian Devil on it, and it came from the Hardee's in Toomsboro. Hardee's was running a special offer: Buy six cinnamon buns and get a free cartoon character drinking glass. Buy a dozen and get not two free glasses, but three.

Mama Sweetie went for the three. She had no need for them, since she had scores of jelly jars that did the job fine. But she couldn't resist Hardee's cinnamon buns. She couldn't resist anything sugary, and she spent half her food stamps on Coke and Twizzlers and fun-size Snickers. She bought cereal and milk for Patrick, and she made him eat tomatoes and squash and crowder peas from their garden, but their house was junk food central.

She was dead now. She died last year from her diabetes. I went to her funeral, but Patrick and I didn't talk.

Anyway, that Tasmanian Devil. I didn't know who he was until Mama Sweetie told me. I just liked how he looked, with his wild eyes and his fur fluffed out all crazy like a puppy after a good shake.

"He's on the show with that Bugs Bunny," Mama Sweetie explained. She worked at the church preschool, and years ago someone donated a used VCR and a cardboard box of old videos. Some were episodes of *Sesame Street*. Others were cartoons. Mama Sweetie played them for the kids at naptime if they'd been good.

"I don't know what he's supposed to be," she went on. "Just that they call him the Tasmanian Devil." She reached over and squeezed her grandson's knee. "You think there's really such a creature, Patrick?"

"Let's go to Tasmania and find out," Patrick suggested. We were in eighth grade, and already he was dreaming up ways to escape.

11

Mama Sweetie chuckled, patting Patrick's knee now instead of squeezing it. Patrick's hand went to hers, and their fingers interlocked.

"There is no such place as *Tasmania,*" I pronounced, knowing no such thing. But good Lord, it sure did sound like a made-up name. I slipped off my flip-flops and poked Patrick with my toe. "Even if there was, how would we get money to get there?"

"We'd get jobs," Patrick said.

I rolled my eyes. Jobs weren't easy to come by in Black Creek, not for grown-ups and especially not for kids.

Undaunted, Patrick said, "Well, then we could invent something. Something good, and we'd save every penny and not spend it on junk, because God helps those who help themselves. Right, Mama Sweetie?"

She ruffled his wheat-colored hair. "One day, baby. Ain't no need to rush." Her gaze was proud, but tinged with sadness, because she knew that eventually Patrick *would* leave. What she didn't know—what none of us knew—was that she would go first.

"Yeah, Patrick, stop rushing," I teased. I captured his foot with both of mine, hooking one behind his ankle and curving the other over the top of his beat-up sneaker. "You're staying with us forever and ever."

Mama Sweetie smiled, because she loved me, too. Not like she loved Patrick, but she didn't love anyone like she loved Patrick. Still, she hugged me every time she saw me, and sometimes she planted loud, wet smooches on my cheeks, forcing me to complain for the sake of my dignity. "Mama Sweetie!" I'd cry. "You *better* not have left lipstick on my cheek."

Patrick saw through me. I knew from the way he'd grin. Some people were happiest when others were unhappy, but Patrick was the opposite. Plus, he knew my family as well as I knew Mama Sweetie. He knew my daddy was a drunk, and that my aunt Tildy was a fine and strong woman, but not one to dole out hugs and kisses.

Mama Sweetie nodded at my glass of lemonade, which I'd halfway drained. "Well, that Tasmanian Devil is a rascal, whatever he is. Spins around like a tornado and gets into every little thing he can." She belly-laughed. "But you wouldn't know nothing about that, would you, Cat?"

"Naw," Patrick said, acting shocked. "Cat wouldn't recognize a whirling dervish if she saw one. Not if she was looking straight in a mirror, even."

I made a face at him, but I secretly took it as a compliment. Back then I *was* rascally. Why wouldn't I be? The world was out there waiting to be explored—and not just waiting, but *wanting* to be explored. So why in heaven's name shouldn't I investigate every nook and cranny?

Anyway, my lemonade glass was better than his, which was decorated with a cartoon pig named Porky, and he was chubby and pink and wore a blue jacket and a red bowtie.

"Maybe I am a whirling whatever-you-called-me, but that's better than being Porky the Pig," I told him.

"Not *the* pig," Patrick said, annoyingly unruffled. "Just Porky Pig, and I think you're jealous 'cause I've got clothes on"—he lifted his piggy glass to prove it—"while you're naked as a jaybird."

"Naked as a *Tasmanian Devil*," I said. "And I am most definitely not jealous, because I'd sure rather be naked than wearing that getup." I giggled. "Good Lord, Patrick. Can you imagine if you showed up at school in an outfit like that?"

"Of course," Patrick said, quirking one eyebrow in a way that drove me nuts. I'd spent hours trying to train my muscles to do that. "I would look *debonair.*"

"Ah, *debonair,*" I repeated, savoring the syllables. Patrick was a few months older than me and had already turned fourteen. He was gangly like a colt, but even so, he *was* debonair.

Not that I noticed, usually. He was *Patrick.* Mama Sweetie said we were kindred spirits. We were different from the rest of the kids in Black Creek, but we were different together, which made it all right. Whenever someone said we were weird, we said, "You just now figured that out?"

We were always getting into stuff. Always asking questions, always wanting to learn everything there was to know. Patrick and I loved reading—we passed our library books back and forth since we were only allowed to check out six at a time— but we also loved being outside.

Sometimes we'd catch bugs and carry them to Mama Sweetie, despite being technically too old for bug hunting. But

Mama Sweetie herself was a little kid when it came to bugs and nature and stuff, so we did it to please her. She taught us to be gentler than gentle, because it was terribly easy to tear a butterfly's wing or pull a leg off a daddy longlegs, she warned us, even if we didn't mean to. Life was precious. Life was fragile.

We'd present her with our treasures, and she'd draw our attention to things we might not have noticed on our own, like how a roly-poly curled up into a ball not to entertain us, but to protect itself from danger.

I'd seen roly-polies do their rolling-up trick and, sure, I knew they did it to guard themselves from harm. Who wanted to be poked by some dumb girl with a stick?

Mama Sweetie made me slow down and appreciate the finer points of the equation. She explained that since roly-polies were small and helpless, God evened things out by giving them the sense to curl up tight if something came along wanting to hurt them. There was a reason for everything, she said. God knew what He was doing, even if we were unable to understand.

Her wisdom applied to more than butterflies and roly-polies, because life *was* fragile. Things happened. Things changed. A girl full of light could get that light snuffed out, and when everything around her was dark, she could roll up into a ball and ignore the whole world, starting with her best friend.

But that was where Mama Sweetie's vision hit a snag, because *why*? What possible reason could God have for letting people treat others like dirt? "Just 'cause we can't see the pattern doesn't mean there ain't one" didn't cut it, not when it came to flat-out cruelty.

My aunt Tildy blamed what happened to me on puberty, an explanation about as helpful as blaming it on the moon or drinking bad water or forgetting to throw salt over my shoulder to keep the devil at bay. But that was Aunt Tildy's way. If there was ugliness to be dealt with, she dealt with it and moved on. If the ugliness left a scar, she brought out her whitewash and got to painting. When the damage was covered, she considered it gone, and it exasperated her to no end that I couldn't forget the rot beneath the surface.

"You can't expect gumdrops to fall out of the sky just 'cause you want 'em to," she scolded me. "No, ma'am. There's gonna be good and there's gonna be bad. That's just the way of it."

"But . . . I don't want it to be like that," I whispered.

"You think that matters, what you want?" she said. "Where'd you get that fool idea?"

Though her words stung, she wasn't trying to be cruel.

"No one ever said the world's an easy place, 'specially for a girl," she went on. "'Specially for a *pretty* girl, and that's just the way of it, too. If you're a pretty girl, you're gonna get . . ."

She pressed her lips together. She couldn't say it, not without scraping off a layer of fresh paint.

"Some things ain't worth dwelling on," she said crisply. "Now help me get the laundry off the line before the rain comes on."

Today, there wasn't a rain cloud in sight. Today, all I saw was an endless blue sky shimmering above the trees at the edge of

Patrick's yard. I pressed the back of my head against the house. My fingers found the grass, and at its roots, the cool soil. I would have been content to sit here for hours, but I needed to get up. I needed to bike on over to church, where Aunt Tildy would be waiting, saving me a seat in a pew and craning her neck to look for me.

Not yet, my body said, heavy with the desire for things to be like they once were.

But that was impossible.

I was sixteen now, no longer that girl full of light and life. No longer Patrick's kindred spirit. If I was like anyone, it was my aunt Tildy with her dogged blindness, because eventually I had adopted her approach to dealing with all things ugly. Blindness, at the time, seemed like my best chance at survival.

So I'd stabbed needles into my eyes and pretended not to see certain things. Bad things. Only by turning my back on certain bad things, I ended up turning my back on my dearest friend, a betrayal I never intended.

Or so I told myself. That was a problem with lying to yourself. Sometimes you got too good at it.

A chill moved down me as I realized how stupid I'd been. By turning a blind eye to the badness, I allowed it to grow. And when it needed more to feed on—*Oh Jesus*—it spread to Patrick.

I should have seen it coming. I would have, if only I'd had my eyes open.

So open them, I commanded myself. I did, literally, and

black spots swam across my vision, making me feel as dizzy as if I was swaying at the edge of a cliff. I'd never been good with heights. I blinked, and the sensation faded. I blinked again, and the trees bordering Patrick's yard faded as well. I looked past them and squarely into Patrick's pain.

I pictured him alone at the Come 'n' Go, my onetime best friend who didn't care for the dark. It would have been pitch-black outside. No one would have been around for miles except pitiful, messed-up Ridings McAllister, who lived in a trailer on the side of the highway. But Ridings would have been asleep, and even if he wasn't, he couldn't save himself from danger, much less someone else. Patrick would have known that. He would have known exactly how helpless he was when whoever attacked him roared into the dirt pull-off outside the store.

Except most likely Patrick didn't feel helpless, not at first. He wouldn't have seen the wolf in redneck's clothing.

I wasn't there that night, but I could imagine how things played out. The shadowed woods surrounding the store. The flickering bulb by the single gas pump. The too-bright lighting within the store, illuminating Patrick as he went about his work.

Then what? A truck engine abruptly cut off? The slamming of doors layered over boisterous, drunk laughter? A male voice—one Patrick knew, if my suspicions were correct—calling, "Patrick. Bro. Get your butt out here!"

And Patrick would have shaken his head and grinned as he pushed through the store's door. He wouldn't have realized how

18

wrong things were until he spotted the baseball bat bouncing against someone's palm.

Then the fear would have kicked in. Too late, he would have grasped what he was up against: a predator, or a pack of predators, there to do what predators do.

Angrily, I curled my hand into a fist and slammed it backward against Patrick's house. The pain helped, but not enough.

I leaned over, flipped the hook-and-eye latch on the door to the crawl space, and jerked it open. I squinted into the gaping hole. It took my eyes a moment to adjust, but then I made out the milk crates, the candles, the tufts of pink insulation drooping from the floor joists.

It was a postcard from our childhood, and it made me ache. Because Patrick wasn't a child anymore, but he wasn't yet a man. Because someone beat him up and jammed a gas nozzle down his throat. Because on top of everything he'd already lost, he was seventeen years old and more alone than I'd ever been, trapped in the deep sleep of a coma.

It enraged me.

But I'd lost out, too, and the realization fed my rage. I lost the strength to face the world head on. I lost my friends, I lost my brother, and I lost Patrick, which was like dying, since losing Patrick was nearly the same as losing myself. And what if Patrick never woke up? What if I'd lost him for good?

My fury sizzled and popped until I wasn't just mad, but crazy mad, as if I'd struck a match and lit myself on fire. What happened to Patrick was wrong. What happened to me was wrong. Every single thing was wrong, and when that great blaze of wrongness reached my core, my heart swelled and roared and cast it back out, leaving behind a white-hot clarity like nothing I'd ever experienced.

What I knew was this: Once upon a time, everything changed. Now things had to change again. Someone needed to track down whoever went after Patrick, and that someone was me.

It had been a week since Patrick was attacked, and Sheriff Doyle hadn't done squat. He claimed he was looking into every lead, but I felt certain he'd buried those leads instead. Slogging around in the muck of our godforsaken town would only bring Sheriff Doyle trouble, especially if I was right about what happened that night.

He would draw out the investigation a little longer for show, but eventually he'd pin the crime on drunk college boys from out of town. That was my guess. "We might never find out who done it," he'd say, shaking his head. "I can tell you this, though. Nobody from Black Creek woulda stooped so low."

But I'd seen things in the week since Patrick's attack that didn't add up, like my brother talking urgently to Beef, only to go dead silent when I approached. Like Bailee-Ann sitting by herself at the sandwich shop, her expression troubled as she chewed on a strand of her hair. Like cocky Tommy Lawson straddling his piss yellow motorcycle at the intersection of Main Street and Shields, thinking so hard on something that he didn't notice the light turn green. Normally, he'd accelerate hard and fast, showing off the power of his BMW's engine, but on that day, an old lady had to tap the horn of her Buick to rouse him from his trance.

I closed the crawl space door. I got to my feet and brushed myself off. My chest was tight, but I looked at the blue sky, clear and pale above the tree line, and said out loud, "Fine, I'll do it." *I* would speak for Patrick. I'd look straight into the ugliness and find out who hurt him, and when I did, I'd yell it from the mountaintop.

"Do you hear that, God?" I said. "Do you see me now?"

A moment passed. Sweat trickled down the base of my spine. Then, out of nowhere, a breeze lifted my hair and jangled Mama Sweetie's wind chimes, which she'd made by hanging mismatched forks and spoons from the lid of a tin can.

It scared me, to tell the truth. It also fanned the flames of my rage.

I lifted my chin and said, "Good."

2

IF YOU LIVED IN BLACK CREEK AND YOU WERE
a good girl, like me, you put on your best skirt and blouse
and went to church on Sunday mornings, and sometimes on
Wednesday evenings, too. Daddy didn't come, and neither did
my brother—so much for Christian being a Christian—but
they weren't girls, so they could get away with it.

Last Sunday, Aunt Tildy let me stay home because I was
such a wreck after hearing about Patrick. But this Sunday, I
rode my bike from Patrick's house to the Holiness Church of
God in time for the "moment of silence," which kicked off every
service. That and the singing were the parts I liked best.

I'd always liked singing, and in the days of hanging out
with Patrick and Mama Sweetie, the three of us would belt

out songs for no reason. Mama Sweetie said you didn't *need* a reason to sing. She said if everyone started off the day singing, just think how happy they'd be. We'd sing hymns from church and songs we'd learned at Vacation Bible School and silly songs Mama Sweetie knew from teaching preschoolers, including a goofy one about a wee-wee tot sitting on his wee-wee pot. Another of our favorites was "This Little Light of Mine," because of how catchy it was. Often, even after biking home from Patrick's, I'd find myself singing it under my breath, until Christian would grab my shoulders and say, "Could you *please* stop singing that dang song! I'm *begging* you!"

Now I just sang in church. After today's service, I filed into the fellowship hall with Aunt Tildy. Then we went our separate ways. She had a Bible study to attend, while I planned on doing some good old-fashioned eavesdropping.

I went to the refreshment table and got myself a doughnut. I even took a nibble or two, so that anyone looking would think, *Oh, there's Cat, eating a doughnut and keeping to herself like always.* Hopefully, no one would try to talk to me, as I had nothing to say. I just hovered on the fringes and listened. In Black Creek, church was as much about gossip as worship, and Patrick's attack was the juiciest thing going.

"I heard from Eunice that he's bound to have brain damage, bless his heart," a church lady named Tammy said to her friend. "Eunice's cousin's a nurse in the pediatric wing, you know."

"They put him in the pediatric unit?" the friend said. "Ain't he too old to be with those kids?" She lowered her voice. "What if he . . . *you know?*"

The flame inside me wanted to burn her up. *What if he turned those kids into faggots?* That was what she meant. Forget that he was in a coma. Forget that his body was beaten to a pulp. Forget that he might have *brain damage,* if Eunice's nurse cousin had access to the truth.

"Naw, they didn't stick him with them sick kids," Tammy said. "He's got a room all to hisself. Got all kinds of tubes and wires and machines sticking out of him."

Machines sticking out of him? I thought. *Really, Tammy?* Tammy worked at the paper mill until it was bought by some Japanese crook who shut it down and sold it for parts. But before that happened, Tammy got full-out scalped when she leaned over too close to the paper rollers. She didn't have her hair pinned up like she was supposed to. To everyone's surprise, her hair had grown back, and now it was just as sparse and stringy as ever, not that she let that stop her from teasing it high and shellacking it till it was as hard as a beetle's shell. I reckoned she was the one with brain damage, *bless her heart.*

I moved on from Tammy and her friend. By the choir room, the choir members were taking off their white robes and hanging them up. I caught the words *wickedness* and *ungodly,* and I turned right around, already knowing where that conversation was going.

I paused in the hallway, my interest piqued by the sight of a timid young woman named Hannah speaking with a plump woman everyone called Zippy. Hannah was new to the church, having lived most of her life in a high-up mountain town called Coonesville. That was where she met her husband, who moved there for a job. But her husband's mama lived in Black Creek, and now she was ailing, so they'd come to be with her.

Hannah had a cute baby I'd taken care of in the church nursery a couple of times. Hannah herself seemed nice enough, and—a big point in her favor—she wasn't from these parts.

I edged closer and fiddled with my shoe, which was, in truth, giving me grief. Dress shoes were expensive, and I'd had these for over a year. They were black with tiny heels, and my toes were wedged in like Vienna sausages.

". . . was a nice boy," Hannah was saying. Her tone was troubled, as if she was looking for reassurance.

"He was," Zippy said. "*Is*, I should say. Ain't dead yet, after all." She barked out an uncomfortable laugh.

"But if he's nice and all, why are folks talking the way they are?" Hannah asked. "It's as if they think he *asked* for what happened to him. I just don't understand it, not one bit."

Zippy eyed her. "Oh, I think you do. I ain't sayin' it's right, mind you. But I've been to Coonesville. I reckon it's not that different from Black Creek now, is it?"

"I couldn't say," Hannah murmured. I snuck a sideways glance at her and saw that she was frowning. "There was one gal I knew—a single gal—and I can't stop thinking about her. Can't stop wondering what *she* would say about this mess."

"She go to your church?"

"No. She didn't go to church."

Zippy tugged at her skirt to adjust it within her rolls of fat. Her expression was disapproving as she waited for Hannah to continue.

"She had herself a lady revolver, and she made sure everyone knew it," Hannah said.

"That so," Zippy said, less a question than a bland acknowledgment.

"I asked her once—her name's Julia, and she's real pretty, not at all what you'd expect—and one day I asked if she was scared of panthers or bears, if that's why she kept a gun. She told me she could handle a panther just fine. What scared her was the thought of a truckful of rednecks paying her a visit."

Hannah kept her wide, anxious eyes on Zippy, which was lucky for me, as a girl could fool with her shoes for only so long. I straightened up and pretended to admire a quilt hanging on the wall.

"She have a man in her life?" Zippy asked, meaning Julia-who-had-a-lady-revolver.

A flush worked its way up Hannah's face. "She was a single gal, like I said. Only . . . not exactly."

"Not exactly a gal?" Zippy said. "Or not exactly single?"

"She was real nice," Hannah said helplessly. "She was a good friend to me."

Zippy snorted. "Oh, I'm *sure* she was."

I didn't stick around for more. I'd been a fool to think I'd gain anything from church gossip, and I was ready to head home.

Unfortunately, I was waylaid by Verleen Cox, who played the church organ and was the worst gossip of all.

"Oh, *Cat*," she said, ambushing me with a hug. She pulled back and regarded me sorrowfully. Her makeup was caked in her many wrinkles, and her wiry gray hair was held back in a ponytail. "I am torn to bits about Patrick. Just torn to bits, and I know you must be, too."

"Yes, ma'am," I said uncomfortably. Verleen had talked to *The Pulse*. She said that Patrick was sexually broken.

"I know how close you two are," she continued. "I always did hope he'd take a shine to you, if you know what I mean. Pretty girl like you could turn any boy's head."

I said nothing.

Verleen clutched my arm. "The gas fumes should have killed him, that's what they're saying." Her color was high with the thrill of talking about it. "They're saying he may never wake up."

"He will," I said. I listened to her yap some more about how upset she was. She just liked tragedy, that's what I thought.

When she swooshed off to find another ear to bend, I went and sat at a tucked-away window nook overlooking the parking lot.

I didn't want to run into another soul on the way to my bicycle, not before I'd had time to collect myself.

When Patrick and I were kids, we didn't have *sexuality*, not that we knew of. We were just kids, running around and catching crawdads and breaking ivy for Aunt Tildy and Mama Sweetie. They used the ivy to make wreaths, which they sold to fancy ladies in Toomsboro. In the winter, Mama Sweetie added holly berries to hers, as well as those pointy holly leaves. Then they were Christmas wreaths.

Patrick and me preferred to use the holly leaves as pretend needles. We'd play doctor, but not like you think. We didn't take our clothes off. We said, "Time for your shot. Be brave so you can get your lollipop." Our lollipops were pretend, too.

Once, in early April, we were out collecting ivy and we got lost in a laurel thicket. Laurel branches grew twisty and gnarled, and if you got stuck in a patch, the overgrowth was so thick you couldn't see the sky. We knew we'd blunder out eventually, but for then, all we could see were laurel branches behind us and in front of us and above us. It was like we'd been spirited into a fairyland—the elf kind of fairies, not the other.

We sat for a bit. There were so many shades of green, it made my head spin. Even without direct sunlight, the green shone down on us and filled us with the promise of spring. I felt as if we were part of the forest, as if the real world no longer existed. Or, if it did still exist, that it no longer mattered.

Maybe Patrick felt the same way. Maybe that's what gave him the courage to open up to me.

We were in the seventh grade. I had a chigger bite on my ankle, and while Patrick talked, I dug at my flesh with dirty fingernails.

He told me he'd been at Tommy Lawson's house the other weekend with some other guys. No girls, just guys. Tommy's daddy was at work, and they'd snuck into his home office, where the computer was.

"Check this out," Tommy said, smirking. Patrick didn't say Tommy had smirked, but I was sure he did.

Tommy sat at his dad's desk, tapped at the keyboard, and pulled up a porn site that showed people doing nasty things without their clothes on.

When Patrick got to that part, my jaw dropped open, and I probably laid off my obsessive scratching. Nudie pictures? Tommy? Tommy was a ninth grader like my brother, and he was the handsomest boy I'd ever seen. He had blue eyes and sun-streaked blond hair, a shade my aunt called towheaded. He wore nice clothes. He smelled good, a novelty among the boys I knew. He smiled easily and with confidence, and though he made mean jokes sometimes, I didn't realize they were mean. Like, he'd say I was fat and pinch the spot above my hip that on all girls is pinchable, unless they're anorexic.

"Shut up, I'm not fat," I'd say, flustered by his touch.

"I'm just messing with you," he'd say. He'd tickle me again to make me squirm. "Just means there's more of you to love, that's all."

In the laurel thicket, where no one could see or hear us, I widened my eyes and whispered, "Omigosh, Patrick. Did you look? Were the girls pretty? Did they have big—you knows?"

Aunt Tildy called them bubbies. My brother, Christian, called them a word that rhymed with "bits." I didn't call them anything, not boobs or breasts or bosoms or hooters. Patrick didn't call them anything, either.

"There were guys, too," he said. "In the pictures."

"*Gross,*" I said, delighted. "Could you see their . . . ?" This time I didn't say "you knows." I just lifted my eyebrows.

The skin of Patrick's neck grew red, and then all the way up his face and out to the tips of his ears. I assumed he didn't like talking about boy parts any more than I liked talking about girl parts. Although actually, I did like talking about them, just not labeling them. And actually, Patrick did, too.

I didn't yet realize that Patrick was as handsome as Tommy, just in a different way. I didn't see it because Patrick wasn't a *boy*. He was my best friend.

Plus, Tommy and Patrick were totally different. Tommy was cocksure of himself, while Patrick was shy, with a habit of ducking his head and looking up slantwise as if he wasn't sure he was supposed to be there. Where Tommy's eyes were blue, Patrick's were green. Not the swampy green of the swimming hole, but a startling bottle-glass green, like a 7UP bottle shot through with light.

"If I tell you something, will you promise not to tell?" he asked me in the laurel thicket.

"Sure," I said. It was delicious telling secrets in the hushed privacy of the forest, where not even the sunlight could cut a path to the leaf-covered ground.

"*Really* promise," he pressed. "You can't tell Gwennie or Bailee-Ann or anyone."

I nodded. Did seeing all those pretty girls do something to Patrick? Was he going to confess a secret crush? Or maybe one of the other guys had confessed which girl he had a crush on. What if Patrick was going to tell me something about Tommy?

Patrick swallowed. "Seeing those naked pictures . . ."

I waited. Above us a bluebird whistled *tur-a-lee, tur-a-lee*.

"I didn't like looking at the girls," he said in a rush.

"Oh," I said. That wasn't what I had expected, but . . . *oh*. "Well, that's fine. In fact that's nice of you, Patrick. That means you weren't being sinful."

"No, I was."

"Nuh-uh, 'cause you didn't pull up the dirty pictures," I argued. Patrick was always hard on himself. He cared about God, and he cared about Mama Sweetie, and he worried about disappointing them. It was my job to assure him he didn't.

"Tommy brought y'all in and showed you, so if anyone was sinful, it's him," I said. "And like you said, you didn't even like looking."

"Except I did," Patrick mumbled.

"What's that?"

He tucked his chin to his chest. "I did like looking. Just . . . not at the girls."

"Oh." This time the processing took longer, but not by much.

Later, when I mulled it over, I realized I'd already known. I just hadn't *known* I'd known.

I told myself it wasn't a big deal. Patrick liking boys was part of who he was, but it was hardly the whole picture.

3

I WASN'T SURE HOW LONG I SAT IN THE WINDOW
nook. When I came back to my body, I found myself gazing at
the windowpane, but not actually seeing anything. I blinked
to wake up—and then *bam*, I was awake all right. My brother,
Christian, hadn't attended this morning's service, which was no
big surprise. But there in the dirt parking lot was his Yamaha,
and parked alongside it were Beef's Suzuki and Tommy's bright
yellow BMW.

Where were the owners? If their motorcycles were here,
then they were, too. A panicked scan told me they weren't in
the fellowship hall, so where *were* they?

I located Christian leaning against the church's brick exte-
rior, over near the kids' playground with its rusty bobbing duck

and a red plastic slide. He was alone. I pressed my lips together, strode to the side door, and pushed into the midday heat.

I checked to make sure Christian was by himself and marched over.

"What are you doing here?" I demanded. My talking skills may have been rusty with the general population, but not with Christian. "You can't just come for the doughnuts, you know. You only get doughnuts if you sit through the actual service."

"I'm not here for doughnuts," Christian said. "Jesus, Cat."

I put my hands on my hips. "That's right: *Jesus*. Jesus is why you're *supposed* to be here. Good for you for learning your Bible lesson."

He gazed at me. He had circles under his eyes, and his hair, dark like mine, was mashed down from his helmet. He needed a shower. He didn't always look this thrashed, but what happened to Patrick had taken its toll on him, too. That as well as something else, I suspected—and it was the *something else* I had my sights on.

"What in the name of creamed corn are you blabbering about?" he said.

What in the name of creamed corn, indeed? When I was younger, I would have laughed at that expression, because it was funny. Christian, if I was being objective, was often funny. But I'd fallen out of the habit of laughing at his jokes.

Anyway, my blabbering wasn't the issue. *He* was the one leaning against the church wall in jeans and a dirty T-shirt. He was the one full of intrigue and secretive, shadowed looks.

"Where're your buddies?" I asked. I called his gang of friends the redneck posse. Their leader was Tommy Lawson, whom I hated. The other main players were Beef and Dupree, and my brother, of course. The girls attached to the group were Bailee-Ann, who was Beef's girlfriend, and occasionally Beef's little sister, Gwennie.

They liked to hang out at the abandoned Frostee Top, drinking beer and smoking pot. Sometimes they raced their motorcycles up to Suicide Rock. They were all about being loud and having a good time, no matter how out of control it got. After Patrick and I stopped being friends, those guys took him in and made a mascot out of him, sort of. That's how it looked. Like, they were always teasing him, and the teasing wasn't always nice, especially with Tommy large and in charge. But they pretended it was all in fun, even Patrick.

"Tommy's helping his grandmother with something," Christian said.

"His *grandmother*," I said scornfully. Other kids had grannies or meemaws; Tommy had a *grandmother*. Ooh la la.

Christian ran his hand through his hair. "Yes, Cat. His grandmother. She needs his help, and he told her he'd meet her here."

"Then where is he?"

"In the front parking lot with Beef, loading stuff into her car."

"Why aren't you helping?"

"There were only two bags. God. And since I know you're

34

gonna ask, here's the answer: What's in the bags are supplies for the new mailbox she wants, the kind that locks."

"A mailbox that locks. How exciting." I did a sweep of the parking lot to make sure Tommy truly wasn't nearby. "So y'all were tearing up the hardware store while I was inside praying for Patrick. That just takes the cake, doesn't it?"

Christian narrowed his eyes. "Lay off, will you? Or else tell me what's gotten you so riled up. One or the other."

I stepped closer. "You were with Patrick the night he got attacked. You ever going to tell me what happened? What *really* happened?"

"Patrick was attacked on *Sunday morning*. He was with us that night, yeah, but everyone was home by, like, one."

"Not Patrick," I said.

"I don't know what you think happened, Cat," Christian said. "It was just the bunch of us hanging out."

"Then why do you and Beef and Tommy keep skulking around? Every time I see the three of y'all together, you're deep in conversation. And every time I come over to say hi, you shut up quick. So what's that about?"

"Cat?"

"What?"

"When's the last time you came over to say hi to me or my friends? Two years ago? Three?"

I scowled.

"I suggest you work on your details before tossing out your conspiracy theories," he said. "You think I'm not broken up by this? You think I'm not mad as hell? Patrick's just about my best friend, even though he is—"

"Gay?" I threw out. The word felt sharp in my mouth, but I'd had it with *you knows* and veiled references.

"I was going to say straight-edge," he said, meaning that Patrick wasn't as wild a partier as him and the others. His tone made me blush because somehow he'd gone and made it seem as if *I* were the one being judgmental.

Yet it was an odd twist of language. Based on the way people usually used the words, Christian was *straight* and Patrick was *gay*. But Christian, when he got wasted, was *gay* if you used the old-fashioned, oh-so-merry definition of the word, while Patrick was *straight-edge* because he didn't drink to the point of passing out.

"You've got a major chip on your shoulder, sis," Christian said.

"Don't call me 'sis,'" I said.

Christian pushed himself off the wall and said, "Hey, there's Tommy and Beef." He raised his voice. "Dudes! Over here!"

My stomach dropped, and I hightailed it back inside the building, where I made a beeline for the refreshment table. That was where the crowd was. That was the best place to hide.

I reached for a cookie I had no intention of eating. As I did, my arm knocked against an elderly woman's frail frame. She turned sharply, and my heart clutched up. It was old Mrs. Lawson, Tommy's *grandmother.*

The entire Lawson clan was as rich as sin, and I figured they stayed in Black Creek just so they could lord it over the rest of us.

They hadn't always been well-off. Tommy's great-great-great-grandfather was one of the first people to homestead Black Creek, way back when it was a decent trading post. Then a railroad was laid between two bigger settlements, and suddenly there was a lot less traffic through Black Creek. The final blow came when the TVA dam was built on Brigham River. The dam cut off Black Creek from the other towns, because who in his right mind would drive an extra twenty miles around the new man-made lake to reach what was nearly a ghost town already?

Tommy's grandfather Merrit Lawson had enough money to get by, but no more. He opened the Come 'n' Go for those who stayed put, and when the feed store went belly-up—due in part to Merrit's ties with the banker, who refused to change the terms of the feed store's loan—he bought it for a dime and turned it into the local Buy-Low, where Aunt Tildy worked as a cashier.

Now there were Buy-Lows all over the state. The Lawsons had built themselves a small empire, and they were too powerful for their own good. That was why I stepped back nervously when old Mrs. Lawson turned from the refreshment table.

"And who are *you*, young lady?" she said.

"Cat Robinson?" I said, hating the way my inflection went up as if I weren't sure of my own name. But good heavens.

Maybe I did maintain a low profile, but Mrs. Lawson knew who I was. There were like five hundred people in Black Creek, period. Everyone knew everyone.

"Tildy's girl?" she said.

"Yes, ma'am. Tildy's my aunt. She works at the Buy-Low."

She clucked. "I know who she is. She needs to teach you some manners."

Oh, nuh-uh. I hadn't been rude. I had accidentally and *lightly* hit her arm with mine. And no one had the right to disrespect Aunt Tildy, not even the queen herself.

Not that I said any of this out loud, because I *wasn't* brought up to talk ugly. But for the record, the prissy outfit Mrs. Lawson was wearing *was* ugly, a powder pink skirt with a matching powder pink jacket. She looked like an eraser.

"I need some creamer for my coffee," she announced in her snooty way of talking. She arched her pencil thin brows, and I realized she meant for me to go get her some.

"Oh. I'll see if they have any in the kitchen," I said, scurrying off.

I returned with a single-serving plastic container, which she regarded with displeasure. "Never mind," she said, her pink lips folding in on themselves. "I'll go without."

She enjoyed making people feel inadequate, and she was good at it. Today, I had a fire in my belly, however. Plus, if I was going to find out what happened to Patrick, I was going to have to talk to a lot of people I'd just as soon not. I might as well start with prune-faced Mrs. Lawson.

"So, um, you know Patrick, right?" I said. "Tommy's friend? Who got beat up a week ago?"

She didn't respond.

"He's still in the hospital, and . . . I was wondering if maybe we could send flowers."

Mrs. Larson's expression remained impassive. I fought not to fidget.

"Or a balloon bouquet?" I tried again. The Buy-Low sold shiny silver message balloons that said things like THINKING OF YOU and GET WELL SOON! "Maybe we could pass around a card for everyone to sign?"

"I suppose you want *me* to pay for them," Mrs. Larson said.

"We could take up a collection," I said. She was trying to make me feel small, and she was succeeding. But I wasn't going to let her make me retreat back into my shell.

She sipped her coffee and grimaced.

"It's just so horrible, what happened to him," I pressed on. "Is there any new information, do you know?"

"Well, it obviously had to do with his . . . *lifestyle,*" she said.

I bit the inside of my cheek.

"I don't want the boy to *die,*" she went on, as if she were speaking of a mutt that uglied up the neighborhood. "But he might just up and do it anyway."

"What have you heard? Has Sheriff Doyle learned anything? Has he discovered any, you know, clues?"

"Grandmother, there you are," Tommy said from behind us. My chest tightened because I'd recognize his voice anywhere.

"I put everything we need into your car. I'll set it up this afternoon."

My instincts said *bolt,* but I was rooted to the floor.

Mrs. Lawson's face brightened. *"Tommy,"* she said. "Now why in the world aren't you wearing that new dress shirt I bought you?"

She smiled at me for the first time. "You know my grandson, don't you? My precious Tommy?"

I read it in his face. First
was I making nice wit
flicker of what ab
interpreted it
then so
as

4

TOMMY WAS A SNAKE—IN EVERY SENSE OF THE
word. A snake and a jerk and a gay-bashing redneck, meaning
he made jokes about how Patrick better not hit on him, how
Patrick ran like a fag, how a man's a-hole was for "exit only."
Tommy wasn't alone in making jokes like that, of course. Black
Creek was no haven for a boy who was "light in his loafers," as
Aunt Tildy put it.

And yet, Tommy was Patrick's friend. That needed saying,
too. Patrick was part of Tommy's posse, though I wondered
how much of a part. I suspected Tommy kept him around for
sport. Tommy preyed on the weak, as I knew.

Seeing him in the fellowship hall made me want to curl
up like a roly-poly. He was none too happy to see me, either.

there was puzzlement, like why
his highfalutin grandmother? Then a
most resembled shame, though no doubt I
wrong. He had every reason to be ashamed, and
e, but more likely he was just embarrassed to be seen
s grandmother's little helper.

"Cat," he said.

I didn't reply. I stared at his cut-down army boots and hugged my ribs.

"Cat thinks we should send flowers to the hospital," old Mrs. Lawson said. "To your friend. *Patrick.*"

Her lips pursed, and I figured there must be a bit of a struggle going on inside her. Jesus said love the sinner, hate the sin, and while I knew old Mrs. Lawson was incapable of loving Patrick, surely she didn't *hate* him, did she? A banged-up boy nearly the same age as her precious Tommy, lying in a coma with no one to stand up for him?

Tommy said nothing. I lifted my gaze, because I had to see what battle of conscience—if any—was playing out on his features.

"Who do *you* think hurt him?" I heard myself say. My words were made of stone, as cold and unforgiving as the outcroppings of granite that rose above the banks of the creek our town was named for.

A flush crept up his neck. "How the fuck would I know? And if I did, wouldn't I say?"

"Tommy," old Mrs. Lawson scolded.

I watched him. He was good looking, the snake, even in oil-stained jeans and a stupid shirt that said 4 STROKE, whatever that meant.

But Tommy didn't look good right now, not with his face twisted up.

"Sorry, Grandmother," he said gruffly.

"You're going against your raising," Mrs. Lawson said. As if to excuse her grandson's behavior, she faced me and explained, "Tommy was with him earlier that evening. That makes it especially painful, of course."

Of course.

"I've got to go," I said, turning on my heel.

"What an odd child," I heard Mrs. Lawson murmur.

Then, from Tommy, "She ain't a child, Grandmother."

"*Isn't* a child," Mrs. Lawson corrected, and I was out the door.

5

AT HOME, I CHANGED INTO MY EVERYDAY CLOTHES, and then Aunt Tildy and I cooked up our big Sunday meal: fried chicken, crowder peas, cornbread, and a mess of green beans. Oh, and tomatoes. Had to have tomatoes in the summertime, picked fresh and lightly salted.

I fixed a plate for Daddy and delivered it to him in his trailer out back. He moved out there when my mama died and had stayed ever since. He took the plate, settled it on the built-in TV tray of his belly, and pulled out the jug of Aunt Jemima syrup he kept under the La-Z-Boy. "You ain't gonna tell on me to your aunt Tildy, are you, kitten?" he said.

That's what he called me, like I was an itty-bitty puffball with a yawning mouth and harmless claws.

He poured the syrup over his food, and I said, "That is just nasty, Daddy."

He laughed, and I could smell the corn liquor on his breath. Also, the sour odor of him needing a bath. Sadness overwhelmed me: for Patrick, for Daddy, for the whole hard lot of everything.

Daddy must have picked up on it, because concern clouded his eyes. "What's wrong, sweet pea?" That was his other nickname for me. I was either a kitten or a sweet pea, each incapable of making a dent in the world's injustice.

Of course, my big smelly daddy was pretty helpless himself. I loved Daddy, but in the way I might love a loyal old dog who could no longer follow me around, just thump his tail whenever I came near.

"Ah, nothing, Daddy." I tried for a smile. "I'm fine."

"You know what you need?" he said as he forked a mouthful of syrup-drenched chicken into his mouth. "Some good clean sunshine. Yessir, that's exactly what you need." This, from a man who spent his days holed up in his trailer, with just his liquor bottles and his TV for company.

"Okay, Daddy," I said.

He wasn't done. "Young girl like you? You should be out stirring up trouble with your friends, not bothering with all them books you read. You know it's them books what make you talk funny."

"Ha-ha," I said, as this was an old joke between us. He poked fun at my *school learnin'*, as he called it. Daddy liked to tease me, but I knew he was secretly proud that I hadn't dropped out of school like so many other kids, including my brother. Patrick and Bailee-Ann and I were the only kids from Black Creek to complete our junior year at Toomsboro High last month, and the three of us were the only ones planning to return in the fall as seniors. We were going to make it all the way to graduation. But with Patrick in a coma, who knew what would happen?

No. I pulled myself back, because Daddy and me had a script that needed following. Otherwise, we wouldn't have a thing to say to each other.

"I don't talk 'funny,' Daddy," I said. "*I* talk *proper.* You just talk country."

"Well, you might have a point there," he said, chuckling. "But don't let that fool you." He tapped his temple. "Your old daddy didn't fall off the last turnip truck, you know."

"Yeah, Daddy. I know." I kissed his stubbled cheek and headed back to the house, where Christian, Aunt Tildy, and I sat down at the table and tucked into our dinners. None of us talked. While I ate, I thought about Daddy's advice and decided I'd take it after all. Tomorrow I *would* go out and stir up some trouble, just not in the way he expected.

monday

6

I'D GOTTEN INTO THE HABIT OF TAKING UP AS little space in this world as I could, which was to say I'd been hiding behind a book or my falling-down hair for basically the last three years. I wished I could go back and change things. If I'd been a better friend to Patrick, I'd have known what he'd been up to recently. Maybe I'd have been with him that Saturday night. Maybe he wouldn't have been attacked.

Maybe, maybe, maybe, and if wishes were horses, I'd gallop straight to Sheriff Doyle and hand over Patrick's attacker. *Poof,* I'd be Patrick's friend again, and *poof,* Patrick would wake up.

Last night as I lay in bed, I thought about Patrick lying alone in the hospital, his body broken and maybe his brain, too. I tossed and turned all night, in and out of sleep, and woke up before first light. I slipped out onto the porch, my quilt wrapped around me, and watched the sun rise from behind the mountains. It was beautiful. That's why Daddy picked this lot, way back when.

"So your mama could be surrounded by beauty," he told me every so often. I'd hug him on those occasions, because talking about my dead mama always made him feel blue. "You sure do call her to mind, sweet pea. My beautiful girl."

A silver mist cloaked the peaks and valleys. Golden sunshine glowed along the horizon, shifting into rosy pinks and a striking, fiery orange as the light pierced the clouds.

I closed my eyes, and still the colors reached me.

I opened my eyes again and turned to the job at hand: to find out who hurt Patrick. I reviewed what little I knew. Patrick was working the night shift at the Come 'n' Go on the night he was attacked, and he was scheduled to open the store the following morning. That's why it was lucky that man from Atlanta came along when he did, although I supposed—if I was trying to think like a detective, though the word *detective* made me feel foolish—that another way of looking at it was, *Huh, what a coincidence he came along when he did.*

Except Sheriff Doyle said Patrick's attack occurred between two and four A.M., and the man, whose name was Dave Tuttle, said he left Atlanta at five thirty A.M. I read that in the *Toomsboro Times.* Every day there'd been at least one article about how the investigation was proceeding, and every article said pretty much the same thing. It wasn't.

But in one article, Mr. Tuttle was quoted as saying that he made the drive from Atlanta to Highlands once a week, and that he always left at dawn. He had a daughter in Atlanta who didn't go with him that Sunday, and she confirmed that yes, he left when he said he did. She could be lying, but I assumed Sheriff Doyle checked out her story, and Mr. Tuttle's as well.

Who else might have been at the gas station late Saturday night or early Sunday morning? I needed to be open-minded. I needed to consider all possibilities. I wasn't convinced by the theory I suspected Sheriff Doyle of pushing, the one about a gang of outsiders attacking Patrick, but I'd be doing Patrick a disservice if I didn't give it a fair shake.

Black Creek had one of the highest illiteracy rates in the state, but if you traveled thirty miles in any direction, you'd hit a college. Not necessarily a good college, but a college. And what did college guys like to do? Besides getting laid and picking at their belly buttons, I mean?

They liked to party, and the Come 'n' Go on Route 34 was nearly halfway between Western State and Toomsboro Community College. When there wasn't a kegger at one of the schools, the college boys would drive to the other, and they often stopped at the Come 'n' Go for snacks. Beef jerky, Monster Energy Drinks, chewing tobacco. Beer.

Patrick wasn't supposed to sell alcohol, because he wasn't twenty-one, but Mr. Lawson, the store's owner, wasn't overly concerned with that law. He was concerned with making a profit, and he told Patrick to go on and sell to anyone with a valid-looking ID.

Unlike Mr. Lawson, Patrick was a rule player, but he had a sweet job and a steady paycheck, so he didn't argue with his boss. He took the "valid" part seriously, however. If a customer's ID looked authentic, then cool. If it seemed sketchy—like if the name listed on the license was "Mario Mario" and the guy sliding it across the counter looked all of eighteen, then Patrick didn't accept it, even though it would have been the easier thing to do.

"Mario Mario?" I said skeptically when my brother relayed this particular story one Saturday night, sitting out on our porch.

"From Mario and Luigi," Christian said. He recited a list of what I assumed were video games: "Super Smash Bros. Mario Kart. Brawl."

"The little dudes with the mushrooms?" I'd seen them on someone's handheld game at one point or another.

"Super Mario Mushroom, baby!"

I wasn't his "baby." I also wasn't drunk, since I'd had zero beers to his, oh, five or six or seven. "That's the stupidest name for a fake ID I've ever heard," I said. "And why Mario *Mario*? Doesn't the mushroom dude have a real last name?"

"I think that *is* his real last name, and yeah, it's dumb as shit," Christian said. "If you're going to make a fake, you might as well try to make it look authentic." He grinned. "But holy goddamn, it made me laugh."

Remembering made him laugh again. Out of stinginess, I didn't join in. My feelings toward Christian were too complicated. Also, I'd promised to help at the church nursery the next day, which meant for an early morning, and which meant I should have just gone to bed.

But didn't. I guess it was nice sitting on the front porch and listening to Christian laugh.

"I'm assuming Patrick turned Mario Mario down?" I said.

Christian filled me in. Apparently, Mario Mario came in with three other guys, all of them dudded out in college-boy button-downs over T-shirts with logos for skateboards and ski wear. They browsed the aisles and plunked their selections on the counter, including two cases of Budweiser. Patrick glanced at Mario's ID to be polite, but, he told Christian later, he'd known from the moment the guys came in that none of them was legal.

"I can ring up the food, but not the beer," Patrick told him. "Sorry, bro."

Mario hadn't liked it. Patrick held firm. So Mario and his friends started ragging on Patrick: calling him a fag, telling him to not to be so gay, checking his plastic name tag and shortening his name to Trish. Normal old normal, and nothing Patrick hadn't endured before.

"Then they laid into Gwennie," Christian said.

"Gwennie?" I said. "What was she doing there? Was she alone?" Gwennie was fifteen years old and too innocent for her own good.

"Uh, *no,* she was with Patrick."

"Yeah, but . . ." I shook my head. "What about Beef? Was he there?" I guess part of me still clung to the belief that big brothers took care of their little sisters.

"Hush up and I'll tell it," Christian said. "Beef wasn't there, just Gwennie. When Mario and his buddies couldn't get a rise out of Patrick, they went off on her."

"How?" I said.

"Just, you know. Making rude comments and stuff."

"Like what?"

He rubbed his neck.

"What did they *say*?"

"Fag hag," he said, shifting his gaze. "But don't worry, 'cause right about then is when me and Tommy came along."

He got his groove back. "Patrick had Gwennie behind the counter with him. The college boys were up in their faces, and we got there in time to see Patrick pull himself tall and let them have it." Christian slapped his knee. "He told them to *exit the premises* or he'd call the police."

"And they did? They left?"

"Well, Tommy and me gave them a helping hand."

"Good," I said vehemently. "I'm glad you were there."

Christian looked at me with a funny expression, which I pretended not to see. Maybe I didn't send love his way all that often, but that didn't mean I couldn't.

As I sat on our porch now and watched the sun rise, I thought about those underage party boys. Maybe they held a grudge against Patrick. Did they return with thoughts of revenge? If so, how could I find out?

I could go to the Come 'n' Go, I supposed. But, no. If any of them had attacked Patrick, they'd never come back.

So, okay. My suspects so far were out-of-town college boys or some random sadist who just happened to be driving along Route 34, and who just happened to brutally assault a guy he didn't know from Adam.

I'd keep those options in mind, but my money was on someone from Black Creek, possibly aided by one or two of his buddies. My money was on the redneck posse, and the only member I exempted was Christian. He wasn't perfect, but I knew with absolute certainty that my brother didn't go after Patrick with a baseball bat. He would never.

It was possible he knew who did, though.

The first order of business was to find out what happened in the hours prior to Patrick's attack. Patrick went out that night with my brother and some others, including Beef and Tommy, and I needed to know what happened when he was with them, before he was beaten up, strung to the gas pump, and left to die.

Christian wouldn't tell me. I'd bugged him and bugged him, and he flat-out denied that anything *had* happened. Yet with every denial, he'd get the same stubborn look I'd seen him wearing all week. One time he said, "Just lay off. It's nothing you need to worry about."

If it was nothing for me to worry about, what was the "it"? If he didn't want me worrying, why not come clean?

There was no point asking Tommy. He'd lie, and a lie was no better than Christian's closed-lipped agitation.

So that left Beef. Beef and I weren't as close as we used to be, but maybe I could get a straight answer out of him anyhow. He was almost a second brother to me, after all. We had a lot of history between us.

Once, when I was a fifth grader, a bigger boy at school told me to move. When I didn't jump to it, he elbowed me in the face and barked, *"Move!"*

Beef found me huddled on the side of the playground with Gwennie, holding a scratchy brown paper towel to my bloody nose.

"Who did it?" he said, his face darkening, and before recess was over, that bigger boy knew never to bother me again.

Another time Beef came over to see Christian and found me crying at the kitchen table.

"Uh . . . what's wrong?" he asked with all the finesse of a farmer in a fancy ladies clothing store. He'd gotten a new buzz cut, and I remember thinking he looked like a baby chick, all scalp and fuzz.

I swallowed and waved my hand to indicate my book, lying facedown on the table. It was *To Kill a Mockingbird.* I'd just finished the chapter where Scout finally meets Boo Radley, who she always thought was scary, but who turned out not to be.

Turned out, he was just scared to death of the world. Even so, he put his life on the line and saved Scout from a *truly* bad and scary man. Afterward, Scout's daddy said to Boo, "Thank you for my children." It killed me every time.

"Just a sad part," I told Beef. "I'm okay."

"Haven't you already read that book?" he said.

"Only a couple hundred times."

"Do you *cry* every time?"

I sniffle-laughed, seeing how he might not understand that sometimes it was good to cry.

He squinted, unsure what to do. He wanted to go shoot things with my brother, but because he was Beef, he didn't feel right about leaving me behind when I was all weepy. "Well . . . wanna rub my head?"

I laughed again. I loved rubbing his freshly mowed head. He knelt on one knee before me, and I moved my palm over his bitsy chick fuzz. Sure enough, it stemmed my tears.

I'd grown up with Beef. I could trust what he told me, and—a big bonus—I could be in the same room as him without wanting to shrivel up and die. But mainly, I needed to get up off my butt and *do* something. Anything.

I'd made a promise—to Patrick, to Mama Sweetie, and to God—and I was going to keep it.

7

AFTER BREAKFAST, I BIKED TO BEEF'S HOUSE.
His dad, Roy, answered the door.

"Well, well," he said. "Look what the dog drug in."

He thought that was funny, but then, he thought most
everything he said was funny—or smart, or clever. He
considered himself to be a pretty big deal, and most of Black
Creek agreed. He wasn't rich like Tommy Lawson's daddy, but
Roy Pierson was the wrestling coach at the high school, and he
was good at it. Beef was the star of the team until he dropped
out.

"Is Beef here?" I asked.

Roy stretched, his shirt hiking up to reveal his abs. His long
hair was in a ponytail, and his frame was lean and mean, though

on the smallish side for a man. Beef was built the same way, but Beef was a good guy, and goodness, rather than meanness, shone through him.

"You wanna see Beef, do ya?" he said, leaning against the door frame. "Whatcha wanna see that sack of shit for?"

I stood my ground.

"Aw, I'm kidding ya." He nudged my shoulder, making me rock back. "What's a fella gotta do to make you smile, dumplin'?"

"I was just wondering if Beef was here," I repeated.

Gwennie, Beef's little sister, appeared behind her daddy, peeking at me from under his propped up arm. Gwennie and I used to spend a lot of time together, and she told me things about how her daddy treated her. Nothing sick, just lots of yelling and hitting and cruel remarks. Just one more reason I didn't think Roy was "cool," like most of Beef's and Gwennie's friends did.

"Cat," Gwennie said from behind her daddy. She was surprised to see me. "What are you doing here?"

The sight of her made a pit open in my heart.

"Hey, Gwennie," I said. Her dishwater hair was shot through with blond and done up in an attempt at fancy. Half of it was falling down, framing her round face. "I like your hair. When'd you do the streaks?"

"'Bout two weeks ago. I used Sun In. You like it, for real?"

Roy grew bored and dropped his arm, making Gwennie have to duck to avoid being whacked. "I'll leave you girls to your girl talk," he said. "I've gotta see a man about a horse."

He moved past me in a way that required I step back. He sauntered to his truck, hopped in, and cranked the engine. He reversed out of the yard and onto the road, roaring away in a cloud of dust.

"He means get more beer," Gwennie said. She stepped aside. "Come on in."

I did, and it brought back memories. Same old linoleum on the floor. Same pictures hanging in the living room. The kitchen, where Gwennie led me, still smelled of bacon, even. Their kitchen always smelled like bacon.

"What's going on?" she said.

"Oh, you know," I said. "Nothing, really."

The lie felt awkward, because Gwennie and I used to be close, even though we were a grade apart and even though she was kind of not so bright. I didn't say that to be cruel. God gave everyone different gifts, that was all, and hers wasn't brain smarts. Something I learned from Gwennie was that being smart wasn't the only quality that mattered in a friend.

Anyway, we used to hang out in youth group and stuff. It was easy to make her giggle, and being around her was just . . . nice. She looked up to me. Then, in the summer after eighth grade, I dropped her cold, just like I dropped the rest of my friends.

"Is Beef here?" I asked.

"Nah, I don't know where he is." She opened the refrigerator and pulled out a plastic pitcher. "You thirsty? I just made some Crystal Light. Want some?"

"Um . . . sure," I said, taking a seat at the table.

She brought me a glass of bright yellow lemonade so fakely sweet it made my teeth hurt. She plopped down beside me, and before I even swallowed, she dove straight into talking about Patrick. She said how awful it was, just *awful*, and a lump rose in my throat. Unlike the Crystal Light, her reaction wasn't one bit artificial.

Most people were shocked and upset about Patrick's attack, but also excited, the way people got excited when they saw a car wreck, and the bloodier the better. But Gwennie had a big heart, same as Beef, despite being raised by her full-of-himself daddy and her hardly-ever-home mother, who was a nanny to some rich kids in Asheville.

She also had a big body. She'd grown *a lot* since we were thirteen. Unlike Beef, she'd always been plump, but now she had to angle her chair out from the kitchen table to make room for her thighs. Her breasts were big, too, and her upper arms puffed out of her tank top like marshmallows. I felt bad, knowing the sort of comments Roy surely made about her weight.

She was doing something about it, though. She told me so after we'd said all there was to say about Patrick. She wiped her eyes, blinked a few times, and pushed a fresh smile onto her round face.

"Guess what?" she said. "I've gone on a new diet, and it's awesome. I think it's really going to work. It's actually more of a *lifestyle approach*. Can you tell?"

Fondness made my lips curve up. A "lifestyle approach."

She must have read the phrase in one of those magazine articles saying only eat grapefruit or only eat steak or don't eat anything at all, just drink diet lemonade all day long.

"Um, yeah," I said. "You look pretty, especially your hair."

"*You* look pretty," she said wistfully. "Gosh, I wish I had your figure. And eyes. And pretty much every single thing about you." She giggled. "Wanna trade?"

"Ha-ha," I said, pretending she was teasing. "How does the new diet work?"

She told me about it, enthusiasm animating her features. She *was* a pretty girl underneath her extra pounds.

". . .which means that in three months I'll have dropped two full sizes," she marveled. "Can you imagine? And then, once I've gone down another couple of sizes, well . . ."

Instead of finishing her sentence, she blushed. A heavy-duty, this-is-serious blush.

"Omigosh," I said, catching on. I shoved her shoulder. "Gwennie, you man-eater. Are you seeing someone?"

"No," she said giddily. She tried to stop smiling, but couldn't.

"Who is it? You know you have to tell me."

She shook her head.

"Gwennie."

She shook her head more, still beaming.

"*Gwenn*-ie," I sang.

"Hush," she said. "And don't you say a word. Promise?"

I lifted my eyebrows and didn't, just for the pleasure of teasing her.

"I'm *serious*, Cat," she said. "You can't tell a *soul*, especially with him laid up in the hospital and everyone and their mama already gabbing about him. Okay?"

My eyebrows came back down as I tried to put together the meaning of what she'd said.

She realized her goof a moment too late. "Never mind," she said quickly. "I didn't just say that. Nobody's gabbing about no one."

I half-smiled, because it was so *Gwennie* to think she could rewind the tape and erase her part of the conversation. Then the humor of the situation dribbled away. Gwennie had a crush on Patrick? How could Gwennie have a crush on *Patrick*?

He was crushworthy for sure, with his green eyes and light brown hair. He was the sweetest boy in all of Black Creek, and probably all of North Carolina. But he wasn't just laid up in the hospital. He was gay.

I didn't know what to say. Patrick and Gwennie would never be a couple. But what would be gained by telling her that?

When she was younger, maybe six, she and Beef came over for dinner along with their daddy. Afterward, we kids went outside while Aunt Tildy did the dishes and Roy and my daddy had a drink. Beef showed off his new .22 to Christian, and Gwennie and I chased after the tree frogs that come out at dusk. She caught one, and she was so happy she squealed. Then it peed on her, and she dropped it. When she lunged for it, she stepped right on it. *Squish.*

"Come on, Gwennie," Beef pleaded when she wouldn't stop

crying and wouldn't stop crying. He threw an anxious glance at our house. If Roy heard Gwennie fussing, Beef would be blamed for not taking care of his sister, and later he'd get a beating.

Gwennie bawled. She scooped up the dead frog and tried to poke it back into shape, until Beef, losing his patience, slapped it out of her hands.

"You killed it, so quit. You can't bring it back to life."

I remembered how Christian came over and put his arm around her. He was in the fourth grade and knew stuff. He had yet to lose the title of best big brother in the world.

"It's in heaven now," he told Gwennie. "If you stop crying, I'll bury it, and then I'll catch a new one for you."

Gwennie went from wailing to sniffling, from sniffling to a few last gulping swallows.

Later, when we gathered on the front porch for dessert, I peeked at Gwennie to see how she was doing. Well, she was gobbling down her slice of Aunt Tildy's homemade pound cake without a care in the world. Not only that, but she was sitting on the floor in front of *my* daddy, leaning against his legs. Her own daddy was one chair away, but she'd taken mine.

"That's some cake, huh?" my daddy said, watching her eat. "We need to get you to the state fair this summer. Sign you up for the pie-eating contest—what do you think of that?"

He said it nice. She giggled.

"Aw, she knows how to pack in the food, all right," Roy said. "Shoulda named her Patty. Fatty Patty."

"She knows good eating, that's all," my daddy said. He rumpled her hair. "Ain't that right, Miss Gwennie?"

It should have been my hair he was playing with, not hers.

I used my pious voice to say, "Well, I'm just glad you're feeling better, Gwennie."

"Huh?" she said.

"About that frog you killed. That poor itty-bitty frog."

Christian kicked me.

Aunt Tildy said, "What's that?"

"Nothing," Christian said.

But Gwennie, she drew her eyebrows together and said, "What frog?" and I have forever after been amazed at how Gwennie erased that dead frog right out of her mind.

Except, did she really? Maybe she was just very, very good at burying things that were ugly. Not that I'd know a thing about that *lifestyle approach*.

I downed the last of my fluorescent yellow lemonade and studied my once-upon-a-time-friend, who was lonely and fat and had a crush on a boy impossibly out of reach. And yet, he'd defended her at the Come 'n' Go, when those college boys called her a fag hag.

"Why are you looking at me like that?" she said.

I didn't know I was. I cleared my expression and moved my hand to hers. It was as if I was watching a movie, only I was the one on the screen. I wondered how long it had been since she'd been touched, not counting being smacked around by her daddy.

64

"Being backhanded, that's the worst," she once told me. She confided in me a lot back when we were kids. I suspected she'd confide in me again, if she had anything to confide.

"You have pretty hands," I said. She did, too. Pale and soft and pretty, nothing bad about them at all. "I wish I had pretty hands."

"You do," she said. "You need a manicure, is all. You want me to give you one right now? Hold on."

She got to her feet, left the kitchen, and returned with a plastic purse filled with polishes and lotions and those thingies you put between your toes to keep them separated.

"Give me your hand," she commanded.

I gave her my hand. She got to work, and it was just one girl painting another girl's nails. Except it was more than that, too.

I told her about running into Tommy at church. I mentioned how he was out with Patrick on the night Patrick got beat up, along with Beef and my brother and some others. I asked if she knew that already, and she said yeah. I asked how late they stayed out. She said she didn't know about the others, but that Beef stayed out *real* late.

"Like, when did he get in?" I said. It felt nice, the way she was rubbing circles into my skin. The lotion smelled like coconut.

"Dunno. I was asleep. But Beef's always out late."

"I wish he hadn't dropped out of school," I said.

"You and me both," Gwennie said.

Beef didn't like school, but he studied enough to get by. He was *this close* to a high school diploma, with a wrestling scholarship to Appalachian State waiting in the wings, when he blew out his knee in a meet and threw it all away.

"I just wish . . . gosh, so *many* things," Gwennie said. "I wish he hadn't dropped out school. I wish his knee didn't get hurt. I wish he'd let me go out with him and the others last week."

The misery in her eyes told me what she was thinking. Like me, she wondered if she could have stopped the bad stuff from happening if she'd been there.

"But Beef wouldn't let me," Gwennie said. "He *never* lets me hang out with him and his friends anymore."

"Christian doesn't like me hanging around, either," I offered.

"But you like being alone. I don't."

I opened my mouth, then shut it, unsure where the truth lay. I didn't like being alone. Being alone was slightly better than having to deal with people, that's all. Or so I'd convinced myself.

"Beef hates it here," Gwennie said. "Hates everything. He used to be fun, but now he's like . . ." She lifted her shoulders. "He's not the same as he used to be."

Gwennie stopped rubbing my hand, though she didn't let it go. "Patrick tried to help him. Tried to remind him of the bright side of things, you know?"

"That's Patrick," I agreed.

Her features softened, and I realized she had it bad for Patrick. She *pined* for him—an old-fashioned word, but the right one. It was as if the ache of it pulled her away from me, leaving her . . . where?

Some place as dreamy and flimsy as a cloud.

"He's such a good person," she said earnestly. "He was always here at the house, talking to Beef and trying to get him out of his depression. But sometimes? When Beef wasn't here? Patrick would stay anyway, and me and him would just talk and talk."

Talk and talk. I knew about that, although surely it was different when it had been me and Patrick.

"About what?" I said.

"Any old thing. Life. Beef. Me and my new diet." She squeezed my hand. "Oh, Cat. We had ourselves such a time when it was just the two of us. And he felt the same way."

I got a twisty feeling, thinking she was being awfully braggy about it. *Too* braggy. I thought of my daddy patting her when she sat at his feet, and the way she looked at me as he did.

She looked at me the same way now, tilting her head and watching me from under her eyelashes. A hank of hair from the messy side of her updo draped the curve of her cheek and kept going, coiling down over her neck like a rope.

"He knows me better than anyone in the world, just the same as I know him," she stated. Her tone was a private, moist thing. "It's true, Cat. We're soul mates."

Maybe I pressed my lips together. Maybe I pulled away from her, just slightly. Whatever I did, it made her features harden up like that special chocolate sauce you pour on ice cream, where it comes out of the squeeze-bottle velvety smooth and then straight away solidifies into a shell.

She released my hand. "You can't steal him away from me, neither."

"Huh?"

"He's not yours anymore, so you don't get no say over it."

"He never was mine," I said, thinking the exact opposite. He *had* been mine once. I cut that tie, so Gwennie was right that I had no say over him anymore. But there was no way that Gwennie, of all people, could have found the loose thread and latched it to herself.

"You don't believe me," she accused.

I didn't contradict her, and her eyes turned mean.

"You ain't better than me, Cat," she said, spitting the words. "You think you are, but you ain't."

I rubbed the headache spot on my forehead.

She saw that I was weary of her, and she jutted out her chin. "Remember when Patrick came to school wearing those pants?" she said.

Those pants. It was a low blow—and not only that, but Gwennie hadn't even been there. She'd been in middle school still, so anything she knew about *those pants* came to her secondhand.

"You helped him pick them out, didn't you?" she accused. "Y'all went to the Sharing House together and went shopping, just the two of you."

Her tone was poison. Was she mad we hadn't invited her? All these years later, was she jealous of the connection Patrick and I once had?

"I'd hardly call it shopping," I muttered.

"What's that?"

"Nothing." Just, you couldn't call it shopping when it was a charity warehouse where every item was free and came from some rich person's throwaway bag.

"Well, *I* wouldn't have let him get those faggy pants," she declared. "I wouldn't have let him, but you did. I bet you said, 'Oh, Patrick, those pants are hilarious. You *have* to.'"

The voice she used for me was awful: husky and flirtatious. And the word *faggy*? It was so wrong.

"You shouldn't say that," I said.

"Why not? It's true."

"No, I meant . . ." My words dribbled off. I stared at the table for a long time.

"You're right," I said. "I'm not better than you."

She launched right in. "Dang straight. If *I'd* been with him, I'd have helped him pick something handsome. You think your poo don't stink, Cat Robinson, but let me tell *you*—"

She broke off as she replayed my confession. If we were in a cartoon, a fluffy question mark would pop up over her head. She squinted at me. "I'm sorry, *what*?"

"You *are* a good person, Gwennie. Patrick, too. He's lucky to have you for a friend."

"O-oh," she stammered.

I rose from the table. "I should get going. Can I use your bathroom first?"

She nodded, a bobble-head Gwennie doll. "Yeah, sure.

69

Anything you need." Color crept from her neck to her face, a darker red than her giddy crush-blush. "And, um, I'm sorry for being nasty."

"You weren't. It's fine."

"I'm just super stressed," she said. "The diet . . . and Patrick . . ."

"It's fine. Back in a sec, 'kay?"

In the bathroom, which needed cleaning, I peed and washed my hands. Then, leaving the water on, I crouched and opened the cabinet under the sink. I felt around until I found what I was looking for: a box of Tampax Pearl Ultras.

Gwennie got her period when she was eleven, and she made me go with her to buy supplies. If she had something private she wanted to keep safe, like a perfume sample or a pretty stone, she'd hide it among her tampons, knowing Beef and Roy would never find it.

I lifted the cardboard flap of the box. Tampons, tampons, tampons. Rows of little white soldiers. Except—*there.* A slim tube of paper, bound with a pink ponytail holder. Carefully, I slid off the elastic and unrolled the paper.

Good golly, I thought as I took it in. It was a collage of pictures cut from magazines, all of models so skinny they looked like skeletons. Bony rib cages. Sharp and dangerous collarbones. Thighs the size of my forearm, forearms like straws.

Worse were the personal touches Gwennie had added. She'd filled every bit of white space with words and quotes meant to motivate her, I guess.

Thinspiration! she'd printed at the top of the page. And then tips, like, *Freeze your food, it makes it take longer to eat.* Or, *Pinch yourself every time you think about ice cream.* Or, *Take a picture of yourself naked and look at it every day, and don't worry if it makes you throw up. Just be sure to brush your teeth after.*

At the bottom of the page, she'd written, *Think thin. Think Patrick!* And then, in loopy cursive, *Mrs. Patrick's Wife.*

Carefully, I rolled up her "Thinspiration" sheet and tucked it back among the tampons.

My heart, as I closed the cabinet and rose to my feet, was a small dead creature. If I could bury it in the woods, I would.

tuesday

8

ON TUESDAY, I TOOK THE BUS INTO TOOMSBORO so that I could go to the public library. I told myself it was to check for new information on the case, but the truth was that talking to Gwennie had left me shaken. I wasn't ready to confront anyone else just yet. I wasn't ready for any more secrets.

The pants Gwennie threw in my face—"candypants," Tommy dubbed them—*did* come from the Sharing House. Patrick and I had taken this same bus to Toomsboro one afternoon near the end of eighth grade, when Patrick was still my best friend and I still thought life was a sugarcoated delight.

At the Sharing House, Patrick unearthed the pants with a cry of glee, and when I glanced over, I squealed, too. They were insane. They were *awesome*. We'd giggled trying to imagine who donated them in the first place, because in our neck of the woods, orangish red wasn't a color guys wore unless it was a vest for hunting season.

But the pants *were* meant for a man. They weren't ladies' slacks or anything, and when Patrick tried them on, they fit perfectly.

"Do I look sharp?" he asked, stepping out from the makeshift dressing room. He turned sideways and admired himself in the cracked mirror.

"*So* sharp," I told him.

"Like someone from L.A.?" He was always dreaming of L.A., where he could cruise around in a convertible and attend movie premieres.

"Totally." I put my finger to the corner of my mouth and acted confused. "Hold on a cotton-picking minute. *Are* you from L.A.?"

He asked the Sharing House lady to bag the pants up for him, and yes, Gwennie was right. I absolutely encouraged him.

Those pants had nothing to do with what happened to me a few weeks later, however. They were in no way connected to the cruelty I myself experienced at Tommy's hand, but in my mind they would be forever linked.

Patrick, the pants, Tommy. Patrick, Tommy, the pants. Me, sitting on the sofa, reading. Aunt Tildy in the kitchen, making blackberry jam.

Tommy found me alone and he messed with me. He *knew* I

wanted him to stop. He didn't, and he was punished. Aunt Tildy made sure of that.

But guess what? I was punished, too. I punished myself every day of my thirteenth summer, slowly shutting down and putting up walls. I quit my chatterbox ways, and I changed the way I dressed, switching out halter tops for the shapeless T-shirts Aunt Tildy hated. And yes, I dodged Patrick's company, but I dodged everyone. It wasn't yet deliberate. It just . . . happened.

Patrick didn't understand. He thought I was avoiding him on purpose, because of something he did.

Not true. I just didn't know how to explain what was going on inside me. Finally, after I'd shrugged and toed the ground and made too many excuses for not doing this or that with him, he asked me flat-out what was up. He biked over one day in July and knocked on our door, and when I slipped out back to escape, he came around the house and found me.

"*There* you are," he said with a strained smile. He tried to act casual, but his muscles were jumpy. "Want to ride into town and get a milkshake?"

In town, there would be people. In town, I could run into Tommy. My mouth went dry, and I said, "Thanks . . . but nah."

"Why not?" He waggled his eyebrows to be funny. "It'd be my treat."

"It's too hot," I said. "It's too hot to even move."

"Ah, but that's where the milkshake comes in." He stepped closer, and I took a step backward. I didn't mean to. I would have done the same no matter who it was.

"Did I do something?" Patrick said. "Whatever I did, just tell me. And . . . I'm sorry, Cat. I swear."

"Please, just go," I whispered. I couldn't look at him. I couldn't bear it that he was apologizing just in case he'd accidentally hurt my feelings. "You didn't do anything. I'm just tired."

He stood there. He was a person, and my friend, yet what I saw from under my eyelashes was a dark shadow that only made me feel bad. I wanted that shadow gone.

"You're just tired," he repeated.

"Yes, I'm tired." Irritation crept in, or desperation. "Really tired, and I don't want to go on a bike ride. Okay?"

I succeeded in wounding him, but he wasn't one to act needy. That was never his style. "Yeah, whatever," he said, and he took off. I didn't see him again until the first day of ninth grade.

With nothing and no one left to distract me, I spent the rest of that miserable summer going from anger to humiliation to wondering if I had it all wrong. What if Tommy liked me, and he'd just been too much of a boy before I was enough of a girl to handle it? What if he ended up being my boyfriend once I learned the rules of how a girl was supposed to be?

I tried to convince myself that things would be better when school started. I'd be a freshman, taking the bus every day to Toomsboro High School. Tommy, as a junior, would never lower himself to taking the bus, not when he could ride his BMW. He called it his crotch rocket, which I thought was gross, but at least it meant I wouldn't be trapped with him for twenty minutes every morning.

I wouldn't be hanging with Patrick, either. Mama Sweetie liked driving him into town herself.

When the first day of school arrived at last, I was a wreck. I stepped off the bus at the high school—a thousand times bigger than Black Creek's combined elementary and middle schools—and focused on not getting lost, not falling on my butt, and not doing something randomly embarrassing that would identify me as a backwoods hick.

But Tommy was always in the back of my mind.

I saw him before he saw me. He was in the hall, shooting the breeze with a couple of his football buddies. The sight of his broad shoulders and easy slouch made it hard to breathe, and I thought, *Well, and why not just head on to your first class now.*

But I didn't, due to a distraction at the end of the hall. It was Patrick, strolling into the fancy townie high school in his orangish red pants. Surrounded by jeans, jeans, and more jeans, his orange pants were a beacon signifying disaster.

Did he wear those pants on the first day of school for a reason? He must have, because pants like that were a statement. He knew they'd draw attention.

Was it his brazen, goofy way of saying, "Yep, this is me! *Hellooooo,* high school!" Or was he possibly—oh, it hurt—trying to reach out to me? To remind me that we were friends, as in, *Remember how much fun we'd had that day at the Sharing House?*

"Holy Mother of Jesus," Tommy said when he found his voice. His teammates laughed, and he laughed along with them. It was then that he must have felt my stare, or maybe he saw Patrick light up at the sight of me, because he turned, and his eyes met mine, and for a second his cockiness wavered. For a second, my ribs loosened and a small seed of hope took root.

"Cat! Hi!" Patrick said, loping over. The pants were brighter than the flames of a popping, crackling fire. They could have been on fire, they were so bright. Had they been this bright at the Sharing House?

"Patrick," I said weakly. I sensed Tommy approaching, and in my head I said, *Go away, Tommy. There's nothing here to see. Nothing for you to mess with.* I thought of Mama Sweetie, who claimed there was goodness in everything and everyone, and I prayed that was true, because Tommy seemed to be teetering on a taut, slender line, capable of falling in either direction.

Patrick struck a pose, throwing his chin high and flaring his hands out from his body. He was being silly.

"Do I look *fabu*lous?" he asked.

My throat closed. Tommy was right behind him.

"You look like a bonbon," Tommy drawled, making Patrick jump. "Isn't that what those candies are called? The ones that come in all different colors and you suck on 'em?"

Patrick blushed, no doubt from being startled, but also from being caught in a moment of play. Then he recovered, grinning as if Tommy meant no harm. Years of practice had made him a pro at laughing along with the kids who laughed at him.

"Not ex*act*ly what I was going for," Patrick said. "But all right. I can work with that." He turned to me. "What do you think, Cat? Bonbon?"

I stayed mute, because Patrick and I both knew that a bonbon was a chocolate, and not a sour ball or whatever candy Tommy was thinking of. Patrick had turned the joke around, so that the two of us could make fun of Tommy without Tommy realizing it.

My gaze skittered to Tommy. His pupils widened, then contracted, and my stomach dropped.

He knew. *Oh God, he knew.* Not about the bonbon, but that I was Patrick's and not his, regardless of how he'd marked me that day in my living room.

If he had been teetering between good and evil, well, he wasn't anymore.

"Yeah, Cat, what do you think?" Tommy said. His voice chilled me with its river stone smoothness. He leaned closer. "And don't worry. I won't tell."

"Won't tell what?" Patrick said.

I swayed, and in a flash, Patrick closed ranks, placing his hands firmly on my shoulders. He dropped his *everything's cool* posture.

"Cat, what's Tommy talking about?" he said.

I gave the tiniest shake of my head.

Tommy chuckled. He sauntered back to his buddies, and when he reached them, he said something that made them laugh. Then he glanced back at Patrick and called, "That's all right, Candypants. You'll get your turn one day."

There was mud in my gut, thick and suffocating, and I pulled away from Patrick before he could ask any more questions.

All morning long, Tommy and his butt-faced football friends had fun with Patrick's new nickname. "Outta the way, Candypants," they said. And "Stay back, Candypants. My lollipop ain't yours to suck." And "Lose the fag pants, Candypants."

Whenever I was within spitting distance of the hilarity, I caught Tommy watching for my reaction. Maybe he expected me to laugh and worship his cleverness, or at least pretend to. But I couldn't. Fear did that to a person.

So Tommy raised the stakes. He was going to force a response from me no matter what, that was what I now thought. Tommy waited until I was at my locker, which was near the water fountain and the bathrooms, and then he and his friends escorted a protesting Patrick into the boys' room. Too many minutes later, Tommy and his goons emerged, hooting and triumphant. Patrick was no longer with them, but *those pants* were.

I never learned exactly what happened in the bathroom, but I knew it was awful. How could it not be, having three guys grunt and struggle as they pulled your pants off? But I never heard the details, because that was the day Patrick and me pretty much stopped being friends.

The candy-colored pants ended up in a Dumpster, way down. That I did know, because I was the one who put them there. In the hall, Tommy tossed Patrick's pants to me with a wink, and I panicked. I didn't push through the crowd and return them to Patrick, and I didn't seek out Beef or Christian, who would have done it for me. Instead, I turned from Patrick's pain. I fled.

Patrick hid half-naked in the boys' room for half an hour until a teacher got wind of it and rustled up a pair of gym shorts. He went home early, but he was back the next day. If he knew *I'd* thrown those pants away, he never said. In fact, he did his best to act as if everything was fine between us, even though it clearly wasn't.

Now Patrick was in a coma, and I was partly to blame, because by turning a blind eye in high school, I'd said, *Go on and hurt him. I don't care.* And by doing that, I'd opened the door to more hurt, because when a person did something wrong and got away with it, he tended to do it again. He upped the stakes. He pushed harder and further, until finally, if no one stopped him . . .

I felt sucker-punched. It wasn't God's fault Patrick had been treated worse than dirt, as I'd let myself believe. It was mine.

9

WHEN THE BUS ROLLED TO MY STOP, I HAD TO
peel myself off the seat, and, once standing, I stumbled like a
drunk to the door. Outside, I blinked in the bright light. I had
a four-block walk ahead of me to get to the library, but that
was good. That meant I had to *move,* and moving would surely
clear the roaring from my head.

I'd read that when surfers were felled by a big wave, the
water pummeled them until they no longer knew up from
down. That was how I felt as I walked along Main Street. I knew
I had to fight my way to the surface; it was just that every cell
in my body was drowning in self-loathing.

But walking got me there. It got me out of my head, and it
got me to the library, sweaty and hot, but back in breathable

air. My feet hurt, however, because I made the mistake of wearing my silver plastic flip-flops with little jewels in the straps. The humidity made the straps rub wrong against the soft flesh above my insteps.

If I'd been in Black Creek, I'd have taken off my flip-flops and gone barefoot. But here in Toomsboro, I felt self-conscious enough already, even with shoes on. I worried that people would look at me and see a hick. Or, as the townies said, a hill girl.

But guess what? If I ever had to go up against a tender-footed townie in a glass-walking contest, I'd be the one who emerged unscathed.

These were the thoughts I distracted myself with as I stepped into the cool, air-conditioned building. When I grew up, my house was going to have air-conditioning, and I was going to crank it down so low I'd have to throw a sweater around my shoulders even in the summer.

Miz Hetty, the librarian, looked up from the reference desk. She was wearing a cute little cardigan over her blouse, and I thought, *See? Like that.*

"Hey, Miz Hetty," I said.

"Well, hey there, Cat," she said. A worry line formed in her brow. "How *are* you, honey?"

Because of Patrick, she meant. Because he and I were both from Black Creek.

"I don't know," I said uncomfortably. "I mean . . . well . . . I sure wish they'd find whoever hurt him."

"I do, too," she said. "More than that, I wish he'd come on out of that coma. I've been praying for him."

I drew my thumbnail to my mouth. I appreciated her concern, but I wished she'd go on and finish up.

She must have seen this, because she arranged her features to tuck away her sadness. "You here for a fresh book?"

"Naw," I said. "Maybe later, but first I think I'll use the Internet some."

I claimed a seat at the row of computers. The guy next to me glanced up, frowned as if I smelled bad, and went back to his typing.

My heart beat faster, because this was my constant fear ever since my freshman year of high school: that in town, I'd stand out as the outsider I was. That people would laugh—or frown. But I was almost 100 percent sure that I did *not* smell bad, because I'd put on deodorant this morning, like I always did.

Discreetly, I sniffed myself. I detected nothing but the baby powder smell of my Suave 24 Hour Protection. Was there something else about me? Something that marked me as *less than*?

A sidelong glance at the guy next to me didn't help. He obviously did belong, and he bore the distinction with a disregard I'd never possess. He was wearing a plaid button-down over a white T-shirt, the standard attire of college boys. He looked a couple of years older than me, so he probably went to Toomsboro Community College.

He might have even stopped at the Come 'n' Go a couple of times. For all I knew, he might have heckled Patrick. He might have heckled Gwennie. He sure seemed comfortable in the role of making others—that would be me—feel inferior.

Whatever. I tried to put him out of my mind. I typed in Patrick's name and pulled up everything I could, but most of it was old news, and what wasn't old news was basically nonnews.

The guy beside me, whom I was supposed to be ignoring, made a fist and banged it on the table. He wasn't having any better luck with what he was doing, apparently. I snuck a second peek at him, and his head whipped toward me.

"What are *you* staring at?" he said. He reached forward and angled his computer screen so I couldn't see it, not that I was attempting to.

I focused on my own computer, embarrassment rolling off me in waves. I could feel that I was blushing, and it made the helplessness I'd felt on the bus rise back up. I breathed faster, *not* thinking about Tommy and *not* thinking about those pants. Not thinking about them so fiercely that the memories sucked me back under, since that was what happened when you struggled against something as grasping and insubstantial as water.

I blinked at my computer screen. I tried a new search, this time on the term *epidural bleeding.*

College Boy exhaled. *"Shit,"* he said, making me flinch.

His presence made me nervous, which, when I thought about it, made me indignant. He was being rude. He was acting like he owned the place, and he was keeping others from doing their work.

"Shit, shit, *shit,*" he cursed under his breath.

Blood rushed so loudly I could hear it in my head. I *wasn't* worth less than this spoiled college boy who threw a hissy when he couldn't make the computer bend to his will. More than that, I couldn't live my entire life letting guys intimidate me just because they were bastards used to getting their own way. I just couldn't.

"Excuse me," I said, my voice wavering, "but this is a public library. Could you be a little quieter?"

College Boy's jaw dropped open. He seemed astounded that I'd dared to go up against him.

"Uh, I *could,* or you could stay the hell out of my business," he said. "You don't even . . . you don't *even* . . ." He floundered, but he was clearly worked up.

"I don't even what?" I said. He didn't know me from Eve, and yet he was acting like he *hated* me. Did he have a problem with people in general, or was his problem just with *me?* "I'm just asking you—nicely—to watch your language." My voice squeaked despite my best intentions. "Like I said, it's a public library. It's for everyone."

"Screw you," he said, shoving back his chair and stalking off. I let out my breath, which I hadn't realized I'd been holding. But then—*crap*—he turned and came back. He stopped at my side. My heart rate zoomed. I could sense him glaring at me, but I was too afraid to look at him.

"Where do you get off being so self-righteous?" he said. He kept his voice low, but it was laced with scorn. "I'm serious. What makes you think you can go around judging people?"

He thought *I* was judging *him*? I mean, maybe I was, but *he* started it. Now I just wanted it to end, because this whole interaction had taken a strange and very freaky turn.

"I asked you a question," he said. "Are you going to answer it?"

I kept my eyes on the table. My chest rose and fell.

"Yeah," he said, as if I'd confirmed something. "I love it when small-minded people can defend their positions. Oh, and I'm sorry you don't like the words I use, because I have a special one just for you." He leaned in close and whispered something in my ear that made my blood freeze.

I stayed immobile as he stomped off, terrified someone had heard. Then, with a *whoosh,* the frozen blood inside me flared to life. I felt hot and cold at the same time.

That college boy—that piss-dumb, psycho college boy—he called me a *mountain nigger,* a term used in the rare occasions when *hill people* or *white trash* wasn't good enough. He said it to shame me, and it did. It slammed me down on the rough grit of my shortcomings and held me there. *I was trash,* my heart said, each beat driving me deeper. *I was worthless. No good. I'd been put to the test, and I failed, so I deserved to be called bad names.*

My eyes welled up, which made things worse, as the jerk had yet to leave the library. He'd just gone over to the periodicals section, where he was reading a magazine. If he glanced my way, he'd think I was crying because of him. Which I was, but I wished I wasn't, just like I wished he'd get the heck out of *my* library. Anyway, I knew he wasn't actually reading that stupid magazine. I knew he was pretending, because he was flipping the pages way too fast to glean any meaning from them.

Fury slid in beside my shame, and I opened myself wide to it. I told myself that College Boy had no idea how good he had it. He probably owned his own computer, or had one at the college he could use. So for real, why *was* he here? He belonged here less than I did. And just because he didn't drive a pickup and shoot deer out of season, did that make him better than me? Just because he had a daddy with a job and a mama who was still alive?

I gripped the edge of the table, very much aware of the transformation taking place inside me. My humiliation had turned to rage, and that was good. But it would take longer still for it to shift into something I could control. Something I could fight back with, not for the sake of my own piddling honor, but for something bigger.

I'd been put to the test with *those pants,* and I failed. But look: I'd been given a second chance. It didn't matter if it was just symbolic. It didn't matter that nobody would know but me. A second chance was a second chance, and I wasn't about to let it get away.

I inhaled through my nose, deliberately searching for a spot above my rage. I knew such a spot existed, because

Mama Sweetie had taught Patrick and me about handling bad emotions. If you breathed deep and set your mind to it, you could rise *above* your anger.

One time, Mama Sweetie drove me and Patrick into Toomsboro for root beer floats, a treat she splurged on maybe once a summer. On Main Street, a man in a Lexus made a left turn without looking, and he would have taken us out if Mama Sweetie hadn't slammed on the brakes.

"Sweet Jesus," she said, breathing hard. "You kids all right?"

We were fine, but the driver who cut us off was fit to be tied. He was the one who screwed up, and yet he laid on his horn, leaned out his window, and yelled, "Learn to drive, you fat bitch!"

To *Mama Sweetie,* he said this!

Patrick and I were only ten, but it made us fume. "Honk back!" we said. "Go call *him* a name, or tell the police on him!"

She didn't. She pulled into a parking space on the side of the road, put her hand to her chest, and sat for a bit. Then she said that the man already knew he was the one in the wrong, and being wrong had embarrassed him. Since he didn't like feeling that way, he unloaded his bad feelings onto her.

"Huh?" we'd said.

"Yes, that man acted ugly," she told us in plain English. "But throwing more ugliness back at him ain't the answer."

As a ten-year-old, I didn't get it. "Still think you should tell the police on him," I'd muttered.

I took something more useful out of Mama Sweetie's lesson

now, even if it wasn't what she'd set out to teach. If I was patient, if I waited until I'd harnessed my emotions, then I might just manage to shame that college boy even worse than he'd shamed me.

I studied him with the detachment I'd use if I was regarding a pile of deer droppings. He was handsome enough, or would have been if he hadn't called me what he called me. He was tan, and he had strong forearms under the rolled-up sleeves of his plaid shirt, which he wore unbuttoned over his white T-shirt. His cargo pants fit the right way, and unlike the guys in Black Creek, he didn't feel the need to let them hang off his butt. Instead of boots or sneakers, he wore flip-flops, which Tommy would have called gay.

I was fairly sure this guy wasn't, though. Gay.

He caught me staring, and this time I didn't look away. His mouth twitched nervously.

That's right, I thought. *You* should *be nervous.*

I smiled, and College Boy increased the distance between us, moving from the magazine display to the *manga* rack. I knew then that I'd shoved my shame down deep enough that I could function without bursting into tears. I knew, too, that he wished he hadn't gone off on me. I could read it in his face. But too bad.

I went over to him. My heart pounded.

"You owe me an apology," I informed him.

"What?" he said, startled.

"I *said* you owe me an apology." I flicked my hair out of my

91

eyes, which were a tawny brown like my mother's. They gave people pause if they got a good look at them, and College Boy got a good look at them now. "For what you called me."

"I don't know what you're talking about," College Boy said. Gone was his attitude, whatever that had been about, and in its place was . . . I wasn't sure what. Remorse?

It threw me off balance, but only for a moment.

"Let me refresh your memory," I said, putting my hands on my hips. "You called me a *mountain nigger*. Now do you remember?"

Heads turned in our direction. Lots of heads, all with shocked expressions. A young mother over by the picture books grabbed her toddler and hustled him away.

Aware of our audience, I held out my arm and twisted it to show both sides. "I'm actually white, but I guess you're too stupid to notice?"

College Boy turned as red as the tomatoes in my garden. "W-wait," he stammered. "No. I just . . ." His eyes darted from one glaring patron to another. "I never said that."

"You never called me a *mountain nigger*?" I said, making the library patrons bristle again. Every one of them was as white as I was, because there just weren't any black people in Toomsboro. But for the most part, these were educated townies, and they didn't like that word any more than I did.

"Um, yeah, you did," I said. "It was after I asked you not to cuss at the computer table, and you got mad and told me to mind my own business."

"What? I didn't—"

"And then you said you had one special word just for me," I went on, wanting the people to hear me and not him. "Is it coming back to you? How you leaned down and called me a . . ."

I broke off, because the little hairs on my arms were telling me I'd pressed my luck far enough. Plus, Miz Hetty was out from behind her desk and striding over.

I swallowed. "Well, I'm not going to say it," I said, even though I already had. Twice. "But actually, it was *two* words. You really are stupid, aren't you?"

College Boy looked scared. I thought, *Ha. See how it feels?* Only it gave me less pleasure than I'd expected.

Miz Hetty reached us, and College Boy's throat worked. He grabbed a graphic novel from the rack and held it in front of him, as if it would protect him. *Fruit Basket*, it was called.

"Cat?" Miz Hetty said.

All at once, I wondered what I was doing. I hoped Mama Sweetie wasn't watching from heaven, because I knew she'd be disappointed.

I covered my face with my hands. My adrenaline drained out of me, and I was just a girl, and it was time to stop. Guys like Tommy, guys like the idiot college boy I'd been so busy humiliating, they did whatever they wanted. I knew that. They said nasty things, and they hurt people, and they never stopped.

But I didn't want to be like them. I wanted to be like Mama Sweetie.

I dropped my hands. Every single person in the library was staring, and my need for vengeance just . . . died.

"*Cat,*" Miz Hetty repeated.

I looked at the college boy, who'd gone pale beneath his tan. I clenched my hands to still their trembling.

"You are what you are, and I am what I am," I said. "And maybe I *am* a hillbilly or a hick or whatever, but I would never use the word you said. Not if a person was white *or* black."

My voice shook just as it did when I first addressed him. This time he didn't smirk.

"I think you should leave," Miz Hetty told him.

The college boy looked at me. His lips parted, and he struggled for words. "Listen," he said. "I, um . . . I really didn't . . ."

"I think you should leave *now,*" Miz Hetty said.

He nodded, defeated. He returned the graphic novel carefully to its rack and walked out of the library. I watched him the whole way, confused by what I was feeling. He didn't look back.

I left not long after, and on the bus ride home, I wondered at what I'd done. It was almost as if a different person had taken over my body—except, was saying that a cop-out? I hadn't been "possessed," after all. Not by an angel or a demon. Maybe there were aspects of both inside me, but *I* was the one who chose which to let out.

I truly *was* a different person now than when I was a kid, however. When I was a kid, I was curious and fearless, and the two qualities were twined together like ivy. I drove Aunt Tildy crazy with "all that wildness," as she put it, and in the summer, when I didn't have school to keep me out of her hair, she would shoo me out of the house as soon as my chores were done. She forbade me to come back till she called Christian and me in for dinner.

But what if I stepped on a rattlesnake? I'd asked. What if a dog bit me, and it had rabies and was foaming from the mouth? What if I saw a baby floating down the creek in a basket made of woven reeds, like little baby Moses?

"No," she said to all of those. "You can only come in the house if you're bleeding, and I'm not talking about a scratch from picking blackberries. If you come bothering me, you better have a whole cup full of blood. And now that I'm thinking about it, if you're bleeding that much, don't you *dare* come in the house. Just stay on the porch and holler for me."

Mama Sweetie, on the other hand, gave me another way to look at myself. She said God had blessed me with an abundance of spirit, and not to ever squash it down. She said there was goodness in everything and everyone, and that it was our job to let that goodness shine out.

"A person does on occasion lose his way," she warned Patrick and me. "We all have our trials. But I'm gonna tell y'all something, something I want you to remember. Can y'all do that for Mama Sweetie?"

"Yes, ma'am," we chorused, giggling and making eyes at each other.

She knew she was being teased, but she didn't mind. She wagged her finger and said, "God loves you even on your blackest days, and He will always, *always* be there to guide you home. All you have to do is look for the light of His love. As long as you remember that one thing, why, then you can cast off the darkness and shine again, can't you?"

I used to believe her. Then, for a while, I stopped. I guess I lost my way.

I wasn't sure I'd found it again, as I hadn't acted . . . exactly . . . shiny at the library. Yes, I was right to defend myself, but I'd gone too far.

Even so, I was proud of myself for taking action at all. I didn't hide or run away or pretend the ugliness didn't happen. I stood up and said something that was true. I said it out loud, and by doing so, I was standing up for lots of people, not just me.

I wondered—and again, I wasn't sure—but I wondered if a bit of God's light was maybe back inside me. If so, it was a dove that might at any moment fly away. But for now, here it was: soft and wondrous in the branches of my soul.

wednesday

10

TEN DAYS HAD GONE BY SINCE PATRICK WAS
attacked, and the police were no closer to finding Patrick's
assailant than when they started. When I was at the library,
I read on the Internet that the North Carolina Bureau of
Investigation had been brought in, since it was a case of "ethnic
intimidation." I didn't see how it was ethnic, as Patrick was gay,
not black or Hispanic or whatever. But because Patrick was
gay, that made the attack against him a hate crime. I gathered
that was the bigger point.

A reporter from Toomsboro interviewed Sheriff Doyle about
the NCBI's involvement, and Sheriff Doyle said it was because
ethnic intimidation cases got more attention than regular old
beatings.

Those were his exact words, by the way. As if "regular" beatings happened all the time.

In the article, Sheriff Doyle also reported that the pump nozzle was wiped clean of fingerprints, the handwriting analysis of the message scrawled on Patrick's chest showed nothing, and that the weapon Patrick was hit with seemed to be a baseball bat, same as they first determined. Baseball bats didn't leave many traces for the forensics team to go after. All paths led to dead ends, according to Sheriff Doyle.

But there was one path the sheriff hadn't gone down, and I reckoned I knew why. I reckoned it would be tricky to bring Tommy Lawson in for questioning while at the same time bowing and scraping to Tommy's daddy, who funded Sheriff Doyle's election campaign. There was surely no conflict of interest in Sheriff Doyle questioning Tommy now, was there?

The *thought* of questioning Tommy myself made me feel sick. There was someone I could question about Tommy, however. Destiny Cooper. Destiny dated Tommy for two years, meaning that for two years she'd been one of the girl members of the redneck posse.

She and Tommy only broke up this past April, and for all I knew they were still in touch, so I hoped she might have some dirt on him and would welcome the chance to vent.

Since I had no legitimate reason to go to Destiny's, I tried to think of a cover. The best I could come up with was that I was collecting donations for UNICEF, like we did on Halloween when we were kids.

Destiny was surprised to see me, to put it mildly. Her eyes opened so wide I could see each and every fleck of mascara on her lashes. Then her expression turned guarded.

"What do *you* want?" she said, holding tight to the doorknob. Behind her, I saw dark colors, low ceilings, and stacks and stacks of all sorts of things, from sewing patterns to old newspapers to sloppily folded clothes.

And hi to you, too, I thought. "I'm, um, here to see if you—"

"Nuh-uh, no way," she said, with a *talk-to-the-hand* gesture. "Whatever you're selling, I don't want it. Whatever you're collecting for, I ain't giving. So bye-bye."

She started to shut the door. I jammed my foot inside.

"Destiny. I'm not selling anything. I just thought it would be nice to come over and say hey."

"Is that so," she said dryly. It wasn't a question. It was her way of saying, *Oh sure, and next you're going to pull out a check the size of a billboard and tell me I've won the lottery.*

"Fine. I want to talk about Tommy," I admitted.

"Girl, that boy's nothing but a hot mess. What're you interested in him for?"

"I'm not," I said. "I know full well that Tommy's a jerk. *That's* what I want to talk about."

"Oh," she said. She pooched out her bottom lip, which was red and shiny with lip gloss. "Well, come on then."

She led me into the living room, where we sat on an overstuffed mauve sofa. I could smell cat pee on it, or maybe the odor came from the carpet, which was filthy. Rubbed-out cigarette butts had streaked entire areas gray. Destiny's parents weren't home, and she told me she was leaving to meet up with friends in just a bit.

"So make it quick," she said.

I opened my mouth. Then closed it. Then said, "I don't like Tommy."

Destiny looked at me as if to say, *Really? That's all you've got?* She stifled a yawn. Her fingernails were hot pink.

"But you know him better than I do," I said. "So I'm curious what your thoughts are."

"On what?" she said. "On how Tommy and all his kin think they're God's gift to creation, and the rest of us are just using up air?"

I appreciated the sentiment, especially coming from her. In her miniskirt and tight pink T-shirt, she was as different from the Lawsons as she could be. Her blond hair was teased and big, and pink cowboy boots finished the look.

"I hear you," I said. "But, I was actually talking more about the hate crime."

She cocked her head. Her left earring, long and sparkly with multiple strands of cut crystals, got caught in her hair.

"What happened to Patrick?" I prompted.

"Ohhhh," she said. She untangled her earring and adjusted her features to show she was with me. "At the Come 'n' Go. Right. It sure was the talk of the town, wasn't it?"

Was the talk of the town? She was as bad as the easily bored reporters.

"When I heard about it, I was like, for real?" Destiny said. "What kind of monster would do that?"

"Exactly. I'm not saying Tommy had anything to do with it, but—"

"*Whoa,*" she said. "Tommy's a dick, but he ain't that kind of dick."

"I know," I lied. "I *know.* I'm just trying to find out everything I can, because he's a really good friend of mine. Patrick, I mean."

She took my words at face value as far as I could tell. Destiny was two years older than me. She didn't have the slightest interest in my social life, and she certainly didn't keep up with who I did or didn't hang out with.

"What do you want to know?" she said.

"Patrick was with Tommy the night it happened. Tommy and my brother. Some other people, too."

"Like who?"

"Um . . . Dupree, for one."

"Mama's boy," Destiny said scornfully. "Pretends to be Mr. Big Bad Businessman, but he'd wet his pants if his mama found out what he was up to."

"Making sandwiches?" I said. "I'd hardly call him a business-man."

She twitched her lips like I was such a dumb bunny. "If that's what you want to think, go right ahead."

"I don't *want* to think it," I said. "I think it because it's true. Dupree works at Huskers with Beef."

"Day job," she said breezily. Then she switched gears. "I'm

not saying I'd throw him out of my bed or nothing. He's got it going on with that lazy smile and those eyes of his. He ain't the marrying type, that's all I'm saying."

"Ah . . . okay."

"That mama of his — you seen how fat she's gotten? Makes me want to puke. But no woman's ever gonna take the place of Dupree's mama, so don't bother trying."

"You don't have to worry about that," I said.

Destiny laughed. She crossed her legs and said, "Who else?"

I frowned.

"At the party," she said. "The night Patrick was beat up. Ain't that what you want to talk about?"

"Oh. I'm not sure it was a party, exactly. But that was mainly it: Tommy, Dupree, Beef, Christian, and Patrick."

"No girls?"

"Oh yeah. And Bailee-Ann."

She made a face. "Watch out for that one. Little cock tease, that's what she is. Tried to steal Tommy from me back when me and him first got together. You know that?"

"Well, she's with Beef now, so . . . yeah."

"I *know* she's with Beef now. I'm just saying watch out."

"Um, okay," I said. "But back to Tommy. I saw him at church, and guess what? He cussed at me even though his grandmother was standing right there."

"Lord," Destiny said, rolling her eyes. "That woman."

"You don't like her?"

"Does *anyone* like her?"

Good point.

"Ever wonder why the Lawsons stay in this Podunk town when they've got enough money to live anywhere they want?" Destiny asked.

"Why?"

"Because *she* refuses to move, that's why. Tommy's daddy is none too pleased about it, believe me. Like, one time Tommy's daddy decided to take his mother to Asheville for a fancy meal, right?"

I nodded to keep her going.

"Me and Tommy went along. I wore a dress and heels and everything. And afterward, we were going to look at houses. 'Just to see,' Tommy's daddy said." Destiny dropped her voice. "I'm pretty sure Mr. Lawson had a retirement home in mind, so he could get her nice and put away."

"What went wrong?"

"Well," she said. "We got to the restaurant, and they had cloth napkins and special glasses for water and little pats of butter in the shape of seashells."

"Seashells?"

"I know. It was classy. We ordered our meals, but when the waitress brought 'em over, old Mrs. Lawson had a cow."

"What did she do?"

"She was all, *'Where* is my *cornbread?'"*

My lips twitched, because Mrs. Lawson sure did love fussing. As Aunt Tildy said, she'd complain if Jesus Christ came down Himself and handed her a five-dollar bill.

"The waitress said they'd run out of cornbread, but that they had absolutely *delicious* homemade yeast rolls," Destiny said. "But nuh-uh, Mrs. Lawson wouldn't have nothing of it."

"Let me guess. She'd ordered green beans for one of her sides," I filled in. My aunt Tildy followed the rules about what made a proper meal, and she would sooner do a hula dance in her underwear than put a dish of green beans on her table without a cake of cornbread to keep it company.

"'Ronald, I would like to leave,'" Destiny said, adopting Mrs. Lawson's snooty tone. "'*Immediately*, Ronald.'"

Destiny uncrossed her legs and recrossed them the other direction. Her pink cowboy boots caught her attention, and she leaned over and rubbed at a scuff mark.

"These are the wrong shoes, aren't they?" she said.

I felt myself frown. "Uh. . ."

"So wrong," she pronounced, springing up from the couch. "Am I going to a rodeo? *No*."

She headed out of the living room. "So anyway," she called over her shoulder, "the whole ride back, she went on about how she grew up in Black Creek and she'd die in Black Creek. She also mentioned how tacky our waitress was, how the iced tea wasn't sweet enough, and how the air-conditioning was turned up too high, if you can believe that."

Her voice was fading. I could make out the words, but it was strange holding a conversation from different rooms. Were we holding a conversation?

"Hey!" Destiny said, louder. I leaned back against the sofa

and craned my neck to see Destiny standing in the door of what I assumed was her bedroom. She had one hand on each side of the doorframe. When our eyes met, she let go with one hand and made an impatient come-here gesture. "What's the problem? You gonna just sit there?"

"Oh," I said. I hopped up and hurried down the hall. On the way to her room, I passed another room crammed floor to ceiling with plastic bins, cardboard boxes, and wire hangers.

"So that's why she's bound and determined to stay in Black Creek," she said, picking up where we'd left off. "Never mind that even here in Black Creek, she thinks everyone's out to get her. Did I mention that part?"

I was distracted, because unlike the rest of the house, her room was spotless. On top of her chest of drawers was a set of nesting dolls, separated from one another and lined up in order of height. Other than that, there was no clutter.

"I'm sorry?" I said.

"For what?" she said.

"No, I mean . . ." I pushed a stray hair behind my ear. "Why does she think everyone is out to get her? Mrs. Lawson?"

Destiny studied me. She made a *hmmph* sound and turned back to her closet. "Supposedly, checks have gone missing from her mailbox, and she saw a *Dateline* report about how *criminals* can do all sorts of stuff with bank account numbers." The way she said "criminals" made it clear she was mocking Mrs. Lawson's concerns. "Whatever, right?"

"Tommy bought a new mailbox for her," I said. I sat cautiously on the end of Destiny's bed, which was twin-size and pink. I didn't want to mess up the covers. "One she can lock."

Destiny straightened up. A pair of black heels dangled from her index finger. "Well, that was nice of him, I guess. Tommy's not *all* bad." She lifted the shoes. "Yes or no?"

I didn't know. I didn't know about shoes or outfits or makeup, and my stomach clenched up. "Yes?" I ventured.

She looked at the shoes, held out one bare foot, and nodded. "Yeah."

As she slipped a shoe on, hopping to keep from falling, I said, "Do you think anyone really stole from her?"

She slipped the strap of the second shoe over her heel and straightened up. "It happens. Freakin' tweakers, coming out like zombies in the night."

Tweakers, meaning anyone dumb enough to do meth. They were zombielike with their gray teeth and pocked skin, if they let it get that far.

"You thinks *meth heads* have been stealing her checks?" I said.

"Oh, who knows," Destiny said, less a question than a worn-out dismissal. "But it happens, sure. They wash the checks with bleach and then write in their own name on the PAY TO line. Voilà, instant money."

It sounded like she knew a lot about it. As she checked her lipstick in the mirror, my eyes strayed back to the nesting dolls. I wondered who gave them to her. How long she'd had them.

I toyed with a question as she applied a new layer of gloss

over her already bright lips. Finally, I went ahead and asked. "So . . . why did you and Tommy break up?"

She smacked her lips, checked her teeth, and drew back from the mirror. "I'm s'posed to be at Sheldon's," she said, exiting her room.

"Just tell me quick," I said, trailing after her. She was a girl once, too. The dolls said as much. If Tommy had hit her or something, I'd have proof that he liked to hurt people in general, and not just me.

Then I realized where my mind had gone—that I was *hoping* Destiny had gotten beat on—and I'd have done about anything to take the question back.

Destiny didn't seem traumatized, however. Just put-out. "You know Willow?"

"Yeah," I said. Willow got pregnant and had a baby when she was sixteen, same age as I was now. She lived with her boyfriend, and they both liked chasing the dragon, meaning they liked to burn their meth and sniff the wispy white fumes. That's what people said.

"Willow and me used to be friends," Destiny said. She passed through the living room and swooped up her purse from the sofa. She continued on to the front door, but didn't open it. "Then Willow got with Darren, and she had her baby, and you know how that goes."

I didn't, but I could imagine.

"I didn't want to just abandon her, so I went to see her one day. To see the baby."

"That's good. I bet she was real glad."

"No, she was real *high*," Destiny said bitterly. "Dumb girl didn't have no job, and neither did Darren. But I showed up at Darren's apartment, and what do you know? They've got a wide-screen TV and a massage chair, not to mention all kinds of crap for the baby. I was, '*Dang*. Where'd y'all get this stuff?'"

"Were they the ones washing checks?"

"*God*, no," she said, like I'd insulted her. "Washing checks takes a steady hand."

"So where'd the stuff come from? Where'd they get money for it?"

"From Darren. Darren's a runner, but he steps on it sometimes."

"*Steps* on it?" I shook my head. "I don't know what that means."

"It means he mixed the shit with talcum powder, but sold it as pure and kept the profits."

"Oh."

"So one day I went over to get a bump, right?"

"I thought you went to see the baby."

"Yeah, yeah." She looked at me hard. "And just so you know, this was before I got my head straight. I don't do that crap no more."

"Um, okay."

"Well, Tommy got there before I did," she said with a sigh. "I was gonna meet him at Darren's, and we were gonna see the baby, and maybe we'd stay for a while. But by the time I arrived, they'd started without me, and every one of 'em was higher than a Carolina pine. End of story."

"What do you mean, 'end of story'? How is that the end of the story?"

She twisted her mouth. She didn't look happy, but her blond hair was shiny, and she didn't have any burns on her face or picked-at scabs on the insides of her arms. She didn't *look* like a user.

"They thought it'd be funny to pull a gun on me," she said. "They were amped out of their frickin' minds, and Darren, he pointed his pistol at me and said, 'Hands up, bitch. We're gonna have to do a strip search.'"

"What *jerks,*" I said.

"'Jerks,'" she said. "That's one way of putting it."

"Does Tommy use meth?" I asked. Tommy was a lot of things, most of them bad. But a tweaker?

Her eyebrows formed upside-down V's. "Um . . . *yeah.*"

Incredibly, a wave of sadness washed over me. I felt like such an innocent.

"So that's what split y'all apart," I stated.

"*And* that's why I won't let him come over or nothing, even though he says he's clean now." She opened the front door. "Called me up and said he didn't want to date me no more, but he did want to apologize for how bad he treated me. Said he'd gone clean for Jesus."

"That doesn't sound like Tommy."

"Tell me about it. Plus I know how easy it is to fall back into

110

that crap." Her features shifted. I couldn't say how, exactly, but the overall effect was to make my heart hurt for her. "And the way he acted when he was high—he did some crazy stuff. Out-of-his-mind kind of crazy. Afterward he'd feel real bad, and he'd go on about how sorry he was, but . . ."

I waited.

She snapped out of it and stepped through the open door. "So, yeah. That's why we broke up."

I stayed where I was.

"Why'd Darren have a pistol?" I asked. Every boy I knew had a rifle or a shotgun, and usually both. Christian got his first rifle when he was six. He killed his first deer a month later and got his picture in the paper, squatting by the carcass and smiling wide.

But handguns were a different story. Handguns weren't for shooting game; they were for shooting people. Plus, unless the rules had changed, you couldn't own one if you were under twenty-one.

"Comes with the job," Destiny said.

"Huh?"

She sighed. "Okay, I'm not trying to be mean, but how clueless *are* you?"

"Pretty clueless," I admitted.

"Well, it's not hard. You want a gun, you're gonna get yourself a gun. Steal it, buy it from a friend, trade some crank for it. Okay?"

"Okay," I said, still trying to piece it together.

111

"You know Wally? Scumbag who cooks up the meth?"

I nodded, happy to supply the right answer for once.

"He gives all his boys handguns. That's how Darren got his, and I'd guess the same's true for Tommy and Beef and Dupree."

I tried not to show my shock, but I couldn't help it. *"Beef?"* I exclaimed. "And *Dupree?*"

"You didn't know they're Wally's boys?" Destiny asked.

I gazed past her. Sunlight glinted on the hood of her pickup.

"You honestly didn't know," she repeated.

"Is Beef a user?" I said, unable to keep my voice from wavering. Tommy using meth was bad. Anybody using meth was bad, and that went for Destiny, too. But Beef? And if Beef was messed up with that stuff—hopefully he wasn't, but just *if*—what if my brother was, too?

No. Never.

I'd heard a saying about meth, that it took you down one of three roads: jail, the psych ward, or death. No matter how smart or careful or under control you thought you were, if you used meth, you'd end up at one of those destinations.

I knew Beef was in a hard place, what with losing his wrestling scholarship and dropping out of school. But how could he possibly think to himself, *Well, I'll just start slamming meth. That'll put me back on the road to glory.*

"If it makes you feel better, Patrick wanted him out," Destiny said. "I don't know much, but I do know that."

"Wanted him to stop using, or to stop working for Wally?"

"Both?" she said.

I pressed my hands over my face.

"Hey," she said. "It *can* be done. Quitting, I mean. Look at me, I'm living proof."

Yeah, only she was heading out the door in a miniskirt and heels. Her lips were bright red, and I was pretty sure she wasn't heading to Sheldon's to play Scrabble.

"But you still party," I said.

"Of course, just no more hard stuff. I can't luxuriate away my youth, see." She hesitated. "Nobody knows this, but I'm gonna own my own beauty salon one day."

I tried for a smile. "That's cool. You'd be good at that."

"I want to learn how to do them Brazilian perms," she said. "You heard of them? They make your hair super straight without even drying it out."

She took a strand of my hair and ran her thumb and forefinger down the length of it. Her touch was steady. "You wouldn't need one, but for people with that super frizzy hair, it could be life changing."

"Destiny . . ."

"Some people do change, Cat. Not many, but it can be done." She prodded me out the door. "I gotta go. If you ever want your hair cut, let me know."

thursday

11

THIS MORNING, I WENT WITH AUNT TILDY TO SEE
Missus Marietta, one of the church shut-ins. She was too elderly
to get around on her own, and she had hardly any visitors. It
was as if the world had forgotten her. It was good of Aunt Tildy
to check on her every month, but that was Aunt Tildy, who
tried to live a godly life. She maybe didn't get it right all the
time, but who did?

A snapshot of Aunt Tildy:

Long brown hair streaked with gray, because she thought it
was vain for a woman to color her hair. I remembered watching
her peer at her reflection and tut, saying, "Lord, I'm not ready
to look like my mama. I'm too young to look like my mama." I
suspected that if Aunt Tildy did get the gray covered, she'd be

as happy as a kid blowing out birthday candles. But she would never. She had rules, and she was big on following them.

The next thing that came to mind was chores, chores, and more chores. Aunt Tildy just loved work, and she loved putting me to work. Christian didn't have to do as much, because he was a boy. She did insist he make up his bed every day, though, and she made him clean whatever deer, squirrel, and rabbit he shot and brought home. "You kill it; you clean it," she told him.

Next on the list? Country music. Aunt Tildy had a radio in the kitchen that she listened to all day. She didn't sing along, because that would be "letting loose," and she didn't do that. She didn't hug me much, either. I figured being prim and proper made her feel safe.

No, that wasn't quite it. It was more like . . . like life was messy, with snotty noses and first periods and girls crying over the things girls cry about. Aunt Tildy didn't like messes, and she would *prefer* to be prim and proper always, but if she absolutely had to step in the muck—if there was no one else to do it, and it had to be done—then she would.

Thinking about that side of Aunt Tildy dredged up other memories. Memories of Tommy. My personal monster-under-the-bed, only it lurked in my heart instead, snapping its sharp teeth when I least expected it.

The few times I tried to talk about it with Aunt Tildy, she just frowned and scrubbed harder on the pot she was scouring. And yes, it hurt, having her pretend it never happened. Aunt

Tildy worked for Tommy's daddy, and she wasn't going to stir up trouble.

Anyway, nursing my wounded feelings was neither here nor there. What mattered were facts, not feelings, and the facts added up to a single, hard truth. Three years ago, Christian saw what Tommy was doing to me in our living room and did nothing. Aunt Tildy, on the other hand, made Tommy stop, and for that I would always be fiercely grateful.

That brought me to the last detail in my aunt Tildy collage. She was my strongest link to my mother. I was two when Mama died, so my memories of her were dandelion wisps fluttering out of reach. Warmth. Safety. A feeling of home.

Aunt Tildy was Mama's older sister, and while she wasn't my mother, she was better than nothing.

Anyway. Missus Marietta loved the rhubarb crumble we brought her. Aunt Tildy was sweet and told Missus Marietta I made it, when really I just did the crumble part. I like lots of brown sugar, so I added twice the normal amount. It looked so pretty when I pulled it out of the oven, the crumbly topping all golden and buttery and chunks of rhubarb popping out here and there, oozing their ruby red juice.

We visited with Missus Marietta for an hour, and I brushed her long silver hair the way she liked. She asked about Patrick, though she called him "that boy, you know the one," and said it was a crying shame what happened to him.

"There's folks in Black Creek who ain't just mean, they were *born* mean," she said in her quavery voice. Aunt Tildy started to reproach her, but Missus Marietta would have none of it. "Now, Tilda, I been living in these parts for near on ninety years. I know what I know."

"But there are also people who are nice," I ventured, surprised to hear myself saying it.

"Yes, there are," Missus Marietta conceded. She gave me her toothless smile. "And all three of us are right here in this room."

On the drive back, Aunt Tildy and I were silent. Just before we reached our house, her hand slid from the wheel, hovered over my leg, and patted me: two quick pats, and then right back to the steering wheel.

"You're doing real good," she said, keeping her eyes on the road.

"I am?" I said.

"At . . . at finally . . ." She frowned. "At growing into a fine young lady." She cut her eyes at me, and if you didn't know her, you'd think she was being sharp. But that was just her way. "I'm real glad you're getting out again."

I felt exposed. But warm, too. "Um, thanks."

Back home, I took a plate of rhubarb crumble out to Daddy, rationalizing that yes, it was dessert, which he wasn't supposed to have because of his heart and being so fat. But at least it involved fruit. It had to be better than fried pork skins and Wally's moonshine.

Then I biked to Huskers, the sandwich shop where Beef worked. Dupree worked there, too. I had yet to find out what happened the night Patrick was attacked, during the before-time when Patrick was hanging with the redneck posse. I wanted Beef to fill me in.

Maybe too, I wanted to see if what Destiny said was true.

I parked my bike on the dying grass between the sidewalk and the sandwich shop. The glass door was smudged, and when I pushed it open, the little bell on the top didn't jingle like it used to. It made one sad *ding,* that's all.

At the narrow counter, I ordered a cherry Coke and paid for it with money earned from our family garden. Every so often I loaded up a wagon with cucumbers and kale and whatever looked good and hauled it to Ridings McAllister, who ran a roadside produce stand. Other folks brought their fruit and vegetables to Ridings as well, and when the mood struck him, he doled out everyone's share of the meager profits.

After ringing me up, Beef reached across the counter and tousled my hair. "Wassup, girl? Looked for you at church on Sunday, but didn't find you."

"Yeah, 'cause you didn't come in the dang building," I scolded him. "You stayed outside where the cars were."

He laughed.

"Come talk to me while I drink my Coke," I said.

"Best offer I've had all day," he said.

Dupree was slapping wax paper between slices of lunch meat, and Beef whistled to get his attention. "Holler if things get busy, all right, homes?"

"Sure thing, hoss," Dupree said, bobbing his head to

whatever tune was running through his brain. Dupree was a stoner, and he was always bobbing his head. Anyway, Huskers was empty except for me, so Beef's services weren't exactly needed.

Beef sat across from me, and we did a brief hey-how-are-ya catch-up. It did my heart good to see him. I told him he had a stain on his T-shirt, and when he ducked his head to check, I reached over and flicked him, just like he used to do to me. We both grinned.

"You better watch it, girl," he said. "You know I always get you back."

"Ooo, I'm so scared," I said.

He slung both arms over the back of his chair, and it reminded me how different girls and guys were. Girls kept their bodies tucked in tight, while boys took up every inch of room they could. Beef especially tried to take up room, because he was on the skinny side. He had muscles, but they were ropy farm boy muscles, and when his jeans hung low, it wasn't for fashion.

I knew he wished he was bigger. That just wasn't the way God made him. And, boys being boys, he got stuck with a nickname that drove the point home.

But, Beef was fine with it. He liked the tough way it made him sound.

"So, about Patrick," I finally got around to saying.

Beef closed his eyes in pain. "Sucks." He winced, because of the nozzle. "Wrong word. But you know."

I did. It was complicated, the way the redneck posse danced

around Patrick, but Beef was the guy who stood up for him when the others took things too far—which they did, especially Tommy.

Like, sure, Tommy escorted Mario Mario out of the Come 'n' Go when he called Patrick a fag. But in real life, when it wasn't an "us versus them" sort of situation, Tommy called Patrick fag names himself. Supposedly, Tommy was teasing, but when pushed too hard, Beef called him on it. He'd get up in Tommy's face and say, "What is that, man? I'm serious. What *is* that?"

Beef was like that. He was protective of anyone smaller or weaker.

"Tell me about that night," I said. "The night it happened."

Beef studied me. I took the time to study him right back. He'd dropped some pounds, and it changed the shape of his face. Made his cheekbones stick out and his eyes look haunted. It also made his scar more prominent, a white crescent cut by his daddy's class ring.

He got the scar in the fifth grade. Back then he had a dog named Daisy, and one time he let Daisy out and forgot to call her back in. He fell asleep on the couch, that's why. Daisy got hit by a pickup truck, and when Roy found out, he punched Beef in the face, leaving a moon-shaped mark that never went away. Then he made Beef dig a hole to bury Daisy in, saying a man has to clean up his own messes.

Beef cried like a baby. Not where his dad could see, but at our house, after it was done.

Beef exhaled, and the sound of it pulled me back to Huskers.

"I don't see the point of talking about it," Beef said. "Why are you so interested? I hear you've been sniffing around, and I don't like it."

I was offended. More than that, I hated the thought of people discussing me, wondering out loud what I was up to. He must have seen it on my face, because he took it down a notch.

"I don't want you getting hurt, that's all," he said. "Why can't you just stay out of it?"

"'Cause I don't want to. 'Cause I want to know what happened." I wrapped my hands around my cup. "Heck, Beef, you know Sheriff Doyle isn't going to do squat."

"Hey. He's doing what he can."

I rolled my eyes. Sheriff Doyle wouldn't know it if his butt was on fire.

"Either way, I've told him everything I know," Beef said.

"But you haven't told me, and Christian won't, either. Come on, Beef."

He tugged at the brim of his baseball cap, which was emblazoned with the logo for the Asheville Tourists. His dark hair curled up from below. He'd always worn his hair buzz-cut short, but now, apparently, he was letting it go—along with everything else. His lips were chapped, and his face was haggard, like he hadn't gotten a good night's sleep in forever. I thought about everything Destiny had told me, knowing her information might or might not have been true. Only one way to find out.

"Do you do crank?" I asked bluntly.

"What?!"

"Someone said you work for Wally. The, um, meth cooker."

"I know who Wally is, Cat. For Christ's sake." He checked on Dupree and lowered his voice. "Who said that? I want you to tell me right now."

"*Do* you?"

"*No,*" he said. "God, Cat. Jesus fucking Christ."

But he was holding back. I could tell because he refused to meet my eyes.

"I know you're lying," I whispered. I didn't, and all I wanted was to be wrong. But I threw it out there, and it stuck.

"I *used* to work for Wally," he finally said. "A little running, a little dealing, all right? But I quit. I *quit,* dammit."

A stone lodged in my gut, because this was my *friend* telling me this, telling me he used to sell meth. It was insane. It was . . . it was a house pet turning inside out, showing itself to be a fox.

"Are you a user?" I asked.

"Goddammit, no. Didn't you hear a word I said?"

The pattern of the plastic table swam in front of me. "Is Christian?"

"Hey," Beef said. "Hey. Look at me."

Reluctantly, I lifted my gaze.

"Your brother's clean. Dang, Cat. You think he would come within ten miles of meth?"

"I guess not."

"But you think *I* would."

"Like I said, I heard some things."

"About who? About *Christian*?"

I rubbed my forehead. "No. Just you, Tommy, and Dupree."

Dupree looked over. "Y'all talking about me? 'Bout how sexy I am?"

"That's right, Dupree," Beef said. "Sexiest man in a five-foot radius."

Dupree laughed, and Beef laughed back—*ha-ha-ha*. When Dupree went back to the slices of meat, Beef made a finger gun and shot him.

"Okay," I said, gathering my courage. I wanted the details, however ugly they were. "So you sold meth for Wally, but you didn't smoke it or sniff it or whatever?"

"I got out, Cat. You gotta believe me." He clasped his hands on the table. "I ain't speaking for Tommy or Dupree. They want to ruin their lives, that's their business. But not me."

"How did you even fall into all that? Was it because of getting injured and losing your scholarship?"

"You know me, king of good decisions," he said, full of bitterness. "Nothing like running meth to get your life back on track, right?"

"I wish you hadn't," I said softly.

"You and me both. You know who else had strong opinions about it?"

"Patrick," I said.

"Yeah. I tried to keep it from him, but he found out, and

once he did, I was done for. *You're ruining your life. You're smarter than this.* Harp, harp, harp. Nag, nag, nag."

"Good for him," I said.

"I know," Beef said. "I owe him my life. He's . . ." His throat clogged up, and he looked away for a long moment.

When he turned back, he said, "I'll tell you one thing, Cat. I *ever* catch you using, I'll kill you." His stare burned into me. "If someone offers you a line? You walk the fuck away."

"Thanks for the tip," I said.

"I ain't playing. You start tweaking, and next thing you know, people'll be dancing on your grave. Hell, you start tweaking, I'll *put* you in your grave."

"Don't worry, Beef. I can take care of myself."

"I'm just sayin'."

"And I'm just saying, too." The moment stretched out. "So, back to that night."

He groaned.

"You were with Patrick," I said. "Who else was with you? Christian? Tommy?"

Beef didn't answer, so Dupree replied for him. Guess he'd been paying attention after all.

"Tommy and your brother both," Dupree said in his lazy drawl. He hopped the counter and loped over to our table. "And don't forget yours truly. We had all our party people with us that night, didn't we, Beef-man?"

Dupree ticked off names on his fingers. "Me, Tommy, Beef,

and your brother. We had a shortage of ladies, unfortunately. Just Bailee-Ann."

Well, of course, Bailee-Ann. She was Beef's girlfriend.

"Where were y'all?" I asked.

"Chillaxing at the Frostee Top," Dupree said. The Frostee Top belonged to Bailee-Ann's parents. Until they went out of business, they sold chocolate dipped cones and milkshakes and stuff. But the Frostee Top went under when the economy went bad, and now it was an empty building with a giant plaster ice-cream cone on the roof. Bailee-Ann and those guys used it as a place to party.

"Oh, and Bailee-Ann's little brother," Dupree said with a stoner's delight in remembering a hazy detail. "Yeah. Robert. He was there, too."

"Robert?" I said. Robert was eleven, scrawny and hyper because of fetal alcohol syndrome. At least that's what Aunt Tildy said. But that didn't matter. What mattered was that he was a *kid*. Why would Robert be hanging out with Beef and Dupree and the others?

"He's a trip, man," Dupree said, chuckling. He reeked of pot. I couldn't tell if he was stoned right then or if it was eau de weed left over from the previous night.

"Why is he a trip?" I said.

"Oh, I dunno," Dupree said. He tilted his chair on its back legs. "He brings it back, you know? Youth. Childhood." His gazed dreamily at a spot behind me. "Not a care in the world."

Uh-huh, whatever. "But Patrick. He joined up with y'all eventually. Was that at the Frostee Top?"

"Nah, we didn't see Patrick till later. We ran out of libations, so Tommy suggested a beer run."

To the Come 'n' Go, that would have meant. Patrick wouldn't sell beer to Mario Mario and his college buddies, but he'd sell it to Tommy and the others. It was the small town code of honor: There were outsiders, like the college boy townies, and there were insiders, like the redneck posse. And the redneck posse *had* accepted him into their ranks, after all.

"I was against it," Beef said. Anger simmered below his words.

"How come?" I asked.

"'Cause he's a big ol' party pooper," Dupree said.

"Shut up," Beef growled.

"Party pooper," Dupree sang under his breath.

Beef shoved the table, driving it into Dupree's chest and tipping over his chair. "*Shut the fuck up.* What about that don't you understand?"

"Ow," Dupree said from the floor. His chair lay on its side. He rubbed his butt and said, "Un*cool*, bro."

My stomach twisted. "God, Beef."

"Don't you start," he warned. "I'm sick of everybody riding me. I'm sick of people thinking I'm the jerk just because I'm not a fucking puppet, all right?" He gave Dupree, who was still on the floor, a hard look. "There are worse crimes than not always wanting to party, bro."

Worse crimes? Oka-a-a-y, that was interesting. As Dupree got up, I pulled a napkin from the dispenser. I folded it into smaller and smaller squares as he made a big deal out of dusting himself off, righting his chair, and sitting back down. This time he planted all four legs on the floor.

"Um, y'all are freaks," I remarked, careful with my tone. I was just a normal, everyday girl scoffing at how ridiculous boys were when they got all macho.

"Whoa," Dupree said. "You don't see me going around tossing people on their asses, do you?"

"I don't usually hear guys using the term 'party pooper,' either," I said. "Unless they're five."

Beef snorted. His breathing had grown more regular, and I felt like it was maybe safe to go on.

I set down my folded-up napkin. To Dupree, I said, "You ran out of beer, so you went to the Come 'n' Go?"

"That is correct," Dupree said stiffly. He sounded like a schoolmarm, but his primness was so deliberate that it crossed over into being a joke. "Patrick's shift was almost over. We sweet-talked him into leaving early."

Beef rolled his eyes. I could see that Dupree was pleased, and I was, too. We were one more step back toward normal.

"Then what?" I said. "Did y'all head back to the Frostee Top?"

"Nah, we decided to take the party on the road." He appraised me from the waist up. "You are looking mighty fine, by the way. Why don't you party with us no more? What possible reason could a lady as fine as you have for breaking the hearts of two handsome bucks"—he thumped his chest—"like us?"

The thumping stirred up some indigestion, or possibly smoker's phlegm, and Dupree fell into a coughing fit. He tugged a napkin from the dispenser, spit into it, and examined the contents.

"It's baffling," I said.

"We picked up Patrick, and we went to Suicide Rock," Beef told me as if he just wanted to get this over with. Suicide Rock was a clearing deep in Pisgah Forest, where the river widened and created an awesome swimming hole. It was good for partying when people were sick of the Frostee Top, because it was far enough off Route 34 that only locals knew of it.

"What'd you do up there?"

"Nothing," he said. "We drank some more and then we went home. Same as I told the cops. All right, Cat?"

"Fine," I said. I'd hoped we'd gotten past the angry spell, but his jaw was sharp. These new moods of his made me miss my chick-fuzz Beef. "I'm not accusing you of anything, you know."

"Feels like you are."

"Well, I'm not. I just want to find the bastard who went after Patrick."

"I hear that," Dupree said. There was something false in his tone, and I turned toward him. He was staring straight at me, his stoner's glaze replaced by a sly intelligence I'd hadn't known he possessed.

"Why?" Beef said.

I was startled. "Huh?"

"Why do you care? You haven't hung out with Patrick in years."

"Yeah, but he's still my friend."

"Oh, really? Since when?" He radiated hostility, and this time it was aimed squarely at me. "When's the last time you hung out with your good friend Patrick, huh?"

My body grew hot, and I hated him. I'd never in my life hated Beef, but I did then. A lump lodged in my throat, and I knew what would come next if I didn't watch out. So I used a trick I taught myself years ago, which was to turn myself off on the inside. There was a girl sitting at a table, and that girl was me, but the switch had been flipped and I didn't feel anything anymore. I could put on a show of being a real girl, but I was somewhere else.

"So you partied at Suicide Rock," I said, as if reading the words off an index card. I looked at Beef, but at the same time not. "You, Patrick, Dupree, and Tommy. My brother. Bailee-Ann and Robert." I paused. "Who drove? How'd everyone fit?"

"Now, Robert didn't come with us up into the forest," Dupree clarified. "Patrick made him go home."

Good for Patrick. Of course he'd be the one to show a lick of sense.

"But Bailee-Ann had her pickup, so we had plenty of room," he continued. "Tommy rode up front with Bailee-Ann, and the rest of us piled into the back. Good times, man. Good times."

A shadow crossed his face. I couldn't tell if it was genuine or for show. "And then . . ." He splayed his fingers and made a sound to represent it all blowing up in their faces.

Uh-huh, I thought. *It's all fun and games till someone gets a gas pump nozzle jammed down their throat.*

The phone rang. Beef stood, but Dupree waved him off, saying, "I got it." He went to the counter and fished for an order pad. Sliding easily into his laid-back persona, he said, "Huskers, tastiest subs in town. What can I do ya for?"

I expected Beef to sit back down, but he didn't. He stood by the table, his hand on the top of his chair, looking lost.

I felt myself letting go of my anger, because this was Beef, and he was hurting, too. We were upset with ourselves for not protecting Patrick, but we were taking it out on each other.

"I'm not attacking you, Beef," I said. "I swear to God. I just want to know what happened."

Beef glanced at Dupree, then gestured with his head, a silent request that I follow him. I did, noting how slim his hips and torso were. He wasn't a man yet, no matter how much he probably wanted to be. He was just a redneck in a ball cap and a T-shirt so threadbare it belonged in the rag pile.

He led me to the back of the store, near the small and filthy restroom/supply closet. He leaned against the cement wall, and I did the same. My eyes drifted to the graffiti scrawled on the supply closet's door. Much of it had been there for ages. *Bailee-Ann luvs Beef. Willow + Darren. Destiny sux cock.*

Out of habit, I lifted my gaze higher, and yep, there it was: *Cat and Patrick, BFFs 4-ever.* Patrick had written the words, because his handwriting was better. I'd used a purple Sharpie to draw a heart around them. A heart-shaped fence that protected neither one of us.

"We hung out, like I said, and then we went home," Beef said. "I'm the one who drove us back into town, because Bailee-Ann was near passed-out. I think Dupree gave her something."

My heart rate spiked. "What do you mean, 'something'?" I said, my brain going straight to *meth-crank-ice-crystal*. "Something bad?"

"Nah, not bad, just something that made her loopy. She was, like, talking to the trees and petting them and stuff."

"Petting the trees?"

The look he gave me said, *Yes, petting the trees. As I said.*

"And then you drove everyone home," I said stupidly. I was going to lose him if all I could do was to repeat everything he'd already told me. I gulped. "Um, who'd you drop off first?"

"Tommy and Dupree. Dupree crashed at Tommy's."

All right, I thought. If Tommy and Dupree were dropped off first, that meant they had the most time to go back out. Hypothetically. "What time was that?"

"Hell, Cat, I don't know. One fifteen, one twenty?"

I wasn't going to let him rattle me again. I focused on the purple heart—that was why I was here, after all—and said, "So you dropped Tommy and Dupree off first. Then who?"

"Then Bailee-Ann, and last of all your brother. Why do you care?"

"What about Patrick?" I said.

He didn't answer immediately. Several seconds passed before he said, with almost no inflection, "I took him back to the gas station after dropping Christian off."

"So he could get his car?" Patrick had inherited Mama Sweetie's ancient Pontiac when she died.

"And so he could finish his closing duties. I was like, 'Dude, it's one thirty. Restocking the napkins can wait.'" His eyes found mine. "But you know Patrick."

I did. The purple Sharpie he and I had used to add our names to the graffiti door had come from school, courtesy of our sixth grade teacher's top desk drawer. When Patrick found out, he made me promise to return it. Heck, he escorted me to Mrs. Padrick's room the next day and watched me do it.

"Jesus, Cat," Beef said. "He could have come home with me. I could have taken him back in the morning. Or I could have helped him with his dang closing duties."

He lifted the brim of his ball cap and rubbed his head. "But no. I left him alone at the Come 'n' Go. Lights blazing, and Patrick inside like a fucking lamb for the slaughter."

"Yo, Beef, I've got a delivery for you," Dupree called. "Hey— what the . . . ? Where the fuck *are* you?"

Beef tugged his cap back in place. He pushed off the cement wall and headed back to our table.

I walked with him, speaking quickly. "You didn't know. It wasn't your fault."

"There you are," Dupree said. "You're messing with my head, man. For real."

"It wasn't your fault," I repeated.

Beef's expression didn't change.

Dupree slapped a sheet of paper on the table in front of him, saying, "Peanut butter and mayonnaise, heavy on the mayonnaise."

"Peanut butter and mayonnaise?" I said. I pulled myself back to the moment, because for a reason I couldn't put my finger on, it seemed important not to reveal anything to Dupree. Not that I had anything to reveal, but Dupree made me want to hold everything in tight. "That's disgusting."

"Ah, but we got customers who swear by it. Ain't that so, Beef?"

"Yeah," he said, grabbing the order sheet.

"We get all sorts of crazy orders," Dupree elaborated. "Peanut butter and mayonnaise, turkey with fried pickles, tongue with spicy mustard."

"Shut up, Dupree," Beef said. "She doesn't care."

Dupree gave me an eyebrow waggle. "You ever tried tongue, Cat?"

"Shut *up*, Dupree."

Beef was himself again, standing up for me like I was his adopted little sister. I was glad. But I was perfectly capable of handling Dupree by myself.

"Yeah, I've had tongue," I said. "You got some you want me to sample?"

"Hells yeah. You want it now?"

"Bring it on. And bring me a knife, one of those sharp ones you keep in the back. I like my tongue cut up real fine."

Dupree's laugh rang out loud and big, and I smiled before I could stop myself. I'd forgotten how fun it could be to sass someone, even if that someone was several-screws-loose Dupree.

"It was good seeing you, Cat," Beef said, already halfway out of the store. "You should come by more often."

I watched him strap on his helmet, kick-start his Suzuki, and roar out of the parking lot. Too late, I realized he'd left with nothing.

"Wait," I said. "What about the sandwich?"

"Huh?" Dupree said.

"The sandwich he's supposed to deliver. Are you stoned, Dupree? For real?"

"Almost always," he quipped. He cracked up. "But dang, you're right. Can't deliver a sandwich without the sandwich, can you?"

I shook my head. Dupree was useless. I headed toward the door, but before I got there, Dupree called out, "You know your buddy Patrick ain't no saint, right?"

I stopped. My radar went off—*ping ping ping*—and I turned around.

"No, as a matter of fact I *don't* know that," I said. "As a matter of *fact,* I'd say Patrick's as close to being a saint as anyone can be."

"Well, I agree that he *acts* saintly. I'll give you that. But there are certain things that a person—a loyal person—should keep to himself. You get me?"

"No."

He smiled. I didn't like it. "Then I'll make it easier," he said. "Nobody likes a tattletale."

"How is Patrick a tattletale?"

He lifted one shoulder. "Hey. Sometimes people bring stuff down on their own selves, that's all I'm saying."

I had to take two full breaths before I trusted myself to speak. "Are you saying Patrick deserved what happened to him?"

"Cat, c'mon. You know me better than that."

"Do I?"

"I ain't happy Patrick got hurt. Don't misunderstand." He searched my face. "There's just one thing I want to tell you, and I want you to actually hear it."

He paused as if waiting for some sort of response.

I made an impatient circle with my hand. "Fine. What?"

"The sun don't shine on the same dog's tail all the time," he said. "That's all I'm saying."

I breathed in and out carefully, trying not to show anything on my face. But I thought about how Destiny said that Dupree was one of Wally's boys: a meth dealer or a runner or both. According to Destiny, Tommy and Beef were, too—or had been at one point.

What if Patrick had known? Would Dupree have seen him as a threat? What about Tommy? What about Wally?

And Beef. If Beef knew the others were muttering about Patrick—voicing concerns about loyalty and the importance of keeping one's mouth shut—what would he have done?

Nobody likes a tattletale.

I left Huskers, because I needed to get away from Dupree. I considered what he said, though. I considered it from various angles, all subject to a variety of interpretations.

One: Dupree was sharper than he pretended to be. His stoner act was just that, regardless of how much dope he actually smoked.

Two: Dupree was not only sharp, but potentially dangerous. Had he *threatened* me before I left Huskers? Was that what his "the sun don't shine" story was about?

Which brought me to three: Wally. Wally was nasty as rotten lunch meat, living out in his trailer with his flea-ridden dogs. His eyes were constantly bloodshot, he had a chronic cough, and he was coated with filth and stink.

All things considered, I was left with a plan of attack that made my stomach lurch. First, I needed to keep Dupree in my sights, whether literally or figuratively. I needed to be very, very careful when it came to that boy.

Second, I needed to talk to Wally. I didn't want to, and I wasn't at all sure I'd find the courage to make it happen. Wally was worse than any fairy-tale witch, and his trailer wasn't made of candy. Just the thought of him terrified me.

I'd think on it. For today, I was done.

friday

12

I HAD CHORES THE NEXT DAY, AND NO WAY AROUND them. Collect kindling, even though fall was a ways off. Water and weed the garden. Laundry, laundry, and more laundry. And finally, tend to the dang green beans so we'd have them ready for dinner.

I hated green beans. First I had to pick them. Then I had to string them, pulling the tough top part straight down the spine of each bean on both sides. Then I broke them. Then I washed them until the water ran clear. Then I cut out the black spots made from bugs. Though fixing green beans was one of my least favorite chores, I stretched it out today. I was working up the courage for what I had to do next.

I knew Wally would talk to me. He liked girls, and the

younger the better. Every winter he came into town for the Christmas pageant, because seeing little kids in angel robes gave him a boner. In the summer, he'd show up at the lake where younger kids went swimming—not Suicide Rock, but a lake with a dock and a lifeguard and a tiny snack shack—and it was the same thing all over again. His thing made a tepee out of his swim trunks, right there in front of God and every living soul.

Once he asked Gwennie if she wanted him to teach her to float on her back. I was ten. She was nine. We'd both known how to float on our backs for years. We wrinkled our noses and said *ewww* and ran off laughing. Gwennie probably should have told her daddy, but she didn't.

When I finished prepping the beans, I put them in a two-quart pan to soak, 'cause Daddy liked them super soft. I threw in a big ol' chunk of fatback for flavor, and also for its grease, and then I went to get my bike. It was a long ride to Wally's trailer, which was deep in the forest. I hoped on the ride over I'd come up with a brilliant scheme to get him to talk to me without arousing his suspicion. I wasn't feeling overly enthusiastic, as this was a man who gave his "boys" pistols. I could well be the most foolish girl in the county.

I was halfway down the driveway when Christian called out to me. I stopped. "Yeah?"

He cut across the yard, looking strong and tough with his sun-kissed skin and his thumbs hooked in the belt loops of his jeans.

"Where are you going?" he asked.

"Why do you care?"

"Because you're my sister."

"Like that's ever mattered before."

"What?"

"Nothing."

"You've been acting strange, Cat." He stood in front of me and took hold of the handlebars. "I'm not the only one who's noticed, either."

"Let go," I said.

"Then tell me where you're going. I'll go with you. We'll take my Yamaha."

I didn't know what he was up to. His shoulders were hunched, his body's way of telling me he was concerned. But why? He didn't care about me. Or maybe he did, but not enough.

To prove it, I said, "You'll give me a ride to Wally's? Hey, thanks."

"Wally? That fucking rock spider? No way!"

"Yeah, well . . . thanks anyway, *bro.*"

I wrenched free and took off, ignoring his cries of "Hey! Get back here!"

I pumped so hard my quads burned. Partly for speed, more to flush out my confused emotions. I wanted Christian back. I wanted him to be there for me. But how could I let him in when I couldn't trust him for fear of being burned?

A few moments later, Christian's motorcycle roared to life, and I heard the pop of gravel on the road to my right. He was coming after me, but guess what? I could cut though the woods and he couldn't, not without getting whacked up by branches and scraping the paint on his bike.

It was coming up on six o'clock in the outside world, with the sun just starting to think about setting. In the woods, it was darker, thanks to the thick overhang of branches and leaves. Everything smelled loamy. The approach of twilight, along with the insect sounds that heralded it, made me feel alone in a way of separating me from all things human. Usually, I liked being in the woods for that very reason, but tonight the chorus of crickets was suffocating rather than reassuring. An owl on the hunt hooted. The hairs on the back of my neck stood up.

I'd never actually been to Wally's before, but I knew I was close when a pack of dogs started barking, drowning out everything else. They were loud and wild. They triggered a deep-seated clench of fear.

Most likely they were chained up, but I decided to continue on foot so that I didn't surprise them, or vice versa. I climbed off my bike and leaned it against a tree. Nailed to the trunk was a plank painted with the words POSTED: NO TRESPASSING. My skin prickled. People who chose to live deep in the woods tended not to be overly social.

I walked in the direction of the barking. My nerves were raw, and I flinched when a twig snapped beneath me. Why had I thought visiting Wally was a good idea? I couldn't for the life of me remember. He was a meth cooker and a lech, and for all I knew, he may have beamed Patrick in the skull with a baseball bat. On top of that, he had dogs. *Big* dogs. I still hadn't thought of what I was going to say to Wally when I saw him, or what he might say to me.

And his dogs—what might *they* do? Eat me?

I reached a clearing, and further ahead, I made out Wally's decrepit trailer. In front of it, three Dobermans snarled and strained against their chains. It occurred to me in the pounding of my pulse—which I could hear in my head, it was so strong—that there was brave, and then there was stupid, and God knew *I* didn't want to end up bound to a tree trunk, something horrid jammed down my throat.

A loud crack made me jump, and my heart tried to fling itself out of my rib cage. I turned on my heel and was fast-walking to my bike when Christian roared up on his motorcycle and stood on the brakes, spraying up dirt and pine needles.

The dogs fell into a frenzy.

"God, scare the crap out of me next time," I said, even as my body went slack with relief. I almost wanted to hug him.

Christian was off his bike and at my side before I realized he'd cut the engine. "You don't belong here," he said, grabbing my wrist.

No, but now that he was here, I was brave again. I headed again for Wally's trailer.

"I mean it, Cat," he said. He scanned our surroundings. "Come on. We need to get out of here."

"Chill," I said. I tried to shake him off, but he stayed beside me, radiating a low thrum of energy. His anxiety cranked up my anxiety, and I took shallow breaths. Something *had* to be going on if Christian was so determined to keep me away.

"Well, *heyyyyyy*, " a man said. Wally. He cracked the door of his trailer with the business end of a shotgun. A bare lightbulb revealed pocked skin, stubble, and a single eyeball. We were several yards away, but I sensed madness in that eyeball, and I remembered what Aunt Tildy had told me about Wally way back when.

"That man's got the crazies," she said. "You stay away from him, you hear?"

Wally used his gun to push the door wider. He nodded at Christian like he knew him, a fact I filed away. Then he took a good long look at me, the kind of look that made me want to cross my arms over my chest. Two of the dogs kept barking. The other grew rigid and growled deep in its throat.

"Aw, now, they won't bother you none," Wally said. He whistled sharply and said, "Down." The dogs dropped to their haunches and shut up.

"So Christian, this your sister?" Wally asked, gesturing at me with that dang shotgun. He leered. "You sure has growed up. Growed up *real* fine. Come in, come in."

I followed Wally into his trailer. Christian was furious. I felt it coming off him. But he followed, too.

Inside, I fought not to gag. I'd seen plenty of filth in my life, but no place as filthy as this. Wally had given up on the notion of a trash can eons ago, apparently deciding the floor was as good a dumping ground as anything. My quick survey showed greasy pizza boxes, crumpled newspapers, and moldy plastic containers. Rubber tubes in random lengths. Empty aluminum foil dispensers, their sharp metal teeth waiting to bite some fool's bare foot.

The room smelled of spoiled food, body waste, and a chemical odor I couldn't identify. Sweet and rotten at the same time.

I must have wrinkled my nose, because Wally laughed.

"Home sweet home," he said, gesturing with fingers that were burned at the tips. He smiled, his lips peeling back from the ugliest set of teeth I'd ever seen. They were yellow, with dark spots of decay. Quite a few were missing. "Now, what can Uncle Wally do for such a pretty gal?"

I couldn't think what to say. I panicked, because *crap,* my ride through the woods hadn't given me any ideas, and now I was a stupid little girl again. *Rock Spider,* Christian had called Wally, because rock spiders worried their way into small, tight cracks. I saw Gwennie and that ratty pink bathing suit she used to wear, with the elastic fallen out of one leg hole so that the fabric rode up and exposed her pale bottom cheek.

"I . . . um . . ." *I was wondering if you'd share your client list with me, and by the way, are you the one who bashed in Patrick's skull?*

Wally stepped closer. He had a limp. With a wink, he said, "Are you two members of our state or federal law enforcement team? I gotta ask, you understand."

"What? No," I said.

"She's not here for that," Christian said tersely.

"That so?" Wally asked me. "You a straight arrow like your brother?" He paused as a coughing spell wracked his pipe-cleaner-thin body. He wiped his mouth with his sleeve. His hands shook and he leaned on his shotgun for support.

"Well, good for you. Mebbe you'll keep your looks after all."

Was Wally saying Christian didn't do meth? If so, thank God for small blessings.

"If you ain't here for that shit, what are you here for?" Wally asked.

"Oh," I said. "About that. I just . . . I guess I just . . ."

Christian exhaled. "Come on, Cat." To Wally, he said, "She was riding her bike. She got lost."

Over Wally's shoulder, I saw a cramped kitchen, with buckets in the sink like the kind Aunt Tildy used when she mopped the floor. Beyond were a short hall and a closed door.

"Can I use your bathroom?" I asked. I figured it had worked with Gwennie, so why not try with Wally?

"No," Christian said.

Wally chuckled. "Sure you can." He pointed. "Down the hall and through the bedroom. You want me to show you the way?"

"I can find it," I said, just as Christian stepped between me and the hall. He took on a soldier's stance, his arms folded over his chest and his feet spread wide.

"You can wait till we get back home."

"No, I can't," I said, slipping sideways past him and fast-walking down the hall.

"Little girls got little girl parts," I heard Wally say to Christian. "Soft and tender, them girl parts."

"Shut up," Christian said.

"Can't do their business in the woods like we can, now can they?"

"Shut up," Christian said, sounding for all the world like the growling Doberman out front.

Wally's bedroom looked like his kitchen, but with bigger heaps of laundry. Near the bed, which was nothing but a mattress on the floor, was a pile of magazines. The top one was called *Barely Legal.* I also spotted a roll of paper towels, a metal clamp, and, inexplicably, a blender.

I took in what I could, careful not to touch anything. But much as I'd hoped for an easy answer, there was no manila folder labeled USERS. No list of names by the phone, which was plugged into the wall and connected to an answering machine.

With my toe, I nudged open the bathroom door. I recoiled from the odor, then tried again, breathing shallowly. There was a pee-crusted toilet with dark stains rimming the bowl. The bathtub was clearly never used for taking baths, as it was filled with funnels, coffee filters, and other items I assumed were for cooking up meth. A pair of rubber gloves lay over the rim of the sink, and those rubber gloves skeeved me out more than anything.

I used my foot to flush the toilet so that it would seem like I'd peed. I was surprised the septic system worked. Beneath the roar of rushing water, I heard Wally's bedroom telephone ring. Just once, then a *beep*. Then someone leaving a message. I couldn't make out the words.

I stepped back into the bedroom and listened for movement. Had Wally heard the phone ring? Was he heading this way?

A red light blinked on the answering machine. My heart matched its rhythm as I pushed the PLAY button. A man's voice was barely discernible, and I squatted by the speaker.

"—so, yeah, still waiting for my hookup," I heard. "You sure it's on the way?"

I recognized the voice, but I couldn't place it.

"'Cause I'm crashing hard, man," Wally's customer continued. "But it's gonna be the good stuff, right? None of that dishwater crank?" He laughed a skittering laugh. "Ah, now, I'm messing with ya. I know you'll take care of me . . ."

"Cat, come on," Christian called.

". . . even if it kills me," the guy on the phone was saying. And God forgive me, I want it to. I gotta get back with Danielle and my sweet little Melody, see?"

My breath caught. I knew Danielle and Melody, or I did before they died.

"Only problem is, Danielle and my sweet Melody are up in heaven, singing with the angels. They *are* angels. But when I die, I know I'm going straight to—"

"*Cat,*" Christian said sharply. I heard footsteps. He was coming down the hall for me. I crossed the bedroom in three long strides and closed the door behind me.

"I'm coming. Jeez," I said. I kept up a stream of words the whole way out, babbling to hide my shock.

From the perspective of gaining information, the visit to Wally's was pretty much a bust. All I learned was that Wally seemed too thin and feeble to go after a guy like Patrick with a baseball bat, and also that Ridings McAllister, the man with the roadside produce stand, was a user. Danielle was Ridings's wife, now in heaven, and sweet Melody was their baby girl, dead before her first birthday.

Maybe that's why Ridings needed a hookup. Maybe he needed it to stay awake when he'd rather fall into an endless sleep.

13

WHEN I WAS TEN, I CAUGHT MY BROTHER DROPPING
his pants in front of the mirror on Aunt Tildy's bureau. It was
summer, and I wanted a piece of ice to suck on, so I went into
the house to get one. I must have entered on silent mice feet,
and that was why Christian didn't hear me. I didn't set out to
spy on him, but I did, and afterward, I felt ashamed. He was
the one who didn't think to close Aunt Tildy's bedroom door,
but I should have tiptoed away when I saw what he was doing.

He never did know, though. I didn't laugh or snicker or use
it against him, because back then, we were tight. Plus, I was
just . . . gosh. *Shocked,* I suppose. My brother's penis was no
longer soft and pink. It was bigger, and it jutted out from his
body in a way that confused me. I shrank behind the door

frame, but I couldn't tear my eyes away. That thatch of dark hair—when did he get that?

We used to take baths together, turning Aunt Tildy's old shampoo bottles into squirt toys and underwater missiles. The first time Christian farted in the bath water, it surprised us both. The next time, he did it on purpose. He caught the bubbles in his cupped palms—or made out like he did—and offered them to me.

"I pooted," he announced, using the dipped-in-grits syllables of Richard from church, a thirty-year-old man with the mental abilities of a toddler.

Oh, man, we laughed. We laughed so hard, Aunt Tildy had to come in and shush us because we were giving her one of her headaches. It wasn't long after that she didn't let us take baths together anymore.

Later, when my own body started developing, I realized Christian had probably been admiring himself in Aunt Tildy's mirror that day, marveling at his manliness the way I would marvel at my tiny soft breasts, turning sideways in the mirror and pulling my shoulder blades together to make them more pronounced.

I guess we all changed. We all grew up, if we lived long enough to. For my whole childhood my brother had been my hero, and now he wasn't anymore. That's what I was thinking as I biked home from Wally's, with Christian stubbornly trailing me on his Yamaha to make sure I didn't go off somewhere else.

It made me melancholy, but mixed with that melancholy

was an unexpected pang of love for my brother. Despite his shortcomings, I was proud of him for staying out of that stupid meth business. Maybe I was being naive, but I'd never smelled that gross smell on him, the one still coating my nostrils. His pupils weren't ever dilated or contracted or anything weird. And Wally himself had called him a straight arrow. Surely anyone doing meth in Black Creek would buy from Wally, at least occasionally.

I missed how it used to be with me and Christian, when he was there for me no matter what. He must have saved me a hundred different times in a hundred different ways back then. Like once, out in our yard, he told me in a scarily calm voice to hold real still and not move a muscle. Then he went and got his rifle and shot a rattlesnake basking in the sun. If I'd gone five inches further, I'd have stepped on it with my bare foot.

He saved me again at Suicide Rock one summer. The day was hot—they always were—and Beef's daddy, Roy, drove a bunch of us up into the forest so we could swim in the river. Patrick was off with Mama Sweetie, but Beef and Gwennie came, and Bailee-Ann and Tommy, too. I was nine, and I had just finished fourth grade. I remembered being so happy on the drive to the swimming hole, because I was happy pretty much all the time. And I *loved* the water.

On the close side of the swimming hole, the bank was flat and level, like a beach made of mud and stones. The stones were smooth, but they came in all different shapes and sizes, and they jabbed the flesh of your soles like nobody's business.

The river water was cool and green, flowing so slow that it was perfect for splashing around in. Or if you were in a different kind of mood, you could float on your back and daydream to your heart's content, the sun kissing your face while the lazy current rocked you like a baby. In the middle of the swimming hole, there was a big old log, sodden and rotting and yet *there*, always there, and I figured it must have been a mighty tree at one point, given how its gnarled roots reached all the way down to the muck of the riverbed and held on tight. I loved that old log. Bailee-Ann and I liked to heave ourselves up on top of it and straddle it like a horse.

On the far side of the swimming hole, there was no bank. Just the straight-up side of the mountain. It was lush with ferns and ivy and laurel trees, whose gnarled branches made perfect handholds for climbing the footpath to the jumping rock—or if you went higher, to the rock the swimming hole was named for: Suicide Rock.

Jumping off the jumping rock gave a good thrill. Jumping from the higher-up Suicide Rock was likely to thrill you right to death. It was because of how the two different outcroppings were formed. The jumping rock stuck out nice and far over the river, like a diving platform. But Suicide Rock was tucked into the cliff and jutted out only a little, not even half as far as the jumping rock. If you stood at the edge of Suicide Rock and jumped off, you wouldn't hit the water. You'd hit granite, break a leg or two, and fall from there to the water, where you'd probably pass out from the pain and drown. Or you'd be unable to swim because of your broken limbs and drown. Or your head would hit the ledge, splattering your brains everywhere, and you wouldn't even need to drown.

Every few summers that very thing happened, usually to guys hopped up on testosterone and beer who decided to play Tarzan, only without the vine. To do it right—meaning, not die—you had to back up several yards into the undergrowth, get a running start, and fling your body out-out-out. You had to clear the jumping rock, otherwise *splat.*

Boys liked their stupid juice, though. What could I say?

On the day Roy drove us up there, the big boys—that was how I thought of them—were showing off for one another by jumping off the jumping rock. They'd leap into the air and whoop as they plunged down. They'd stay under water for longer than I liked before bursting out of the green-brown water like playful, boisterous seals. I only thought they were big because I was small. I didn't know what *big* meant, not then.

I wanted to jump off the jumping rock, too, I decided. I was tough. I could do it. I waded into the swimming hole until it got deep enough for swimming, and then I used my clumsy breaststroke to head for the far side.

"Cat!" Bailee-Ann cried. "What are you doing?"

I didn't turn back. Gwennie went for her daddy, who was half-drunk and baking in the sun, and I guess Gwennie dripped cold water on him, because he got pissed. He told her she was a baby and that I could do whatever the hell I wanted.

I climbed all the way to the jumping rock, though it took about a year. The rocks along the side of the cliff were slippery, even when they didn't look it. The fine mist from the river kept them wet, and the moisture grew a near-invisible moss that was as slick as ice. If you slipped, it was a guaranteed twisted ankle. Or your foot could get wedged into a crack and you could break a leg when you fell, since the rest of you had to obey the laws of gravity regardless.

I got up there, and I made the mistake of looking at the water, despite the warnings of the big boys.

"Whatever you do, don't look down," Beef called, treading water in the deep center of the pool.

"And now that you're there, don't think. Just jump," Christian said.

Even Tommy gave me advice. At twelve, he was all about skipping stones and sluicing river water through his front teeth. He was an expert jumper, so he was happy to coach his best friend's little sister.

"When you leap, clamp your legs together tight," he told me. "And when I say tight, I mean tight. So tight you couldn't get in there with a crowbar."

Beef laughed, and Christian said *dude*, like a guy-scold.

Tommy grinned, but didn't push it. "You gotta be an arrow, that's what I'm saying. Point your toes, and hold your hands straight up over your head. Otherwise, you'll smack the heck out of your arms."

"I know," I said, trying to sound sure of myself despite the fear pulsing in my veins. I hadn't expected to be scared. I hadn't had a clue what being up so high would do to my breathing, or to my balance. Dark flecks messed with my vision, because turned out I wasn't so good with heights. I didn't know it till then. Wasn't that odd? All the stuff that went into mind and body and soul, and so much of it left buried unless the right situation came along to unearth it.

On the bank, Gwennie bit her nails. She had *her* legs clamped together, like she had to pee really bad and was holding it in, but just barely. She was so tiny down there.

"Come on, Cat!" Beef called.

"You can do it!" Tommy added.

But I couldn't. My palms grew sweaty and my heart raced and my lungs squeezed themselves so tight I would have been afraid of fainting, if I'd had room for fearing anything other than *how'm I gonna get down oh God can't do this gonna die can't breathe can't move can't—*

And then Christian appeared, materializing out of bright air. He'd climbed up to me. The other boys hooted things like "Oh, my *hero*!" and Christian yelled for them to shut up.

"Come on," he said roughly. I think I was shaming him just as much as I was shaming myself. Or maybe *he* was scared— not for himself, but for me.

Since I couldn't get my muscles to work, he took my arm and led me off the ledge. I didn't remember the particulars, just that he didn't *talk* me off the ledge. He somehow *carried* me off that ledge, and back down the rocks until, finally, I was in the swimming hole again. My bathing suit was torn up, and snot was running out of my nose, and Gwennie and Bailee-Ann dog-paddled over to lead me out of the water and fuss over me. Christian grunted in disgust and went back to play chicken with his buds.

Or maybe he grunted because he was glad it was over.

saturday

14

THIS MORNING, I WENT TO THE HOSPITAL TO VISIT
Patrick. I knew it would be ugly, and I knew it would hurt. Most
of all, I knew I should have visited him days ago. I'd pulled an
Aunt Tildy by avoiding it this long.

But when I got there, the nurse turned me away. "Sorry,
hon," she said. "Family only."

I stared at her. "But . . . he doesn't have any family."

The nurse, who was young and probably straight out of
nursing school, regarded me sympathetically. "I'm sorry. It's
the rules. But he'll be allowed to have visitors if he comes to,
so keep checking on him, 'kay?"

"*If* he comes to?" I said. I felt wobbly.

"When he comes to," the nurse said fast. Her name tag said KELLY. She took my hand and squeezed it. "Just pray for him. It's in the Lord's hands now."

I nodded, but I was in a daze, and I walked off in the completely wrong direction. I didn't come out of my fog until I heard someone else asking about Patrick at the nurses' station. A guy.

"So, uh, can I see him?" I heard him say.

The back of my neck prickled, and I turned around as Kelly, the nurse, explained the "not unless you're family" rule. The guy was lean and well built, and his khakis fit him just like khakis should. His shirt was a striped oxford, nice enough for church.

It was the guy from the public library, here to see Patrick. Why?!

Well, march over and ask him, I told myself. *There is no reason on God's green earth for him to be here, and you need to find out what the heck is going on.*

So I did, doing my best to ignore the tree frogs jumping around in my stomach. I walked up behind him and said, *"Hey,"* so loud it made *him* jump.

He whipped around. "How . . . why . . ." He blinked. "What are *you* doing here?"

"Wrong," I said. I was vaguely aware of Kelly behind us, her sweet face concerned. "The question is, what are *you* doing here?"

He didn't reply, and my brain started working overtime trying to supply answers. Did Patrick know this guy? Were they friends? If so . . .*why,* given that he was such a jerk?

Except I knew the answer to that one. Patrick was friends with Tommy, after all. That's just how Patrick was. Accepting.

But any thought I had was pure speculation, which meant I was wasting my time, since what I needed were answers. Plus, the look library guy was giving me made me uncomfortable. It wasn't that he seemed pissed or wanted to throttle me or anything. He looked . . . well . . . remorseful.

I didn't want to talk in front of Kelly, so I strode away from the nurses' station and motioned for him to follow. There was a red vinyl sofa next to the hospital elevator, and I dropped down into it, leaving plenty of room for him. He sat. He was very obedient. Or maybe just in shock.

I was certainly in shock. I never expected to see him again, and now here he was.

I gave my head a good hard shake. "So. You know Patrick?"

"Yeah," he answered cautiously.

"Are you friends with him?"

He started to speak, but hesitated.

And then, finally, it dawned on me. When we first met, I hadn't gotten the vibe that he was gay. But that was at the library, and now here he was at the hospital, asking to see Patrick.

"Are the two of you, um, together?" I said.

"Are we . . . what? *No.*"

I didn't believe him. I didn't not believe him, but I didn't believe him.

He raked his hand through his hair, which was long enough to fall in his eyes, and said, "Two things."

"Okay."

"One, Patrick already has a boyfriend. And two, I'm not gay."

"You aren't?" I said. And then, "He *does*?"

"Uh, yeah, and I'd think if *you* were his friend, you'd know that." His eyes narrowed. "So are you?"

"Am I what?"

"His *friend.*"

"Yes," I said. "Are you? Because in all your counting, you never said."

He fell silent, and I felt like a fool. Given his low opinion of people who lived in backwoods towns like Black Creek, of course he wasn't Patrick's friend.

In that case, what did his visit mean? Did he come to the hospital to mess with Patrick some more? To admire his handiwork? To finish what he'd started?

"Tell me how you know him," I demanded.

"Tell me how *you* know him," he said.

"I go to school with him. We live in the same town." Feeling a need to defend myself, I added, "And obviously, I know he's got a boyfriend. I just haven't met him yet."

He slumped back on the hospital sofa.

"He wouldn't tell you, either, huh?" Under his breath, he muttered, "God, I'm such a dumb shit."

I was confused.

"I want to talk to the guy, that's all," he said.

"To who? Patrick? You can't, because he's in a coma."

"No, I want to talk to his boyfriend. His *undercover lover.*"
He didn't use air quotes, but his intonation achieved the same
effect. "If I could find him, I could see if he knew anything."

Undercover lover, I repeated silently. I could imagine
Patrick referring to a mysterious boyfriend like that. He would
have liked the cheesiness of it, the delicious rhyme of the words.

"Maybe he knows something, but he's scared to come
forward," the guy from the library went on. He pressed the
back of his head into the cushion behind him. *"Fuck."*

A lump formed in my throat. He was a jerk, but he *did* care
about Patrick. Any idiot could see that.

I thought about what was best for Patrick, what was best for
getting to the bottom of things. I swallowed my pride and said,
"Then we need to find him."

"'We'?" he said.

"Fine, *I* need to find him," I said, my face heating up. I stood,
went to the elevator, and jabbed the button.

"Wait," he said.

The elevator doors opened. I stepped inside, and he leaped
forward to join me.

"What I said at the library . . ." he said. "The name I called
you . . ."

I stared at the indicator lights for the different floors. There
were only three of them. *Come on, come on,* I silently chanted.

164

"I owe you an apology," he said stiffly.

"Great," I said. It didn't escape me that an *actual* apology failed to come.

"Look, here's my number and my email addy," he said, fumbling in his pocket. He pulled out a pen and a crumpled receipt and started scribbling. "I'll tell you if I find out anything, and you can do the same." He gave me the scrap of paper.

I stared at it. His name was Jason. Jason Connor.

"Now you," he said, and I glanced up to see him holding his phone, ready to punch in my info.

I folded the scrap of paper and shoved it into my pocket. "Don't have a cell. Sorry."

"You're shitting me."

"Nope. No cell."

"How can you not have a cell phone? Everyone has a—" He broke off, and I saw that he'd figured it out. White trash kids don't get the same toys as rich kids.

"Yup," I said, adopting Daddy's countriest twang. "It's a dang shame, but all my money goes to moonshine and dirt."

The elevator doors slid open, and I quick-walked out, my heart beating fast.

"Wait," he called. "I don't even know your name!"

"Bye, Jason," I said, tossing the words over my shoulder. "Have a nice life."

15

AUNTY TILDY HAD MY FAVORITE MEAL WAITING for me when I got home: chicken and dumplings. She knew I'd gone to the hospital, and I guess she was worried I'd be upset when I got back home. I would have found more comfort in a hug, or a few simple questions about how the visit had gone, but no. That was what the chicken and dumplings were for.

Though I didn't have much of an appetite, I cleaned my plate to please her. I sensed Christian watching me as I ate. I kept my eyes cast down.

I was frustrated, because I seemed to be gaining more questions than answers. Who was Patrick's boyfriend? How on earth did Patrick get to be friends with a Toomsboro snob like Jason? And on a whole different level, the Wally/meth mess, with Beef, Dupree, and Tommy mixed smack up in it. Tommy and Dupree, I could buy. But Beef? I couldn't wrap my head around it, even though he admitted he used to be involved. Even though I'd seen the possibility of continued involvement in his eyes.

I hadn't learned much from Wally other than that he'd trapped poor Ridings McAllister in his spiderweb. Tommy was the only one of "Wally's boys" I hadn't spoken to, aside from our brief exchange at church. But I couldn't face him. Not yet. That left the one tagalong member of the redneck posse: Beef's girlfriend, Bailee-Ann.

After dinner, I dragged a brush through my hair, pulled it into a ponytail, and headed out of the house. Bailee-Ann and I used to be tight. Patrick was my true best friend—my kindred spirit—but Bailee-Ann was my best female friend.

Our friendship fizzled out in high school, just another smoldering by-product of my amazing disappearing girl act. But Bailee-Ann never treated me with spite, because she wasn't like that. She was more . . . more like a fawn, with creamy, freckled skin and big brown eyes and a gentleness that made people not want to hurt her.

Well, made *me* not want to hurt her. Sometimes I worried about Bailee-Ann, because what one person saw as tenderness, another might perceive as an opportunity to get in and do some damage. But with Beef looking after her, Bailee-Ann would be okay. I wondered if she knew that Beef had worked for Wally? I'd have to talk carefully, in case she didn't. But maybe I could get her to tell me what happened the night of Patrick's attack.

Twilight had come and gone by the time I grabbed my bike from the side of the house. The stars weren't out yet, but the sky was bluish-purple. It would be dark soon.

When Christian saw me throw my leg over my bike, he called out, "Hey, where do you think you're going?"

Aunt Tildy followed him out on the porch, and he turned to her. "I don't want her going out again."

"Well, too bad you don't have any say in it," I said.

"You two, stop fussing," Aunt Tildy said.

"She's been out too much already," Christian insisted. "She needs to stay put."

"Needs to stay put?" I echoed. "What am I, a dog?"

"It's late. You shouldn't be out when it's dark."

Christian had been a warm body to stand by at Wally's, and I appreciated it. But this big brother protective act of his was making me nervous. It opened up old wounds.

I rolled my eyes and said, "It's hardly late. I'll be back in, like, an hour. All right, Aunt Tildy?"

"I already said *no,*" Christian said.

"And just when did you become the boss of me?"

"You're sticking your nose where it don't belong," he accused.

"Sticking my . . . ?" I gave Aunt Tildy a baffled look. "I just want to go to Bailee-Ann's. It's Saturday night, and I thought it would be nice to see her." I shrugged. "I miss her."

"Bullshit," Christian said, making Aunt Tildy inhale. I glanced at her with wide eyes to say I didn't know what had gotten into him, either.

Christian's nostrils flared. "It's because of Patrick. She's going around asking questions about Patrick, and she needs to stop."

"I don't know what he's talking about," I told Aunt Tildy.

I turned to my brother. "Honestly, I have no idea what you're talking about." I kept my tone the same, but the look Christian got said, *If you'd answer my questions yourself, I wouldn't have to.*

A flush worked its way up his face.

"Anyway, you go to your friends' houses all the time, so why can't I?" I said.

"Because you don't have any friends, that's why!"

Aunt Tildy whapped him with her dishcloth.

"*Ow,*" he complained.

"That's enough," Aunt Tildy said. "Now, Cat. There is no reason for you to be"—she pursed her lips—"getting involved with what happened to Patrick."

I pulled my eyebrows together. "But, Aunt Tildy—"

"*However,* I know you're smarter than that, and I'm glad to see you getting back with sweet Bailee-Ann. You been keeping to yourself for too long. So yes, you may go to her house."

It was Christian's turn to protest. "But, Aunt *Tildy*—"

Aunt Tildy whapped him again. "*Nossir.* You leave your sister alone."

"Yeah," I said. I smirked, as smirking felt called for, but in truth my emotions were more complicated. I felt choked by them, as if someone's thumb was pressing into the hollow of my throat.

Maybe he's changed, I thought. *Maybe he's stronger now. Maybe he* will *be there if I need him.*

But what a dangerous game to play. He would always be my big brother. I would always be his little sister. There would always be a part of me that ached to believe in him the way I used to . . . but it was a temptation I couldn't afford to give in to.

So I biked along the dirt road to Bailee-Ann's house, which was closer to town and nicer than ours. It wasn't fancy, but her daddy kept it up as best he could, with a fresh paint job and a newly mown lawn and a split-rail fence around his wife's flower garden. Wildflowers were what Bailee-Ann's mom liked: larkspur and violets and lady's slippers, which Mama Sweetie called moccasin flowers.

Bailee-Ann welcomed me with a hug, which caught me off guard.

She pulled back. "You okay?" she said, her blue eyes full of concern. Most people, when they looked at me, didn't really see me, but Bailee-Ann did.

She led me to a purple sofa patched with duct tape, which someone—probably herself—had colored with a purple marker in an attempt to make it match. On the sofa, as well as the coffee table in front of the sofa, were knitting supplies:

balls of pink and blue yarn, needles, and what looked like the beginning of a leg warmer.

"It's Patrick, isn't it?" Bailee-Ann said. "That's why you're here?"

I moved a skein of yarn and sat beside her, amazed we'd gotten to the heart of the matter so quickly. My eyes teared up, and I nodded.

"You two always were close," she said. "Have you gone to visit him?"

"No," I said. "I tried, but they wouldn't let me. His condition has to be more stable or something."

"Well, my mama just knows he's gonna be okay," Bailee-Ann said. Her mama worked for the hospital cleaning crew. "She says the doctors are taking good care of him, and the nurses, too."

"They think he'll regain consciousness?" I said. "For real?"

Bailee-Ann put her hand on my knee. "*Yes.* It's something about his brain waves looking good, that's what the nurses are saying. I wish I could grow up to be a nurse, don't you? And we could wear those cute shirts with the little teddy bears on 'em?"

"Scrubs," I said, still drinking in the news about Patrick. Hope fluttered in my chest for the first time in days.

"Huh?"

"Scrubs. That's what the nurses' outfits are called." I paused. "Or that might be just the doctors."

"Oh my God," she said. She picked up her knitting project

171

and hooked a loop of yarn with one needle. "I am *so* marrying a doctor, and when we have our first baby, we won't need the free hat." She held up what she was working on. "I'll have already made it!"

"That's a baby hat?" I said.

"Not yet, but it will be." She pushed up on one knee, reached behind the sofa, and came back with a plastic bin. "Like these, which I'll get Mama to take to the hospital next week. See?"

Inside the bin were five tiny hats: three blue ones and two pink ones. They had pom-poms on top and were utterly, absolutely adorable.

"You made these?" I marveled. I picked up a blue one. "You're good, Bailee-Ann. Like, *really* good."

She was pleased, but tried to play it off. "Oh, hats are easy. Anyway, the hospital gives me the yarn."

"And then the hats go to little babies? That's so cool."

"I think so, too. That's why I said yes when the head of the volunteer program asked me to do it. I want to be a better person, you know?"

"That's awesome," I said. "But you're already a good person."

She got busy with her needles. "But I could be *better*. I could work harder at school and not do bad things."

"Bad things?" I said. I returned the hat to the bin.

"I want to be, like, the best me ever, and then maybe I *could* grow up to marry a doctor. I'll give him babies, and he'll give me drugs." She giggled. "Kidding! He'd only give me the legal kind, and only if I needed them. I might need them a lot is all."

I saw *her* for just a moment, the real her, just as she'd seen through to the real me. I saw her weariness, which she tried to hide with sparkly eye shadow and berry-colored lip gloss. I also saw that she'd been pulling out her eyelashes again. Back when we hung out, she pulled out her eyelashes when she was nervous.

What was she nervous about now? And I wasn't going to ask again, but what sort of bad things was she no longer going to do?

"There's no reason you couldn't marry a doctor," I told her. "You could *be* a doctor, even. Or a nurse."

She smiled. Not bitterly, because Bailee-Ann didn't do bitter. It was more just a hat-knitting smile that said I didn't need to lie.

"But, Bailee-Ann, why would you want your doctor husband to give you drugs?"

"Um, because they're fun?" She looked up from her work. "Not street drugs. God, I would never. But Beef knows this guy, and sometimes he gets Vicodin from him. Beef had his own prescription once, from when he blew out his knee, but it ran out."

"Oh."

"And actually, I'm trying to quit. That's one of the ways I want to make amends. But have you ever tried it?"

"Vicodin? No, I don't do that stuff."

"*Riiight,*" she said. "You're better than that. I forgot."

Something shifted. It happened as quick as the click of her needles, and it made my skin tingle.

"No, I just don't like feeling out of control," I said.

"Oh. *O*-kay." She hooked another loop of yarn. *"So that's* why you dropped all of your friends, including Patrick. Including *me*. It wasn't because you're so much better than us. It was because you felt *out of control*, like maybe you'd accidentally catch a case of the stupids from us. Thanks for explaining. Now I totally understand."

Whoa. Apparently Bailee-Ann *was* capable of doing bitter.

"Bailee-Ann . . ." I said.

She glanced at me. Her eyes held pain, but also a sliver of hope.

"I . . . I never . . ." *I never thought you were stupid,* I wanted to say. *I never stopped liking you.*

"Son of a goddang," she cussed, looking back at the little hat. "Missed a stitch. Gonna have to do the whole row over."

I felt awful. She'd let herself wish, and I failed her, and so, all right. Back to normal Bailee-Ann, who would take her disappointment and pretend it had to do with the dropped stitch instead of the dropped friendship.

My heart felt like lead, but what was done was done. I needed to regroup.

"Did Dupree give you Vicodin last Saturday?" I asked. "When y'all were at Suicide Rock?"

"I wish," she said. Then she closed her eyes and gave herself a moment. She opened them, saying, "No, I don't, because I'm quitting. I truly am. But anyway, all Dupree had was some herbal something-or-other. We put it under our tongues."

There were old-timers all over the mountain earning a meager existence by selling herbal "remedies." Aunt Tildy warned me and Christian to stay away. "If you can't buy it at the store, don't buy it at all," she said. "Who knows what goes into their tinctures and potions?"

"You should be careful about that stuff," I said.

"I know, I know. It didn't do nothing but make us loopy, anyway." She put down the little hat, balancing the needles on top of it. It was so small. I was that small once, and the thought blew my mind. I was that small, and so was Bailee-Ann, and so was Patrick. So was Patrick's attacker.

"You wanna watch TV?" Bailee-Ann said. "Never mind. Set's broke. Duh."

I bit my lower lip. "Bailee-Ann, don't take this the wrong way . . . but you don't do meth, do you?"

She cut her eyes at me. "No, Cat, I don't do meth," she said, enunciating her words as if addressing someone very stupid who was also hard of hearing. "Meth eats your brain. Haven't you seen those commercials?"

"Well . . . good. But some kids *are* using it. Here in our own town."

"Kids are doing meth in every town in the country, Cat. Dang. Get your head out of your butt."

"Do you know when it started? Um, people in Black Creek doing meth?" *Beef* doing meth?

"I don't know," she said. "When the paper mill shut down and all those folks lost their jobs, I guess. That's when my mama started seeing more tweakers showing up in the ER. She said the Mexicans were running it through Atlanta, and from Atlanta to here."

"The Mexicans?" We didn't have any Mexicans living in Black Creek. I didn't know that I'd even seen a Mexican, period.

"I don't want to talk about it. It's depressing," Bailee-Ann said.

"I know. It's just—"

"And anything I *do* know, I know from my mama." She looked at me hard.

I nodded. "Of course. Yeah."

"Well, I guess what they were selling was crap, and then the dealers in Black Creek—down-and-out mill workers, what have you—they got the stuff from Atlanta and watered it down even more. Not *watered* it down, but you know."

Yeah, I knew. They'd *stepped on it* by adding baby powder or something. Destiny had taught me well.

Bailee-Ann found a stray piece of yarn and pulled it repeatedly through her fingers. "It wasn't good business, so eventually people in Black Creek learned to cook it themselves."

"Wally," I supplied.

Her face registered slight surprise. "Among others. Apparently, it isn't that hard."

"Until you blow yourself up."

"Yeah. But until then, it's easy money."

"And that's why people got into it," I filled in. "People from here. People we might even know."

The yarn in Bailee-Ann's fingers grew taut. "Maybe. But like I said, this is all secondhand."

"Must be a lot of gossip at the hospital, huh?"

"Almost as much as at church," she said.

I laughed. It broke the tension. "I sure wish you'd come back to church, speaking of." She rarely came these days, because her mama had Sundays off and wanted to sleep in. "Without you, I don't have anyone to pass notes with."

She half-smiled, perhaps remembering all the scribbling we used to do on the church bulletins. It perked her up, and she said, "Hey. Wanna go to Tommy's and catch a movie on his flat-screen?"

I shifted. "Um, thanks for the offer, but movies aren't really my thing."

Her half-smile turned into something worse: a false smile. "Of course they aren't," she said. "Silly me, whatever was I thinking?" She wound the piece of yarn into a neat bundle, placed it on the coffee table, and said, "Well, it was nice chatting. Thanks for stopping by."

I felt my cheeks heat up. I got awkwardly to my feet.

"Why *did* you stop by?"

"To talk about Patrick."

She raised her eyebrows, wanting more.

"I'm trying to make sense of it, that's all. And I guess I was just wondering . . ."

"Spit it out, Cat," she said dryly. "I promise I won't take it the wrong way."

I splayed my feet so that my weight was on their outside edges. I stared down at them and said, "Beef said he drove y'all home. On Saturday night."

"And?"

"He said he dropped Tommy off first, with Dupree. Is that true?"

"Yeah. *And?*"

"So Tommy was home by one thirty."

"Oh my God," Bailee-Ann said, blinking her patchy eyelashes. "Is that what this is about? Seriously?"

Adopting a dumb blond voice, she said, "Tommy was home by one thirty, and I was home by one forty-five. Beef made me feel like a slut when I kissed him, because he pushed me away and said I smelled like a brewery. But he made sure my truck was back in my driveway by the time I woke up the next morning. He even washed it for me. Wasn't that sweet?"

"If you say so," I said. I hesitated. "Are you and Beef doing okay?"

"Of course. Why wouldn't we be?"

Well, let's see. Because he quit school, and because he was possibly selling and/or using meth. Most of all because of the "slut" reference Bailee-Ann threw into her recitation.

"No reason," I said. Anyway, Bailee-Ann didn't say Beef actually *called* her that, just that he made her *feel* like that.

"Don't listen to me," Bailee-Ann said. "I'm just weird. I'm sure Beef didn't kiss me because Patrick and your brother were waiting in the truck."

"Uh, okay."

"He hadn't dropped them off yet. It would have been gross to make out in front of them. Plus, Beef was mad at them in a *big* way. That's why—"

She broke off, zipping her lips together so purposefully that I understood where that expression came from, *zip your lips.*

"That's why what?"

She shook her head.

"Bailee-Ann. I know something went on that night, something more than getting high and petting trees. Just tell me."

"Who said anything about petting trees? I didn't pet no trees. You think I'm so starved for love I'd pet a dang *tree*?"

"Why was Beef mad? Was there a fight?"

Seven or eight years ago, some older boys went at one another up into the forest, and things went south fast. One guy had a knife. The other had broken beer bottle, its edges jagged and sharp.

Bailee-Ann stared deliberately past me, but her eyes defied her, sliding to mine for one quick second.

My heart gave a peculiar double beat. Bailee-Ann was scared. *That's* why she was keeping mum.

"You can tell me, Bailee-Ann. I swear."

She leaned forward and got back her piece of yarn, winding it tightly around her index finger. I watched her fingertip go from red to white. "Tommy and Patrick had something they wanted to . . . *discuss* with Beef. Your brother was in on it, too."

"In on what?"

"But Beef wouldn't listen. He felt ganged up on, I guess. He wanted them to lay off, but they wouldn't, and finally Beef lost it. He told Tommy and Christian to go play with their vaginas, though he didn't use that word, and he called Patrick a fucking pansy. Nice, huh?"

"Wait. Beef called Patrick . . ." I shook my head. "*Wait.* In front of everyone, Beef called him that?"

Bailee-Ann cocked her head, and my mouth went dry. Beef was Patrick's champion. Beef was every underdog's champion.

Disoriented, I sat back down on the sofa. Different explanations vied for a toehold: Bailee-Ann was lying. It was Tommy who called Patrick that, not Beef. Or maybe Tommy said something worse and Beef lashed out without thinking, his words meant to hurt everyone in the redneck posse, not just Patrick.

There had to be more to the incident than Bailee-Ann was telling me. Everyone knew how stressed Beef was; whatever the guys wanted to discuss with him must have made him even more so.

"It's probably losing his wrestling scholarship," I whispered.

"You think?" Bailee-Ann said sarcastically. "Do you know the full story of that, by the way?"

"The full story of Beef losing his wrestling scholarship? I think so. He got a knee injury. I don't know *how,* or what kind of knee injury, only that it's in his . . ."

". . . knee," Bailee-Ann filled in, making me feel like a

baby. "But it wouldn't have happened if he'd had his head on straight."

My own head was muzzy. All I could think was, *Beef called Patrick a pansy? Beef did that?*

Then, for Patrick to be attacked only hours later . . .

I understood why Christian was being so close-mouthed about it. *Means, motive, and opportunity*—I knew those terms from various mysteries I'd read over the years, and Beef could be seen as having all three.

I now understood Beef's hostility at Huskers, too. It wasn't hostility. It was fear and guilt and self-loathing, all smashed together and coming out as hostility. Because, God, how terrible. It was like a kid lashing out at his daddy for something dumb like not getting to have an ice-cream cone. Like if the kid said, "I wish you were dead," and then, the very next second, the daddy collapsed from a heart attack.

Bailee-Ann was talking, using wrestling terms and gesturing with her hands. I did my best to tune in.

". . . could have pinned him right then," she said. "It was a done deal. But no, he let him back up in order to humiliate him some more."

I'd missed a big chunk of the story, but I didn't want to let on if I could help it.

"So Beef took him down *again*," Bailee-Ann said, unwrapping the yarn from her index finger and moving on to the next. "He put the legs on him, like maybe he was planning a guillotine. Only he never got the chance to lock it down

181

because the guy from Woodward grabbed hold of Beef's foot and cranked it."

Bailee-Ann said "the guy from Woodward," and Woodward was in Asheville, so now I knew where the other wrestler was from. I didn't know what "putting the legs on someone" meant, however, and though I knew what a guillotine was, I suspected it was something different in a wrestling match.

"Is that bad?" I asked. "Grabbing someone's foot?"

"Not if you do it legal. But if you pull back on it until you break the other guy's ligament, then yeah. That's bad."

I went over it in my mind. Beef had his opponent almost pinned. He let him up just to take him down again. To humiliate him. Only it backfired, and Beef ended up with a blown knee.

"Why didn't the ref step in?" I asked.

"He was on the wrong side of the mat," Bailee-Ann said. "He couldn't see what was going on till it was too late."

"Oh. And why did Beef want to humiliate the Woodward guy again?"

Her expression was incredulous.

"I know, I know," I apologized. "Just explain it one more time?"

"What's to explain? He called Beef a crotch-sniffing faggot."

I winced.

"Then when they were facing off, he wiggled his fingers and said, 'Come on, sweetheart.' And he made smoochy noises."

"That's so stupid."

"You think?" she said. She was silent for several seconds.

"There'd been jokes," she filled in. "Stupid jokes, like you said, about him and Patrick being friends."

"That's nothing new. Beef's never let it get to him before."

She shrugged.

"Did Beef even know the guy from Asheville?"

"Does it matter? He didn't like being called sweetheart."

It made me think. As Patrick's defender, Beef had been on the receiving end of plenty of stupid comments over the years. Patrick got it ten times worse, yet I wondered, for a guy, which was worse: to be called a fag when you *were* one or when you weren't.

For the first time, I also wondered if Beef ever got sick of standing up for Patrick, sick of being sprayed by mud just because he was standing in the wrong place. Maybe that was why he lost it at Suicide Rock. Maybe he slipped, like we all did at times, his anger lowering him to the level of guys like that Asheville jerk.

"Anyway, that's how he hurt his knee, and that's why he lost his scholarship," Bailee-Ann said. "It's sad. It's extremely sad. But how long is he allowed to punish everyone else because of it?"

"Good point."

"One day, everything's great—*Whoo-hoo! I love life! Let's party, girl!*—and then there's one little wrinkle in his universe and, suddenly, everything sucks."

I started to reply, then stopped. Then did anyway. "Pretty big wrinkle."

"I *know*," she said, like she didn't need me explaining it to her. "And then he has to go and be all *sweet*, washing my truck for me or bringing me one of those cookies I like from the sandwich shop. Those butterscotch ones. You ever had one?"

I shook my head.

She leaned back into the sofa, looking bone tired. I knew she'd said all she was going to say about Beef.

We were pretty much done after that. Only later did I realize that she never did tell me exactly what happened at Suicide Rock. She said Tommy and my brother and Patrick wanted to "discuss" something with Beef, but she never told me what that something was.

16

I STEPPED INTO THE PITCH-BLACK COUNTRY NIGHT. Certain parts of town had streetlights, but not in this neck of the woods. I thought about how Christian would disapprove of my being out here alone, and to tell the truth it *was* spooky. Then someone said my name, and I nearly jumped out of my skin.

"Robert, what the heck?" I said, peering into the shadows to see his weaselly face. *Weaselly* wasn't a nice word to describe him, but it was accurate. Robert was an eleven-year-old trapped in a body that was scrawny by nine-year-old standards, and what he lacked in size, he made up for in hyperness. I felt bad for him, because it wasn't his fault. His mama drank too much when he was in the womb. These things happened.

But there he was, scrawny and hyper, and just because he wasn't to blame didn't mean people forgave him for it.

"Ha-ha, got you good," Robert said, practically dancing around me. "I saw your bike, and I sat here and waited. Passed the time by throwing pinecones at that there tree"—he jerked his chin at a dark blob among other dark blobs—"and I woulda hit it, too, if I wanted. I just didn't wanna."

"Uh-huh, that's great, Robert," I said. I took hold of my bike and toed up the kickstand.

"You come here about Patrick?" he said.

I didn't know what to make of his question.

"I listened in," he bragged. He laughed and did a sideways nod at the open windows. "I'm good at being sneaky, ain't I? I hear all sorts of stuff."

"Like what?" I almost said, but at the last moment, I avoided the trap. Robert would talk my ear off if I let him, boasting about one thing or another, and none of them more interesting than pinecones.

"Yes, Robert, you're good at being sneaky," I said, swinging my leg over the frame. "And now, I gotta go."

"Naw, wait," he said. Mucus snaked out of his nose. He sucked it back in while at the same time stepping closer, as if along with his snot he wanted to suck every ounce of attention from me that he could. "I like Patrick, even if he is a spoilsport."

"Huh?"

"He made me go home when it wasn't even my bedtime. I don't even *have* a bedtime. Duh."

I cocked my head. "Are you talking about the night your sister and everybody went to Suicide Rock?"

"Everyone but me," Robert complained. "I've never gotten to go there at night, not even once. And the others didn't care if I went. But Patrick was all, 'Robert's too *little*. Robert has to go home.'"

"He was just looking out for you," I said.

"Only I don't need him looking out for me," Robert said. He flipped his wrist. "And ain't it just like a fairy to get his panties in a wad over something that's none of his business."

"Robert, don't."

"What?"

"Don't call him that."

"A fairy? But he *is* one."

I was too tired for this. Most everybody called Patrick names, so it wasn't as if I was going to change Robert's way of thinking.

"*Ohhhhh,*" Robert said. "You think it's one of those hate words."

"It *is* one of those hate words," I said. "And you just said you like Patrick, so why would you call him something hateful?"

He hawked a loogie and rubbed dirt over it with his bare foot. "I like him well enough. I don't wanna be kissy-kissy with him, but I didn't clonk him in the head with a baseball bat, if that's what you're asking."

That wasn't what I was asking. Robert was a kid, and an undernourished, puny one at that. He didn't have the strength to clonk someone in the head.

"Well, I like Patrick, too," I replied. "Your sister says he's gonna be okay. That's good news, isn't it?"

"If you say so," he said fake-mysteriously. "Only if I were you, I wouldn't go around believing everything Bailee-Ann says."

I lifted my eyebrows. "And why's that?"

"'Cause she lies, that's why."

I glanced at the house with its open windows. Then I put down my bike's kickstand and stepped further into the shadows. He scampered behind me, and I groaned inwardly, knowing I was wasting my time.

Robert was what you'd call an *unreliable narrator*, that was the book term for it. The kind of kid who was never wrong about anything, who always had a reason for why the pinecone didn't hit the tree.

"All right, Robert," I said when we were out of Bailee-Ann's hearing distance. "What do you want to tell me?"

His face lit up. He liked the low pitch of my voice, the intimacy of sharing secrets. He stepped close, put his lips right up to my ear, and said . . . nothing. Just inhaled deep, like he was breathing me in.

"Robert." It was a matter of will not to pull away from him. As I said, it wasn't his fault, but he was a boy who ate his boogers and didn't bathe often enough. Who without provocation said things like "I gotta go drain my willy" because he was under the mistaken impression that it made him seem manly.

"You smell like raspberries," he said, his breath warm. He burrowed into my hair, and I drew away.

"Eww, Robert, gross. It's called shampoo. You buy it at the store. Now, do you have something to tell me or not?"

His face closed over. "You don't have to be mean about it, bitch."

"What'd you just call me?"

"I called you a *bitch,* bitch."

My mouth fell open. I used to kiss Robert's boo-boos back in the day. I probably even changed his diapers once or twice, seeing that he wore those pull-ups way longer than a child should.

"Robert Wayne Boxberger, you go inside and wash out your mouth with soap," I told him.

"Who's gonna make me? You?"

"Good Lord," I muttered, heading back toward the house.

"Cat! Wait!"

I climbed on my bike and pushed off. Rocks popped up and dinged my fenders.

Robert ran after me. "Don't you wanna hear what I got to say?"

"Nope."

"I'll tell you, I swear. And you ain't a bitch, okay?"

"Gee, thanks," I kept pedaling, and eventually I escaped the pounding of his sneakers. All I heard were the bumps and crunches of my tires on the dirt road, blending with the dark noises of the forest. But it wasn't the forest that scared me. It was the people who lived and prowled within them.

sunday

17

CHURCH WAS A MISERY.

Something happened last night at the hospital, that's why. Verleen had the most information, because her sister was married to Deputy Carl Doyle. She told a circle of ladies all about it before the service started, her shellacked hairdo bobbing as she spoke.

"A *perpetrator* jimmied open the window to Patrick's room," she said. "He sliced the screen too. Carl said it hung off the window frame like a flap of skin."

"Oh my," a church lady named Dottie said, putting her hand to her heart.

"Uh-huh. Carl don't know *why* someone was trying to break in, just that they was. The only reason they didn't make it was because of the night nurse doing her rounds. She musta scared him off, Carl says."

"Well my goodness, Verleen. That is just *terrible*," Dottie said.

"Uh-huh. It is. Now Carl has to do round-the-clock surveillance, sitting outside that boy's room with his pistol in his holster." Verleen pursed her lips. "I reckon I'll bring him a ham sandwich later on."

I felt ill standing on the fringes of the crowd and listening in, but I couldn't make myself leave. Verleen said the reporters were back in flocks now, milling around the hospital and hunting for information. Only, there wasn't much to go on. There was a single set of footprints in the dark soil below Patrick's window, but no fingerprints, and no hints as to what the *perpetrator* had in mind to do if he'd gotten in.

The worst part was that all the commotion affected Patrick's "stability."

"Carl heard that from Dr. Granville," Verleen said. "People in comas can be aware of their surroundings, you see."

Hannah, the young mother from Coonesville, nodded. "That's why you're supposed to talk to them. Same with plants."

"The doctor said he won't wake up if he don't feel safe," Verleen said.

Dottie clucked her dismay.

"That poor boy," Hannah said. "I wish they'd caught him, that fella at the window. I wish they'd just catch him and put him away."

"*I* wish Patrick hadn't gotten himself into this mess in the first place," Verleen said. "Can you imagine poor Aurelia having to deal with such a mess?" Aurelia was Mama Sweetie's given name.

"It woulda killed her if she weren't dead already," Dottie said. "Bless her heart."

The ladies gave a moment of silence to Mama Sweetie's memory.

A middle-aged woman spoke up. She was in the choir, but I couldn't recall her name. She had a birthmark the size of a stinkbug under one eye. It pooched out like a mole, only it was the reddish-purple of the grape juice we drank at communion.

"Could have been anyone who attacked him," she pronounced. She nodded at Verleen. "I know your Carl thinks it's an out-of-towner, but I wouldn't stake the farm on it."

"Carl is doing the best he can," Verleen said, giving the choir woman a look.

"Well, of course, he is. We all know that." The choir woman patted Verleen's arm. "I'm just saying—" She broke off and scanned the room. "Well, you know what I'm saying. You all do. And to think that here we are, talking about it in the house of the Lord."

The ladies tutted. I wanted to smack them all. I wanted Aunt Tildy to smack them all, or break up the group in some other way, like by telling them that in that case, they *shouldn't* be talking about it in the house of the Lord. But Aunt Tildy was busy in the church kitchen, arranging doughnuts on a platter.

"Sounds to me like someone don't want Patrick waking up," Hannah said timidly.

The ladies nodded.

"That's why I think it was a local boy, and a smart one at that," the choir woman said. "One who ain't interested in getting caught."

"We might even know him," Hannah said with wide eyes.

"He might go to this very church," Dottie said. "He might be in this very room with us right now."

Everyone glanced around, myself included. I spotted old Mrs. Lawson sipping a cup of coffee, but Tommy wasn't with her. None of the members of the redneck posse had dragged themselves out of bed for church this morning, not that I was surprised. The congregation lacked guys in that age group, period. Still, the group of ladies tightened their circle.

The choir woman eyed the ladies, her gaze coming to rest, inexplicably, on me. A bolt of alarm shot through my bones, and with it came the recollection of her name. Obedience Burwell. She went by Biddy.

"People say you're hunting for the perpurtrator yourself," Biddy said. She'd learned the word from Verleen, and it didn't set comfortably on her tongue.

"No," I said. My chest went up and down, up and down.

Biddy stared at me. Her birthmark stared at me, a fat, blood-filled sac. "If I were you, I'd leave it."

The ladies nodded as a single unit. A flock of hens.

"Cat!" Hannah said anxiously. "Oh my gracious, you can't

go poking around in something like this. Not when it involves criminal activity!"

"He don't want to be found," Dottie chimed in. She stepped closer and squeezed my shoulder. I pretended to be a statue. "And *you* don't want to be the one who finds him. Believe me, hon."

"You could get sliced up, like that window screen," Hannah said. She blinked rapidly. "Or worse."

Verleen said, "Now, Cat, I can't believe you'd act as ill-afformed as that, getting into business that ain't yours to get in. Surely you have more sense."

"I do," I said in a panicked, breathy voice.

But Verleen wasn't done. "If you *are* poking around, it stops today. You hear? You leave that business to Carl and Bubba."

"Yes, ma'am."

"That gasoline nozzle," Hannah whispered, looking at me like I'd already gone and gotten such a thing stuck up in me.

"All right, I think we've said enough," Biddy said, although I swear to God she was pleased with what she'd made. "I think we all need to be careful. A perpuhtater like that, we don't none of us want to come face-to-face with him."

She'd changed her pronunciation. *Purple tater*, I thought. *Purple tater, purple tater.*

"And we won't," Verleen said. "He's wily enough to wipe his prints off the windowsill, he's wily enough not to get caught."

"Oh my," Dottie said. "Verleen, hon, you might be bringing Carl sandwiches for a long time."

18

WHEN IT WAS TIME FOR THE SERVICE, I DIDN'T
file into the sanctuary with the others. Instead, I snuck into the
church office. I used the slow-as-molasses computer to see if I
could find out anything more about the hospital break-in.

I didn't, but I did learn more about comas and other medical
stuff. I tried to educate myself as best I could, because Patrick
was *not* a plant, and I couldn't believe that Hannah—who
had a baby! an itty-bitty, crying, and smiling baby!—had said
something so thoughtless.

Patrick probably had blisters erupting around his mouth,
that was one thing I read on the medical sites I pulled up.
Because of the gas fumes. And I learned a new word: *hypoxia*.
It meant lack of oxygen, and sometimes people recovered

completely from a hypoxic hit to the brain, and sometimes they didn't.

I also found an online Toomsboro Community College student directory, and guess whose information was listed in it? Jason Connor's, that's whose. He was a college boy, just like I'd suspected. He opted to "share his contact information with prospective students," so now I had his email address as well as what dorm he lived in . He was taking summer classes, I guess. Whoop-de-doo for him.

I could take the bus into town tomorrow morning and be at Braiden Hall by nine. If he was asleep, I'd wake him up. If he was in class, I'd wait outside his room. If he never showed up at all, I'd knock on every door of every dorm room until I found someone who could lead me to him.

Given what happened at the hospital, it was time for me and Jason to have a true and real conversation.

monday

19

I WAS ON MY WAY TO TOOMSBORO BY EIGHT THIRTY the next morning. There weren't many other people on the bus. A man wearing overalls, maybe going into town to do yard work. A woman wearing an ankle-length skirt, her hair in a bun. I didn't have a clue what her story was. Was she a day care worker? A member of one of those old-fashioned basement churches where the ministers traveled from house to house and the females weren't allowed to wear pants?

Oh, and there was one other passenger: Robert.

Yep, scrawny, hop-about Robert was heading into Toomsboro with me. He must have been hiding a couple of yards from the bus stop, because he wasn't in sight when I got there.

Then the bus came rumbling around the bend and wheezed to a stop. Its doors sighed open, I climbed aboard, and *woosh.* He was like a squirrel darting out of the scrub brush, hyper and gloating as he dashed on behind me. He didn't have to pay any fare since he was only eleven.

"Robert," I said, exasperated. "What are you doing here?"

He grinned and tried to sit down beside me. "Goin' on a bus ride. With you. Scooch and make room."

I blocked him by planting one foot on the floor and pressing the other against the back of the seat in front of me.

"Aw, now, why you gotta be like that? I just want to talk to you."

"Talk to me another time. And get off the bus."

"Ain't have to if I don't wanna. I got just as much right just as you do."

The bus driver hit the gas, and Robert stumbled backward.

"Young man, sit down," the driver commanded.

Clinging to the seats, Robert tried to haul himself back to where I was. It was like watching a fish try to swim upstream.

"Now," the driver growled.

Robert plunked himself down three seats behind me, on the opposite side of the aisle. He whispered, "Hey. *Hey!* Just talk to me, will ya?"

There was so much wrong with that boy, I didn't know where to start. Following a girl five years older than him onto a bus? Hiding in the dang bushes so I wouldn't spot him till it was too late? Poor kid must have been awfully lonely to go to all that trouble.

"You know I didn't mean it, Cat," he said. "What I called you the other night."

I faced forward. "I know, Robert. Now leave me alone."

"Can't I come sit with you?"

"No."

"Why not?"

"Because once you pick your seat, you have to stay put, or they'll kick you off."

"For real?"

"Safety regulation. And if they kick you off, the next time you try to get a ride, they won't let you."

He thought about that.

"How would they know it was me?" he said.

"Because they'd take a picture of you and tape it up where the driver sits, on every single bus. Now will you please stop bugging me?"

"Yeah. Okay. But I have a secret to tell you, remember?"

I twisted to look at him. He grinned, squirming with the pleasure of being noticed.

"Okay, Robert. Tell me your secret. I'm dying to know."

"You don't sound like you're dyin'."

"I am. Believe me."

"It's real good, the secret. You're gonna be real happy when you hear it."

"Why don't you prove it by telling me?"

More grinning and squirming. He needed to be medicated—like that was ever going to happen.

"Robert? We're almost to my stop, so if you're going to tell me, tell me now."

"If it's your stop, it's my stop, too," he said.

"Um, *no.*"

"Yeah-huh."

"Robert, I am here on business. You can*not* bother me."

He huffed. "Why you being so cold to me? Why's everybody turned so cold all of a sudden, acting like I'm a kid when I've got chest hairs and everything?"

I snorted. I didn't mean to, and if I could have stopped myself, I would have. It hurt his feelings.

"Fine," he said. "I ain't gonna tell you my secret after all, so fine." He slammed his body against the back of his seat and sulked.

We rode like that for the next few minutes. As we approached the college, I attempted to smooth things over.

"Hey, Robert," I said. "You ready to talk to me yet?"

He angled his body toward the bus window, presenting me with his skinny back. I saw the knobs of his spine through his threadbare T-shirt.

"Well, don't go wandering off in Toomsboro by yourself," I told him.

"I'm eleven years old. I can take care of myself."

"I know, but still." I doubted Robert would ever be able to take care of himself.

The bus rolled to a stop. The doors *shushed* open.

"How about this," I said, standing up. "Meet me back here in an hour, and we'll ride back together. Can you do that?"

"Can you do that?" Robert mimicked.

"Well, can you? It's like . . ." I tried to think how to put it. "Like the buddy system."

"Don't need no buddy, especially you."

"Well, all right, then."

I got off the bus. He followed. I headed for the college, and he trailed behind me. He was as sneaky as a rhinoceros.

I found Braiden Hall, and miraculously, Robert didn't enter the dorm behind me. When I glanced to check, he was gnawing his thumbnail. Perhaps he felt as intimidated by the fancy campus as I did.

"Stay," I told him, like you'd say to a dog.

He looked caught out. Then he said, loudly, "I think I'll sit here by this tree. I think I'll just sit here and enjoy the morning air."

I went inside the dorm. I found a student list stuck to a row of metal mailboxes and saw that Jason resided in room 101, so that's where I went. I rapped on the door, trying to act braver than I felt. I banged louder.

"One sec," a guy said groggily, and my heart jumped into my throat. There were footsteps, and then the click of a deadbolt. The door opened, and there, in the flesh, was Jason. It really was him. He was wearing loose pj pants with brown monsters all over them, and his hair was messy. He wasn't wearing a shirt.

"Whoa," he said. I jerked my gaze from his chest to his face. "Uh . . . *whoa*. What are you doing here?"

You have monsters on your pj's, I wanted to say. *And they're cute. Cute little monsters. Who are you to be wearing pj bottoms printed with cute little monsters?* I caught myself noticing his build and looked away. I wasn't here to notice the fact that he happened to be . . . well . . . *built.* Good heavens.

"I need to know about Patrick," I said. "You gonna let me in?"

"Uh, yeah, sure. I guess." He opened the door wider. "How do you know where I live?"

"Don't worry about that," I said. "Would you please tell me how you know Patrick? For real?"

He didn't answer, so I used the time to take in the details of his room: the boy smell, the posters of indie bands, the stacks of books. The one and only bed, which I sat down on. Guess he lucked out and got himself a single.

Jason scratched his bare chest, which must have made him aware of the bareness of it, because he blushed and yanked a shirt from a hanger in the closet. He slid it on and went to work on the buttons. "Seriously. Why are you here? How'd you know where to find me?"

I gave him the basics of how he shouldn't post personal information on the online college directory if he didn't want people reading it. While I spoke, he rolled up his sleeves. I had to pull my eyes from his tan forearms.

"Anyway, you may not be aware of this, but last night

205

someone may or may not have tried to break into Patrick's room in the hospital," I said.

He blanched.

"Was it you?" I demanded.

"What? *No.*" He went from confused to pissed, and he said a lot of things about was I crazy? and what was wrong with me? and how could I even think something like that?

I chose not to respond. I just folded my arms over my chest.

He pulled his desk chair over near me and dropped into it. "Tell me more," he said. "Tell me exactly what happened."

I told him what I'd heard, and his face darkened. Then, because nothing in life was free, I returned to my question: *How did he and Patrick know each other?*

"From the Come 'n' Go," he said, dazed. "*Fuck.* Who would do something like that?"

"That's what I'm trying to find out," I said. "What do you mean, from the Come 'n' Go? Did you buy beer from him?"

He dropped his head into his hands. "Sometimes. Except, no, because he wouldn't sell to us. Um, we bought snacks. Junk food."

"Did you give him a hard time? Call him girly names and make fun of him for being light in the loafers?" *Light in the loafers,* my God. I'd channeled Aunt Tildy rather than mustering the confidence to say the word *gay.*

Jason nodded, and I felt a stab in my chest. Maybe because I'd started to change my opinion of him after seeing him in the hospital? Maybe I wanted him *not* to be one of those Mario Mario jerks?

"But I don't treat him like that anymore," he said.

"Wow, you should be so proud."

He stared at me, part hostile and part hurting. The hurting part must have won out, because he started talking, and he didn't hold back. He told me that yeah, his college buddies were assholes, and yeah, so was he. But Patrick took it like a man, and Jason couldn't help but respect him for it.

Over time, Jason started driving to Black Creek on his own, leaving his buddies at the dorm. He quit harassing Patrick. One night, he spotted one of Patrick's philosophy books by the cash register, and it was a book Jason had read, so they talked about it for a while. It got to the point where Jason and Patrick would hang out at the Come 'n' Go for hours. They'd argue about philosophical issues, or they'd just shoot the breeze. Occasionally, according to Jason, Patrick wouldn't be in the mood to talk, so Jason would leave.

"He'd act like nobody could possibly understand how *hard* his life was, and that got old," Jason admitted. "But no one's perfect. He's a good guy."

"I know."

"He didn't deserve what happened to him."

"I know." I looked Jason straight in the eye. "Do you know who did it? Was it one of your friends?"

"No," he said. "The guys I hang with . . . *no*. They're dumb

207

shits, but they're not . . . they would never . . ." He rubbed the bridge of his nose. "They drink. They smoke a little weed. They go to parties and hit on girls, and that's all life is to them, one big kegger."

"Were you with them that Saturday?" I asked. "What if they were partying and wanted some beer and drove to Black Creek to try and buy some? And the store was closed, and Patrick wouldn't open it back up, and things got ugly?"

"No," Jason said.

"Well, what if they knew from the get-go that Patrick wouldn't sell to them, and they drove to the Come 'n' Go looking for a fight? Boys can be like that, you know."

"No. Not those guys."

"How can you be sure?"

"Because all their lives, they've been given whatever they want," he said, anger flashing across his face. "Because I doubt any one of them's been in a fistfight, even. They're soft and they're spoiled and they don't know the kind of ugliness we know. Okay?"

I grew silent. How did Jason know what kind of ugliness I knew or didn't know? And since when did him and me become a "we"?

"You live in Black Creek, right?" he said. "Same as Patrick?"

I hesitated, then nodded tersely.

"Yeah, well, I'm from Hangtree."

My eyebrows went up, because Hangtree was even more backwoods than Black Creek. Think toothless hillbillies and cousins marrying cousins and corn liquor distilled with battery acid. That was Hangtree.

"But in the library, you called me . . ." I didn't finish. The point was, being from Hangtree meant he was even more white trash than me.

He looked ashamed. "Yeah, and like I said at the hospital, I'm sorry."

"Actually, you didn't."

"Yeah, I did."

"No, you didn't. You said you owed me an apology, but you never gave me one."

"I didn't? Well, um, I'm sorry. I'm really sorry. What I said was uncool."

"You think?" I said.

"I was in a bad place. I'd heard about Patrick, and I was so angry I couldn't think straight. I was so angry I didn't even go to the college computer lab, because I wanted to see what I could find out about Patrick, and I didn't want some asshole coming over and saying, 'Hey, bro, whatcha doing? *Whoa,* you reading about that faggot? What's up with that, man?'"

His eyes were full of despair, and I had the craziest urge to hug that fool of a boy, the way a mama would hug her rascally toddler after he rammed his trike into her pot of petunias and broke the thing to bits.

It's all right, the mama would say. *Shhh, now. Quit your crying. We all mess up. It's what we learn from our mistakes that matters.*

But Jason wasn't three. And I wasn't his mama.

"I'm sorry," he said again, and this time he took those words and owned them. "I was a complete tool."

We sat with it. Or I sat with it, and he let me, until at last I said, "Well, I'm sorry, too. For embarrassing you in front of all those library people."

He exhaled through his nose. "Hell, I deserved it. But, man. When you get fierce, you get fierce, don't you?"

No comment, I thought. I liked the way he saw me, though. I tried it on . . . and it actually kind of fit. I was fierce, or getting there. I sat up a little straighter.

"Did you find anything when you were doing your research?"

He pushed his fingers through his hair. "No. It had been a week. A *week,* and Patrick was still unconscious, and the sheriff's department didn't have a clue who worked him over."

"They still don't," I said.

He nodded. "That day at the library . . . I don't know," he said. "I figured it was a good ol' boy from the hills who hurt Patrick. Some ignorant redneck filled to the brim with 'Jesus Saves' and 'Adam and Eve, not Adam and Steve.' I guess I wanted to punish someone."

"So you saw me, and what? Thought you'd punish me for being an ignorant redneck?"

He hitched one shoulder. "You were kind of crawling up my butt."

"I was not," I said, making an *ew* face. "Anyway, you're more country than I am. You just don't look it."

"Whatever."

"How'd you peg me as being country?"

It wasn't like I'd worn overalls or anything. It couldn't have been my accent, either, because I was just sitting at the computer, minding my own business. Plus, I didn't talk like most folks in Black Creek did. I made a point of it.

He muttered something unintelligible.

"Come again?" I said.

His whole face was red, along with his neck. "Patrick pointed you out once. You wouldn't remember."

I didn't remember. He was right about that.

"Did he introduce us?" I asked.

Jason shook his head.

"Then how do you know it was me?"

"You're right, maybe it wasn't," he said, giving in too easily.

"*Oka-a-a-y,* then why'd you say it was?"

He sighed.

I waited.

"It was this past winter," he finally said. "We had half a foot of snow dumped on us the night before, but the next day, the sun came out. You were taking a walk."

My skin tingled. I had no recollection of seeing Jason, but I did remember that particular day. I remembered the glint of the fresh snow, so bright it hurt to look at. I remembered how amazing the sun felt after months of being cold.

"It was the first warm day of the year," I said.

Jason nodded.

"Patrick honked," I said slowly. "He was in his car. He drove past me."

"There was a film festival in Asheville," Jason said. "My car wouldn't start, so he picked me up, and afterward we drove back to Black Creek. Patrick saw you and pointed you out. He wanted to stop the car and offer you a ride. I told him no."

"Gee, what a gentleman," I said. My mind was somewhere else, though. I was surprised Patrick would have pointed me out to a friend after three years of getting little more from me than quick nods of acknowledgment.

"I didn't want to bother you," Jason said. "You were in your own world. You looked . . ."

I tilted my head.

"Happy," he said. "And then Patrick honked, and you jumped, and your expression changed."

"Ohhh," I said, the details falling into place. I'd been daydreaming about the book I was in the middle of, and when Patrick honked, it *did* startle me. There was a time when I would have recovered with a laugh, but that was the old me. The pre-Tommy me. The girl Patrick honked at was someone else entirely.

And yet . . . was it possible that the real me still existed, buried beneath snowdrifts of hurt?

Jason and I talked for a long time. I finally told him my name, which I'd managed not to up until then, and he said it suited me.

I asked him why, and he said, "I don't know. Because cats are smart? Because they know how to track things down?"

I laughed. "Things like you? Believe me, it wasn't that hard."

"Well, because of how they keep to themselves, then," he said. "Dogs like everyone. Cats choose who to like."

Hmmm, I thought, mulling that over.

We talked more about Patrick, and he told me he was here on campus the night Patrick was attacked. He and his college buddies were at a party at someone's apartment. He showed me pictures on his cell phone, and I told him he looked like a frat boy. He snorted.

I told him about Wally the meth cooker, and he said meth had spread like poison ivy through his hometown, too. His sister-in-law lost her kids to it. A cousin had nubs for hands because of a meth-cooking explosion. Even so, she was still a user. She gripped a tiny silver spoon between her pawlike hands while her boyfriend held the lighter beneath.

"Have you done it?" I asked, thinking *please say no, please say no.*

"No, and I never will," he said. For a moment, his vehemence transformed him into the angry Jason from the library. "That's why I'm here. I had to get out of that fucking hellhole. Once I get my degree, I'm going even further. Maybe Nashville, maybe Atlanta." His throat worked. "I'm never going back."

I was awed by his conviction, and I felt a pang that unlike Jason, I'd be stuck in Black Creek forever.

Only . . . did it have to be like that? What if I came here after I graduated? My grades were good. Maybe I could get financial aid?

I ducked my head and drew into myself like a stupid snail. Maybe the president himself would fly to Black Creek to offer me a full scholarship, and while he was at it, maybe he'd buy some of my homemade corn relish. Then he'd ask Aunt Tildy for the privilege of killing a chicken so she could fry it up and serve it with dumplings, and as she was making dinner, he'd pop out to the garage and offer Daddy a job so he didn't have to be a drunk anymore.

But forget all that. I was glad—very glad—about Jason not being a tweaker.

I shared bits and pieces of my life, too, especially the parts relating to Patrick. I told him about Beef, explaining that he was Patrick's best guy friend, and Jason said yeah, that Patrick had mentioned him. I swallowed and told Jason how I'd found out about Beef's involvement with meth, and I gave him the details about Beef and Bailee-Ann's problems in the romance department. I also told him about Gwennie, who appeared to have a thing for Patrick despite the fact that Patrick was gay.

I described the other members of the redneck posse: Dupree, a meth runner who possibly did some on-the-side dealing as well; my brother, the coward; Tommy. I told Jason almost everything, and he listened.

Scooching back on his bed and leaning against the cinder

block wall, I even told him about Robert, whose neediness worried me and irritated me in almost equal measure.

"He keeps saying he's got a secret to tell me, but he won't say what it is," I said. "Oh, and he's here, by the way. He ambushed me on the bus and followed me."

"He's here?" Jason said. "Where?"

"Lurking outside the dorm, I reckon."

Jason went to his window, hiked it up, and leaned out. "Skinny kid in baggy shorts? Pacing around and talking to himself?"

"That would be him," I confirmed dryly.

"You should buy him an ice-cream cone," Jason said. "He looks hungry."

I told him I didn't have money for anything other than bus fare, and he fished out three dollars from his wallet.

I held my hands up and said, "Uh, *no*. I'm not here for handouts."

"For God's sake, Cat," he said. "You said he has a secret, so take him out for ice cream. I bet he'll open up."

Still, I hedged.

He said, "I'm Patrick's friend, too. Let me help."

He helped more than that. He threw out a theory about Dupree and Tommy, based on the information I'd given him. Destiny had said that Dupree would freak out if his mama found out about his drug life, and Dupree said Patrick wasn't a saint, but a tattletale. What if Patrick was blackmailing him?

"Blackmailing!" I said. "If you think Patrick's the sort of

215

guy who blackmails people, you don't know him as well as you think you do."

"Think about it this way," Jason said. "We know Patrick was upset that Beef was involved with meth. What if Beef hasn't gotten out of the business? Maybe Patrick was trying to enlist Tommy and Dupree's help, you know?"

"No," I said. If Jason knew Tommy and Dupree, he'd understand that *enlisting their help* was a scenario that would never play out.

"Try it this way," Jason said. "Maybe Patrick *suggested* to Tommy and Dupree that it would be a good idea for all of them to quit working for Wally. Patrick would have brought up Dupree's mama, which would have made Dupree wet his pants. And from what you've told me about Tommy, I'm guessing he would have been shitting at the thought of his family finding out their golden boy was committing a felony. Am I right?"

If Tommy's father found out that Tommy was tarnishing the family name, he'd kill Tommy. So yeah, I'd say Tommy would do almost anything to keep his reputation clean.

As for Patrick being a blackmailer . . . It sounded low described like that, but in theory, having a long talk with Tommy and Dupree would be the right thing to do. Patrick might well have convinced himself that he'd be sinning if he *didn't* help his friends get out of a sinful situation.

After going over everything we knew, the one missing piece of the puzzle was Patrick's boyfriend. Who *was* he? Was he a good guy? A jerk? Was he involved in Patrick's attack? Did he know anything about Patrick's attack? So many questions would be answered if only we could talk to him.

"But you're positive he has one," I said.

"According to Patrick, yeah. He talked about him a lot, but he never used his name."

"That's weird," I mused. "And why hasn't he visited Patrick at the hospital? The boyfriend?"

"How do we know he hasn't?" Jason countered. "Plus he'd be turned away the same as us."

"What if it was Patrick's boyfriend who tried to break into his hospital room? Not for a bad reason. What if he just, you know, wanted to see Patrick's face for a minute?"

Jason shrugged. With no name, we had nothing to go on.

"You see what you can find out from Robert," he finally said. "I'll . . . I don't know what I'll do." His jaw tensed. "What should I do? What *can* I do? *God,* I hate this. I hate being so fucking helpless."

But you are helping, I thought.

"You really don't have a cell phone?" he said.

"I really don't have a cell phone," I replied.

"You can call me from your landline, then. Or a pay phone." He snagged a Sharpie from his desk and grabbed my arm, turning it so that the top of my forearm faced up. My heart beat faster.

"Call me any time," he said as he wrote his number. "All right?"

I nodded. He'd given me his number already, the day at the

hospital, but I didn't remind him. His fingers easily circled my wrist, and I liked that he was bigger than me. I liked the fine hairs between his knuckles.

He lifted his head, and we gazed at each other. It was a gaze that lasted for a long while, but I felt safe within it and didn't look away. It was strange, but wonderful.

"Um, hey," he said seriously. "There's something I want to tell you."

My stomach tightened. "Okay. What?"

"Nothing. Never mind."

"No way," I said, knowing that if he left me hanging, I'd worry about it forever. "Whatever it is, just tell me."

He half-smiled. Then he gave a quick and decisive nod, as if committing to do something scary, like jumping off a rock into water far below.

"You have pretty eyes," he said.

They widened, my pretty eyes, and I knew I was blushing. "Oh," I said, flustered. "Um, you too. And thanks. And . . . yeah."

I wasn't any closer to finding out who hurt Patrick, but I felt like I was. I wasn't just *me* anymore. I was half of a *we* . . . I was no longer alone.

20

HERE'S TO JASON AND HIS BRIBE MONEY, BECAUSE a double scoop of mint chocolate chip—combined with my complete attention—was just the encouragement Robert needed to tell me everything I wanted to know. It made me ache for him, something I didn't see coming. It was unfair how the kids who were starving for attention tended to be so annoying that people had no inclination to give it to them.

Like Robert, shifting about once we sat down in our booth and saying, "Dang, woman. I got a wedgie."

"I am so glad you shared that with me, Robert," I said, making him giggle.

He was as twitchy as a dog's hind leg, though. He kept sliding back and forth on his side of the booth, chattering about bugs and guns and dinosaurs, until out of the blue, he said, "You wanna talk about Patrick, don't you?" he said. "That's why you brought me here. Right?"

"Well, yeah." I shrugged, seeing no reason to lie. "You said you had something to tell me."

He nodded, pooching out his bottom lip as if he was thinking it over. "All right, then. I heard what Bailee-Ann told you when you were at my house the other night, but Bailee-Ann's a big fat liar." He took a big lick of mint chocolate chip, getting ice cream on his face.

"Use a napkin," I said, jerking one from the container and handing it to him. Instead of taking it, he tilted his face as if I should do the wiping.

"Robert, you can wipe your own mouth," I said. "You're a big boy."

"I sure am," he said, waggling his eyebrows.

I was taken aback. He was *eleven*, and in all of three seconds he'd gone from acting like a baby to tossing out a suggestive comment, or whatever the heck he was going for.

"Just tell me about Bailee-Ann," I said. "What'd she lie about?"

"Lots of stuff."

"Such as . . . ?"

"Well, she lied about that Saturday night, for one. I mean, Beef *did* drop her off. She didn't lie about that. But guess who was back half an hour later, throwing pebbles at her window?"

"Beef dropped the others off and then came back?"

"No," Robert said scornfully. "*Tommy* came and got her, and they went off together."

Tommy and Bailee-Ann? I was confused. "Why would Tommy and Bailee-Ann go off together?"

"Just because," he said coyly.

"Just because why?" I grabbed a napkin and wiped his dang mouth off. He grinned.

"All right, I'm gonna tell you something I ain't told nobody else. You listening?"

I nodded.

"I thought maybe it was Beef who done it. Who beat Patrick up."

I drew back. "Robert. Beef's Patrick's *friend*," I said. I heard in my own ears how doggedly insistent I sounded, and it frightened me.

"Duh," Robert said. "I know that *now*. But Beef doesn't like homos, even though he's got a buddy who's one, and so that's why I thought that." He leaned in. "Beef's teaching me how to be a man, see. We've had all kinds of talks. I don't know if you know this, but I'm, like, his best friend, practically."

Robert was not Beef's best friend. Robert was eleven. But maybe all of his hanging out with older kids had made him think he was older, too. Maybe that explained his waggling eyebrows and stupid innuendos. Maybe being with Beef and Tommy and Bailee-Ann, with their drinking and kissing and all that, had made Robert not just hyper but hyper-sexual, if there was such a thing.

Best friend or puppy dog tagalong, I didn't want to hurt Robert's feelings like I did with his nonexistent chest hairs. So I said, "Oh. That's nice."

"Yeah, only now he's dogging me, and it's pissing me off." A shadow crossed his face. He did an odd head-thrust to clear it.

"Anyway, he told me about faggots and no tears for queers and all that," he said. "So when I heard about Patrick sucking on that gas nozzle, what was I s'posed to think?"

What was he supposed to think, indeed? *Faggots? No tears for queers?* I thought Beef's calling Patrick a fucking pansy had been a onetime slip.

"So what made you decide he didn't?" I asked. My heart was beating faster than I would have liked.

Robert shrugged. His shoulder blades were as narrow and sharp as pigeon wings. "I just plain out asked him. I said, 'Hey, homes, you beat up that faggot?'"

"Good glory, Robert. What'd he say?"

"He said, 'No way, homes. Beating on people ain't cool,'" Robert recited. "I said, 'Not even homos?' And Beef said, 'Not even homos. Ain't right to beat on anyone.'"

I loosened with relief. "He's right," I said. "It isn't."

Robert was in his own head. "I figured he was playing," he said, "so I was like, 'Uh-huh, I hear ya. You're not gonna smack Bailee-Ann if you find her being humped by some other guy?'"

"Robert."

"But Beef was serious. He said he'd drop her sorry ass, but he wouldn't hit her, 'cause it ain't right to hit a girl."

"Good for him. And anyway, would you *want* him to hit your sister?"

He dragged his tongue around his ice cream. "So *then* I said, 'Lemme see if I got this straight. It ain't right to hit a homo. It ain't right to hit a girl. Who *am* I allowed to hit?'"

I put my elbow on the table and propped my cheek on my fist. I was glad Beef was teaching him not to hit homos and girls, but Jesus, this conversation was just plain depressing me.

"He said I ain't allowed to hit *no one*," Robert replied, his voice hiking up in disbelief. "Said it ain't right to hit, *period.* So I'm like, 'Not even guy-on-guy?' And he's all, 'Not even guy-on-guy.'"

I closed my eyes and pressed the heel of my palm against my forehead. "Maybe he wants to set a good example for you," I said at last.

"Whatever," Robert muttered. "Still think Beef should knock Bailee-Ann around for being such a slut."

I recalled how Bailee-Ann had described herself using that word, and I felt a pang, because now I got it. She'd acted mad at Beef for not making nice with her, but really, she'd been mad at herself for cheating on him.

"Robert, I know you don't believe that," I said. "Bailee-Ann isn't a . . . what you said she is."

"Is too, the way she wears those halter tops and lets her boobs hang out. And she's stepping out on Beef! With Tommy!"

I didn't understand how Bailee-Ann could cheat on Beef, either. Still, Robert was being disrespectful. He was supposed to look up to his big sister, not call her names and talk about here boobs.

Christian wasn't much as far as brothers went, but he didn't do that.

"Have you told Beef about Tommy and your sister?" I asked.

"Not yet," he said. He looked troubled. "But that's how I know Bailee-Ann was lying that night you came over. She said she was in for the night by one forty-five, but she weren't."

It took a moment for the implication of what he said to sink in. Then came the adrenaline. If Bailee-Ann wasn't in for the night by one forty-five, then neither was Tommy.

"Hey, Cat," Robert said as if he'd just had a new thought. "You think *Tommy's* the one who beat up Patrick?"

My heart hammered. "Do you?"

"I don't know. He sure told lots of fag jokes. Wanna hear one?"

"No thanks."

"How does a fag change a lightbulb?"

"I said *no*," I snapped.

Robert peered at me with concern. "I didn't understand it anyway," he said. "I hardly ever do."

"Did Tommy tell jokes like that around Patrick?"

"Sure." Robert pulled his eyebrows together. "So maybe he *did* beat up Patrick, huh?"

I felt sick, hearing it out loud. But I didn't deny it.

"Only if he did, Bailee-Ann wouldn't have been part of it,"

Robert said firmly. "She ain't *that* messed up, and anyway, she can't fight for shit." His face broke into a smile. "She hits like a damn girl. *Ha.* That's funny."

"What if Tommy did it and Bailee-Ann just watched?" I asked. I curled my toes within my flip-flops. "Would she stop him, or would she just . . . ?"

Robert licked his ice cream, considering. "Nah," he said at last. "She don't like seeing things get hurt. She helps baby birds and stuff, like if they fall out of their nest. She found one outside our house once, and she kept it alive in a shoebox for a week. Then it got better and tried to fly through the window, so it got dead all over again."

Sadness made him scowl. "Stupid baby bird."

"Okay, let's just think for a second," I said, talking to myself more than to Robert. "If Tommy *did* do it, he wouldn't have done it when Bailee-Ann was around." I pushed my fingers against my temples. "But she left y'all's house with Tommy, which means they were together, which means she was with him the whole time."

I slumped against the back of the booth. "Which means Tommy *didn't* beat up Patrick, not if you're right and Bailee-Ann wouldn't have let him. There's no way."

Robert looked at me like I had a bug crawling out of my ear. "I don't know why people say you're so smart. You sure seem dumb to me."

"Excuse me?"

"You think my daddy lets Bailee-Ann have sleepovers with boys?" He laughed. "What would they do, put that mud stuff all over their faces and paint each other's nails?"

"Robert, you're making no sense. Talk normal."

"Tommy got Bailee-Ann, and Tommy brought Bailee-Ann back," Robert said, real slow like he was explaining it to a potato. "She was in her bed the next morning, so she didn't spend the whole night with him. So where'd Tommy go after he dropped her off?" He gestured with his cone. "See?"

My fingers got fidgety on the table. The adrenaline was coming back. "How long were they together? What time did Tommy bring Bailee-Ann home?"

"Dunno. She must have stepped over me."

"Huh?"

"I slept under her window. She was s'posed to wake me up, but the sun did instead."

"You slept on her *floor*?"

"And when I woke up, Bailee-Ann was in her bed. *And* I got a crick in my neck, and it still hurts."

"So don't sleep on the floor."

"I had to, so I'd know she was back home and not with Tommy no more. But hey, least she's not a dyke."

He wanted a reaction, but all I could think about was Tommy.

"That's the word for a girl faggot, if you didn't know," he informed me.

I think we're done here, I was fixing to say, but Robert got in before me.

"If she ever *did* try to be one, I'd stop her, because no tears for queers, like Beef said. He told me not to go down that faggot path, not ever, 'cause one way or another, faggots get what they deserve." He hesitated. "Even the nice ones, like Patrick."

Robert stopped puffing his chest out. *Be nice to fags. Don't hit 'em. Don't call 'em that. But say they do get beat up, and they land in the hospital with burns all around their mouths and deep down in the pink of their lungs. Well if that happens, don't waste your time crying for them, because they had it coming.*

"I don't think Patrick deserved to get hurt," I said.

Robert searched my face. "Yeah?"

"I don't think Beef thinks that, either. In fact, I'm sure of it."

Robert looked uncertain.

"Maybe he just feels like he has to *act* tough, or the other guys'll give him a hard time," I suggested.

"Whatever," Robert said, drawing an invisible line on the table with one finger.

I remembered what Robert had said earlier, about Beef dogging him of late. "Plus he's busy with work, and plus he's just got a lot on his mind. He's not ditching you, Robert."

"Did I say he was?" Robert said. *"No."*

"Well, good." I paused. "The two of you got any plans coming up?"

"Like you said, he's busy," Robert said defensively. "Real busy. *Super* busy."

"Too busy to make time for you?"

He flushed a violent red.

Nice, Cat, I told myself. To make amends, I said, "He's too busy for me, too. Just for the record." Not that I was yapping at his heels, but I saw no need to mention that. "When y'all do hang out, what do y'all do?"

He shrugged. "We go to Suicide Rock sometimes. He likes it there."

I frowned. Robert plus rocks and water wasn't a good combination. Add in Robert's inborn need to show-off, and maybe it was for the best that Beef had stopped giving him attention.

"You *do* know to only jump from the jumping rock, right?" I said just in case. "You can't jump from the one that's one higher up."

"Not yet, but I'm gonna. If Beef can do it, so can I."

"*No*, Robert. Absolutely not." There was no way Robert could launch himself far enough to clear the rock below. There was no way Beef would let him try, either. Still, I shivered as if someone had walked over my grave.

"I want you to give me your word that you won't," I said. "Will you do that for me?"

"Yes, Mama. Thank you, Mama." He rolled his eyes. "I think I can take care of myself just fine, *Mama.*"

I let it go, knowing that ordering Robert not to do something was probably the best way to make sure he did. "What else do you and Beef do besides going to the swimming hole?" I asked.

"Sometimes me and him go to Asheville," Robert said. "That's another thing we do, just the two of us. But he ain't come for me in forever." He looked at me squint-eyed. "You think maybe I done something? I knocked over his motorcycle that one time, but it weren't my fault. He parked it bad is all, and anyway he never said I couldn't *touch* it. He never did say that. Anyway, he wasn't there, so how does he know if I did or not?"

"Whoa," I said. "Slow down. When was this, and where was Beef?"

"We were in Asheville so Beef could run an errand. That's my job, to watch his Suzuki."

"While he does what?"

"One time we rode up to some rich folks' house, one of those mountain houses where the people only come up on the weekends." His enthusiasm returned. "It was *awesome*."

"Oh yeah?"

"They had these cement animals in their yard. Bunny rabbits, frogs, all kind of stuff. Even this big fat pig. That pig was funny." He smiled. "They were hidden in the grass and by the porch and stuff. I don't know why, but they were."

"Probably just for decoration," I said, not liking the idea of Robert and Beef trespassing on some rich folks' yard. "Or to hide a key. Sometimes people hide keys under those things."

His eyes brightened. "Ha! So *that's* how Beef got in!"

"Beef broke into their house?" I said. This was not the Beef I knew. Why would he break into someone's house? Unless . . . did it have to do with a drug run, maybe? Or that guy who hurt Beef's leg? The wrestler? He was from Asheville.

"We stole one of them animals," Robert went on. "A lamb, like in the Bible. Beef let me keep it. He had to go run some errand, and so he left me there with my lamb."

I opened my mouth to protest. He didn't give me the chance.

"Relax, the house people weren't there. Anyway, Beef said they'd never know the lamb was gone, and it was my payment for being such a good friend."

I raised my eyebrows. "Friend" was a funny word for an eleven-year-old playing lookout for a high school dropout.

"He said I could do whatever I wanted with it, so wanna know what I did? I smashed it on the driveway, that's what. *Bye-bye, lambie-pie.*"

"You did not," I said.

"Did so."

I looked at him. Within half a minute, his eyes went jittering away. I reached across the table and took his sticky hands, surprising us both. "I don't believe you."

He tried to pull away.

"I think you put it back," I went on. I watched his face. "Maybe you told Beef you broke it, but you gave that lamb back, didn't you?"

"Nuh-uh, I smashed it to bits," he insisted. "I threw it over a wall at the end of their yard. I threw it over that wall, and it smashed on the rocks below. Then I took another rock and banged it to dust."

"I thought you smashed it on the driveway."

He tried harder to get his hands back. "You shut up. And if you tell Beef, I'll . . . I'll . . ."

I released his hands. He fell against the back of the booth.

"I'm not going to tell Beef about the lamb," I said. I slid out of my seat. "I *am* gonna tell him about Tommy lying, though."

Robert went pale. "You better not!"

"I won't tell him the Bailee-Ann part, and I won't tell him it was you who told me. I just think Beef should know that Tommy lied about where he was the night Patrick was hurt."

I adjusted my shirt with a tug and flipped my hair over my shoulders. "And Robert? I'm real proud of you for being straight with me, and for not smashing those people's property. You're a good kid."

Color spread from his neck to his face to his sticking-out ears. "Ain't a kid."

"Tough. I'm proud of you anyway."

Robert got up and said stiffly, "I am going to the john to drain my willy, and you better just . . . you better just . . ."

I waited.

"Don't leave without me. Promise?" He stalked toward the bathroom, and I closed my eyes and pressed the heel of my palm to my forehead.

Good Lord.

21

ON THE BUS BACK TO BLACK CREEK, ROBERT LAY down on the seats across the aisle from me. I guess all that sugar did him in.

"Will you scratch my back?" he asked.

I sighed and scooched over so I could reach him. With my fingernails, I drew circles on top of his shirt.

"Under?" he said.

Oh, whatever, I thought, moving my hand and slipping it under the fabric. His skin was soft, which shouldn't have surprised me, but did. He was so skinny I could feel his ribs.

"So did you tell me everything you wanted to, or do you have any other *secret knowledge* you think I should know?" I asked, half-joking.

"Well, there's Ridings and that whole mess," he murmured into the seat.

My hand stilled. At Wally's trailer, Ridings was the "customer" I'd heard leaving a message.

He twitched his shoulder to make me start scratching again. I complied and said blandly, "What about Ridings? What whole mess?"

Several seconds passed.

"Robert?" I said, slowing the pace of my circles.

"'Cause of that cow," he said.

What cow? I thought. But I held my tongue.

"But Beef's daddy fixed it so Tommy wouldn't get in trouble, even though Tommy's a douche."

"*Tommy*? What did Tommy do?"

"When he was out shooting with the others," he said, like surely I knew this story already. "You know how they get wasted and go and shoot at road signs?"

Boys and their guns. I snorted.

"Well . . . Tommy shot Ridings's cow."

I froze mid-scratch. *"What?!"*

"The one with a bell around her neck. That one."

Well, of course, *that one,* 'cause Ridings only has the one. And Tommy *shot* it?

"Did it die?"

"Maybe," Robert hedged. "But you can't tell no one. And Tommy did pay to have it butchered. Butchering a cow costs a *lot* of money."

233

Ah, crud. Ridings loved that dumb cow like a pet. Not just that, he *needed* her. A man can get by on milk and cheese and a decent vegetable garden, even a dead-broke junkie like Ridings. Why on earth would Tommy shoot Ridings's cow?

"I mean it, Cat. You can't tell," Robert said. He turned his head to look at me. "No one knows 'cept me and you, okay? Well, and Tommy and Beef and Roy, since Roy told Tommy how to fix it."

"How to fix it?" I said. You couldn't "fix" a dead cow. How did you fix a dead cow?

"Anyway, it was an accident, and anyway, it *might* have been lightning. So stop looking at me funny!"

If I was looking at him funny, it wasn't on purpose. I was just trying to figure things out. Could a dead cow have anything to do with Patrick? Was there any possible way the two things were connected?

"Did Patrick know?"

Robert chose not to reply, which I interpreted as a "yes." In a town like Black Creek, dead cows were hard to bury, even just the bones and scrap meat of them. The fact that I *didn't* know showed how out of the loop I was.

We were quiet. Robert laid his head back down and straightened his stick-thin legs in his ridiculous shorts, and I resumed the back scratch. On the edge of consciousness, he mumbled, "You're nice, Cat."

Then he fell asleep. His eyelashes were dark and long, a detail I noticed only because he was finally still.

I saw Robert safely home, and since I was there anyway, I went inside to see if Bailee-Ann was around. If she was, I planned on questioning her some more about the night Patrick was attacked.

I agreed with Robert that Bailee-Ann wouldn't have played a role in anything violent, but maybe she saw something when she snuck out with Tommy. Or heard something. She obviously lied to me for some reason.

Bailee-Ann wasn't there. No one was. Robert's face fell, and I could see he didn't want to be left alone. When I was his age, I had Patrick, and Mama Sweetie, too. When I was his age, I didn't know what loneliness was.

So I stayed for a bit. We played slapjack. I let him win. He talked nonstop—mostly more hero worship regarding Beef— and I listened with half an ear.

After a while, he said, "I'm bored. You're too easy to beat. I think I'll go to Huskers and see Beef. Wanna come?"

"No, thanks." I wasn't in the mood for Huskers. Who knew who all might be there?

"Will it make you feel bad if I go anyway?"

"No," I said, smiling ruefully.

He shoved his chair back from the rickety kitchen table, and I did the same.

"Tell Beef hi for me," I said. "But, Robert . . . be careful what you say to people about all of this. I don't want you getting hurt."

Robert gave me the finger, so what the hell, I gave *him* the finger. For an instant, he was shocked, and then his face lit up and he laughed, the little rat.

I laughed back. I hated to say it, but he was growing on me.

22

IT WAS FOUR O'CLOCK BY THE TIME I GOT HOME. Dinner wouldn't be for a few hours, so I stopped by our garden and picked the best-looking tomatoes, which I lay gently in the basket I'd rigged to the back of my bike. There were green beans ripe for picking, so I put those in, too. I'd take them to Ridings and see if I could figure out how—or if—he fit into all of this.

As I started down our bumpy driveway, I heard our screen door slam.

"Cat!" Christian called. "You just got here. Where the heck are you going?"

Another voice chimed in. "Is she leaving? Tell her to come back. Tell her we need to talk to her."

My blood ran cold, and my fool head turned like a puppet's on a string, even though I knew that voice as well as I knew my own nightmares.

Tommy Lawson, in my house. Tommy Lawson looking for me. *Tell her to come back. Tell her we need to talk to her.*

"Hey, Cat, hold up," Tommy called, the devil himself standing beside my brother. He was strong and broad-shouldered and handsome as a movie star, most people would say. "I want to talk to you."

Yeah, only I had no desire to talk to him. I rode hard and fast toward Ridings's place, and while the burn in my muscles didn't banish Tommy from my thoughts, it helped. It made it so I could force Tommy back and think about matters closer to the surface.

Once upon a time, Ridings had a house, just like once upon a time he had a pretty wife and an even prettier baby girl. He worked at the paper mill and brought in enough to live on. They were happy. Then a tornado came and sucked the happiness right out of him, and so much for fairy tales really being true.

When I arrived at his ramshackle roadside stand, I saw just how far he'd fallen. There was a basket of rotten peaches on the fold-out counter, and there were fruit flies buzzing everywhere. Also, Ridings himself was a hot mess, as Destiny would say, and he had BO that nearly knocked me over, even from yards away.

"Well, hey!" he called from the metal folding chair he'd set up alongside the lonely highway. He smiled, showing teeth in desperate need of dental care. "You bring me some veggies? That's great, that's great. Bring 'em on over and sit for a spell, why don'cha?"

Normally, I wouldn't give a second thought to sitting and chatting with Ridings for a bit. But Ridings's eyes were glassy, and his words were too fast, and there was no one around but the two of us. A car might drive past in the next hour, or it might not.

But I unloaded the beans and tomatoes and leaned tentatively on the wooden stand he'd set up for his vegetables. Remarkably, it didn't collapse.

"What's going on, gal?" Ridings said energetically. He scratched his arm, then his other arm, and then the back of his neck. The skin all over his body was raw, with blisters and gashes everywhere. "Durn chiggers. Worst summer I ever seen. Them bugs crawled up under my skin, that's what I think. Burrowed in and laid their durn eggs."

"Ridings, can I ask you something?" I said.

"Yeah, 'course. Ask me anything at all." He scratched his scalp. "You wanna buy some peaches? My little girl, she loved peaches. Juice just dribbled down her chubby cheeks. You ever meet my little girl? You want to see her picture?"

"I've seen her picture," I said. "She's a cutie, all right."

He was already digging into the front pocket of his jeans, hiking up one bony hip to get in deep.

"Oh yeah, here we go," he said. He flipped to the first

battered photo, which showed Ridings and his wife and their little girl, Melody. They were sitting stiffly in front of a blue background, all of them wearing crisp white shirts. Ridings wore jeans, his wife a denim miniskirt, and little Melody a teensy baby miniskirt. She had one of those baby headbands for when babies didn't have hair yet, the kind that went around the baby's forehead and had a bow on the front.

"It's a beautiful picture," I said. I tried to smile. "So, I wanted to ask—"

"They're gone now," he said. "My Danielle, she was at the Piggly Wiggly when the wind started picking up. She shoulda stayed put, but she wanted to get home to me and the baby."

"She loved you, that's why," I said, feeling as if I was being sucked into quicksand. "She wanted to be with you."

"A tree knocked out the windshield, right in our driveway. They say she didn't feel no pain. That's good, don't you think?"

I sighed. I'd heard all this before. Everyone in town had. The first few times, it was heartbreaking. Then it was just sad. It never stopped being sad, but it was a broken record sad, playing again and again on endless repeat.

I'd hoped to skirt around it today, but watching Ridings rock back and forth in his folding chair, clutching that beat-up picture, I knew that wasn't going to happen.

"I think it's real good," I said, referring to his wife's pain-free death.

"And Melody . . . my baby girl—" He choked up. "I tried my

best. You know? I put her in her car seat. She took naps in it sometimes. I figured it would keep her safe."

"I know. That was good thinking." And it was. What else were you supposed to do when a tornado touched down right on top of you? Go to the basement, sure. But what if you didn't have a basement?

"I strapped her in her car seat, and I put the car seat in the bathtub," Ridings said. "And then I got in the tub with her. I lay my whole self on top of her."

He shook his head. His eyes were red, and his sallow skin hugged his skull. The meth Wally had cooked up for him had gotten him bad.

"She died, too," he whispered.

"I know. I'm so sorry."

"Just a little baby. A tiny little baby."

His lips were dry and cracked, with blood showing where some of the cracks had split open. Less than a year ago, he'd been handsome in his redneck, crew cut way. Then that tornado lifted his baby girl right out from under him, tossing her high and dropping her in a field three hundred feet away. She was still in her car seat when Ridings found her. No broken bones, just the life sucked right out of her.

"Why would God take a little baby?" Ridings asked, fixing his meth-addled eyes on mine. He answered his own question. "He needed another angel, I guess. She was too good for this world, her and Danielle both."

"Um . . . Ridings?" I ventured.

"Yeah?" he said, the entire word a sigh.

If there was a right way to do this, I didn't know it. So I said, "Didn't you used to have a cow?"

His gaze drifted. It seemed like he was looking into the forest, but when I angled my head, I saw an open field. At the edge of the field was the shack where Ridings now lived, and also his pickup truck.

"I did," he murmured. "She died, too."

"How?"

"Lightning."

"Lightning?!"

"Don't that beat all? No insurance for an act of God, not when it comes to cows and lightning." He thumped his bony chest. "I thought it was foul play, that's what I thought at first. But nope, it was lightning."

"Lightning. Wow."

"I got her cut up into steaks and such, though I hated to do it." He tugged on his ear, his face as scrunched and bewildered as a baby's. "Least, I think I did. Man's gotta eat, right?"

I had no response to that. Tommy killed his cow. Then Tommy had it butchered and got the meat to Ridings, either because Roy told him to or because his sins got to gnawing at him. Was Ridings's brain so riddled with holes that he no longer remembered anything?

Ridings stood up from his folding chair. He came right up to me, and his confusion dropped away, replaced by a feverish intensity. I thought fleetingly that a person could do whatever he wanted if he knew he wouldn't remember afterward.

"You're a good girl, Cat," he said. "A real good girl, just like my Melody. Don't you let the world beat you down, you hear? Don't you take no peanut butter and mayonnaise sammiches, 'even if someone gives 'em to you free, 'cause there ain't no such thing as a free ride. Maybe they're free at first, but then comes the strings. There's always strings, and them strings, they tie you up and pull you right down to Satan hisself."

I tried to step backward, but I couldn't, because I was up against his produce stand.

"Bad things happen. *Evil* happens," Ridings said. "Evil's out there. I seen it riding right by me, like the riders of the apocalypse."

I inched sideways. My bike was a foot away. I just had to get to it. Once I had the handlebars clenched in my hands, I felt a heck of a lot better.

"I'm real sorry about your cow, Ridings," I told him.

He went still. Slowly, the feverish light left his eyes, and his body lost its rigidity, so that he was no longer up in my face. He scratched his arm and said, "Damn chiggers."

"So . . . yeah," I said. "Guess I'm going now." I hesitated, thinking about evil. "Hey. You know Patrick, right?"

"Sure I do," Ridings said. "He used to come talk with me."

"He did? About what?"

"Just whatever. Tomatoes. The weather. Stuff like that."

"Oh. Well, he got hurt, like *bad* hurt. Did you know that?"

"I sure did." His eyes were mournful. "Satan."

The highway Ridings set up his stand on led to the Come 'n' Go. It didn't get much traffic, but it did get some.

"Did you notice anything . . . odd?" I asked. "Not this past Saturday, but a week ago Saturday? The night Patrick got beat up?"

Ridings looked at me like I was speaking gibberish. Maybe I was, or maybe he couldn't think back that far, what with his brain eaten up from Wally's home cooking.

I thought about Wally's cooking, and then I thought about peanut butter and mayonnaise sandwiches, and my brain put them together in that way brains sometimes do: pairing ideas that shouldn't be paired, yet nonetheless were.

Don't you take no peanut butter and mayonnaise sammiches, even if someone gives 'em to you free.

We get all sorts of crazy orders. Peanut butter and mayonnaise, turkey with fried pickles, tongue with spicy mustard.

Shut up, Dupree. She doesn't care.

Ridings's brow cleared. "Oh. You want to know did I *see* something. Something suspicious."

"Yeah, did you?"

"Naw. I packed up my stand, then went home and watched the stars some. Saw Beef pass by in his girlfriend's truck a few times, driving folks around. I guess I watched the stars some more and called it a night." He made a sound that for him might have been a laugh. "'Course the sun was coming up all red and teary by then. You ever notice how swollen the sun is so early in the morning? Like it got no sleep, either?"

Beef driving everyone home. That was all he'd seen.

Ridings yawned, his eyes closing. He opened them again and looked at me, his eyes glazed. "Hey. You ever meet my little girl? You want to see her picture?"

It was time for me to go, because just as sure as God made plump, juicy peaches, Ridings had left already. And just as sure as God made peaches, I knew he wasn't coming back.

23

I SCREAMED WHEN I SAW IT: A SEVERED TONGUE on my pillow. It was jagged at the end, like it had been sawed off with a knife. There were bumps on the surface, like on a human tongue, but it was too big to be human. It was a cow's tongue, flaccid and damp and *on my pillow.*

I screamed, and Aunt Tildy came running, Christian right behind her.

"What? What is it?" Christian demanded.

I tried to speak, and he grabbed my shoulders, because maybe I wasn't making words come out so well, or maybe I'd gone pale. I was shaking so hard that he had to hold me up.

"Good Lord in heaven," Aunt Tildy said when she saw. She peered closer, then drew back as if she'd been stung. "Why do you have a cow tongue on your pillow? Is that a *note* under there? Cat, what have you done?"

What have I done? I thought. *What have I done!?*

Christian eased me to the floor, my back against the end of my bed for support. He looked into my eyes and said, "You're okay. You hear?" He stood and strode to my bed. "Aunt Tildy, move."

I heard rather than saw what happened next. Footsteps as he strode to the front of my bed. The rustle of the paper as he grabbed the note. Then a whole stream of cussing before he came back into view. His face was stormy as he crumpled the piece of paper. "Who did this, Cat?"

"What does it say?" I said. I tried to rise, but I was lightheaded, and my balance was no good.

Christian was at my side in a flash. He squatted and pushed down my shoulders. "Sit down. Good Lord."

"Give it to me," I said.

"I don't think so," Aunt Tildy said, her voice high. "Whatever it is, it's no good, and just . . . give it to *me*. I'll burn it."

"Give me the note, goddammit," I said to Christian.

Aunt Tildy gasped. "Cat! *Language!*"

I dug at Christian's closed fist, and at last he relented, because that was the code of siblings, even when the relationship was fractured. We might keep secrets from our daddy or our aunt, but not from each other.

Stop flapping your tongue, or I'll cut yours out, too, the note said. The block letters were as dark as congealed blood.

Christian grabbed it back and shook it. "Was it Tommy? When he was here, he said he wanted to talk to you, but then he claimed it was nothing important. Was he the one who fucking wrote this?"

I blinked.

Christian was furious. "I didn't see him go into your room, but I guess the piece of shit could have slipped in when I wasn't watching. So did he, or did some other piece of shit climb through your window and leave this trash on your pillow?"

I flinched and cried, "How am I supposed to know?"

Aunt Tildy shifted into efficiency mode. She disappeared into the hall, came back with one of the rags she uses for cleaning, and scooped the tongue up. Then she fast-walked to the front door and stepped out into the yard. I guess she flung that piece of meat as far as she could, because I heard it land, a faint *plump* in the woods.

"Thanks," I said weakly when she came back to my room.

"It has to do with Patrick, doesn't it?" Christian said. "I told you to leave it alone. But did you? *No.*"

"It's late," Aunt Tildy said. "You children ought to be in bed."

"Should we call the police?" I said. "Get Deputy Doyle out here?"

"Why on earth would we do that?" Aunt Tildy said.

"To tell him what happened. About the note. About . . ." I swallowed, unnaturally aware of my own mouth's inner workings. A wet thick muscle, that's what it was. "About the tongue."

"What tongue?" Aunt Tildy said. "It's gone, et up by a fox."

"But, Aunt Tildy, we all saw it."

"Et up by a fox," Aunt Tildy repeated stubbornly.

"There ain't no point in calling anyone," Christian said angrily. "Deputy Doyle's either passed out at the hospital doing guard duty, or else he's at the snack machine, stuffing his gut with those damn cheese crackers he loves. He ain't gonna drive out here, not for a high school prank."

"You think it was a *prank*?" I said.

"Hell no," Christian said. "But that's how he'd see it, or that's how he'll *say* he saw it. Deputy Doyle ain't gonna do nothing." He slowed the pace of his words. "So if you know who did it, if you even *think* you know, then fucking tell me so I can take care of it."

My eyes went to Aunt Tildy. She wouldn't meet my gaze, but instead fixed her stare on floating, invisible dust motes.

Christian, on the other hand, did look at me. His eyes burned so fiercely into mine that I felt a physical jolt, and the sheer force of it seared me and threw backward into the past. Time shifted invisibly and deeply, dropping me three years back to when Tommy got me alone on our living room sofa. The dead tongue spoke to me from the woods, insisting in the horror of the moment that ugly things couldn't be thrown away so easily. They had to be dragged into the light, or they'd keep growing.

The ugly thing—*the bad thing*—happened when I was thirteen. It was a week before my eighth grade graduation, and Christian was outside burning the old smokehouse that had been next to our house since before I was born. Nobody'd smoked meat in it since my granddaddy was young, and we no longer had hogs to slaughter even if we'd wanted to. We once used the smokehouse as a shed, but that was when Daddy still kept the place up and needed somewhere to store the lawn mower and other tools.

By my thirteenth summer, the smokehouse was beyond repair, listing to the side like a carnival fun house. A feather drifting lazily from the sky could land on it wrong and make the whole thing collapse. So Christian decided to burn it to make room for a new shed. His Yamaha was old, and it would last a little longer if he could keep it out of the elements. Plus, a covered shed would give him a place to coax it to life on rainy days.

Beef was out there with him, both of them sitting in lawn chairs and sipping moonshine from mason jars. Aunt Tildy thought they were too young to be drinking, but Daddy let them, so Aunt Tildy couldn't do a thing about it.

I was out there, too, sipping lemonade. I tried to make a case that I deserved a glass of shine, too, since I'd be turning fourteen in two months. I wasn't a kid.

"The hell you ain't," Christian said. "And quit asking, 'cause the answer's no."

I didn't care. I just liked being with them. We were shooting the breeze and watching the fire, Beef telling me jokes that made lemonade come out my nose, when Tommy roared into our drive on his blue BMW R1200C, the make and model of which I knew because he bragged about it so much. Not a ding on it, and no doubt worth more than our house.

He did a power slide into the dirt yard and stopped a few yards from our chairs, his rear tire pointing our way. Then he clamped the front brake and cranked the throttle, spraying a rooster tail of dirt and grit on the flames. Some got on us, too, with Beef getting the worst of it.

"What the hell?" he cried, grabbing the metal arms of his chair and scrambling out of Tommy's range.

Tommy laughed and cut the engine. The smell of motor oil hung in the humid air.

As Tommy toed down the kickstand, Christian said, "Hey, bro. You might want to park your Beemer somewhere else."

He was offering friendly advice. He didn't want Tommy's fancy motorcycle that close to the burning shed.

But Tommy didn't like being told what to do. "Don't get your panties in a wad," he said. "How long you think I'm gonna be here?"

It was a put-down, but Christian didn't take the bait.

"Well, pull up a chair, man," he said, and Tommy did. He grabbed a lawn chair and slung it down between me and Christian, and I giggled, because I thought Tommy was cute.

Christian poured Tommy a jelly jar full of moonshine, which Tommy accepted, drained, and held out straight away for a refill. I held my lemonade out and asked for a splash, too. Christian didn't bother to respond.

The guys talked, and I listened. I felt shy around Tommy, that was why I clammed up.

After a while, Aunt Tildy came outside and said hey to the boys. She turned to me and told me to go put on my graduation dress, which she'd bought months earlier because it was on sale.

"Why?" I said.

"To make sure it still fits."

"But why now?" I didn't want to leave.

"'Cause I'm fixin' to make jam, and once I get the berries boiling, I'll have to stand watch over them."

"But—"

"Don't you backtalk me," she snapped. "Your ceremony is next weekend. If the dress needs altering, I gotta know."

"Okay, okay," I said, wishing she hadn't shamed me in front of Tommy.

I went inside to change. When I came back out, Beef whistled. I smacked him on the head. I liked the attention, though. Of course, I did.

Then Aunt Tildy said, "Oh, Cat," like I'd done something bad. She was looking pointedly at my chest, so I looked too. There were buttons down the front of the dress, and the cloth gaped open between them. My breasts had grown, that's why. I could see the dark of my nipples, and how the fabric strained over them. I supposed this was bad in terms of having to let the dress out, but I didn't yet know to be ashamed.

"What?" I said.

"You had to go and grow you some bubbies, didn't you?" she scolded, and all the boys laughed, including Christian.

Then I knew. I blushed, though I don't think Aunt Tildy meant to embarrass me. I realized *Tommy* was staring at my chest, and it made me feel tingly in a strange and particular way. I crossed my arms over myself, pulling my shoulder blades in to make a C-curve out of my spine.

Aunt Tildy remained clueless. In her mind I was still a little girl, and Christian's friends were playful, rowdy boys who shot at street signs, tussled like pups, and drank a gallon of milk a day.

She clucked impatiently. "Now, Cat, put down your arms so I can see how much letting out I gotta do," she said. "Come on over here so I can do a measure."

I took an uncertain step forward, just as Tommy said, "Or you could come over here. I'd be more than happy to measure those *bubbies*."

And just as clear as a bell, Aunt Tildy realized what she'd done. She'd asked me to stick my breasts out, and me with no bra on. I was a tomboy. I wore Christian's hand-me-downs and ran around with Patrick, catching crawdads in the creek, so what'd I need a bra for?

Yet Aunt Tildy had stood me up in front of three hormone-addled boys slouched in lawn chairs by a burning shed. One of them was my brother, but the other two weren't. There was liquor. There was the reek of gas and oil from Tommy's motorcycle. And there was me in my too-small dress, my nipples poking tents in the fabric without my having any say over it.

I'd been to livestock auctions, the calves mewling as farmers pried open their mouths. Right then, I was that dumb calf.

"Cat, go inside," Aunt Tildy said sharply.

As I scurried toward the house, I heard Tommy say something real low. And then Christian was on him—I heard a chair tip, and scuffling, and angry words from my brother— and then Tommy saying, "Get off me, man! Beef—a little help?"

"No way," I heard Beef say. "That's Christian's sister you're talking about. You're outta line."

"Jesus," Tommy said. "I didn't mean nothing by it, all right? Just that she's hot."

And then Beef and Christian *both* went after him, and Aunt Tildy was shooing me in the house and closing the door.

"Ain't nothing good ever come from trash talk," she said. "You go get changed. Put the dress on my bed—I'll take care of it before your ceremony. Right now, I got other work to do." She disappeared into the kitchen, muttering under her breath.

So I changed back into my cutoffs. *I'm hot,* I thought wonderingly. *Tommy thinks . . . he thinks I'm hot.* I reached for the oversize T-shirt I had been wearing, but at the last second I dug around in my bureau and pulled out a baby blue camisole instead. I'd never worn it before, thinking it too girly, but Aunt Tildy had brought it home from the Sharing House one day.

She presented it to me proudly and told me it was a real find, and not one stain on it.

I didn't put on a bra, because I didn't own a bra. But I brushed my hair. I pinched my cheeks the way I'd seen Bailee-Ann do, and I leaned in close to the mirror and gazed at myself. My black hair framed my sun-kissed face. My eyes shone. Was I pretty? Was I hot?

Back in the living room, I plopped down on the sofa and pretended to read *Black Beauty,* the part where Black Beauty was a colt frolicking in the meadow. But really, I was watching the boys. I saw the three of them stand up from their chairs, and my heart beat faster. Were they coming inside?

No. A few minutes later, I heard the sound of bullets hitting tin cans. They'd left the shed still burning and gone around back to do some shooting. I felt disappointed.

I despised myself for that now.

Aunt Tildy had the radio on in the kitchen, set to the country station she liked. I could hear her singing along. I went back to my book, and after a while I fell into it for real. I propped my feet on the beat-up coffee table made from a plank and two cinder blocks, and I went off with Black Beauty, who was fighting against the bit his master stuck in his mouth. I didn't hear Tommy come in. He must have eased the screen door shut, because all of a sudden, there he was, dropping onto the sofa beside me. He sat so close our thighs touched.

I thought Tommy was the handsomest boy I'd ever seen. Yes, he was cocky. Yes, he was sometimes a jerk, especially to

Patrick. But he'd grin afterward, as would Patrick. I figured they were boys being boys.

So I was thrilled he'd come inside to sit with me. I was even more thrilled when he draped his arm over my shoulder and gave me a squeeze.

"Hey, Cat," he said, leaning toward me. I started giggling and couldn't stop. I couldn't even look at him. I kept my eyes glued on my book, fiddling with it until he took it from me, closed it, and set it on the cinder block table.

"Tommy! You lost my place!" I protested.

"You looked hot in that dress," he said. His hand slid beneath the strap of my cami. He rubbed my shoulder, then right away dipped further, his fingers tracing my collarbone.

"Tommy," I said, pushing his hand away. I told myself he was just playing. My stomach clenched up, but I tried not to listen.

"You ain't wearing a bra," he murmured. His hand went back to my collarbone and kept on going, a tadpole slipping beneath a rock, that easy and quick. He squeezed my breast, grazing his thumb back and forth over my nipple. His voice grew husky. "You like that, huh?"

My eyes widened. I liked him sitting next to me, yes. But his hand where it was? No. *No.* It was private, the part of me he was touching. Plus he'd never even taken me for a ride on his motorcycle, or sat with me on the porch, or brought me fresh strawberries from his grandmother's garden.

My breaths came short, making my chest rise and fall.

He laughed, saying, "You're so cute." He shifted so that his body was angled toward me, and I felt trapped, even though I wasn't. Why didn't I call out? Why didn't I push him away?

"Tommy," I whispered. I wanted him to understand without my having to say it. I didn't want to hurt his feelings.

His right hand squeezed my breast, and his left hand tried to work my knees apart. When that didn't work, he slid his hand up my thigh and under my frayed cutoffs. I gasped, because he touched my panties. He went that far.

"Tommy. Don't."

"Hush now." His breath smelled like my daddy's corn liquor. He fumbled at the elastic of my panties, but my cutoffs were tight, and he couldn't work his fingers to where he wanted. "C'mon now, Cat. Lemme feel how wet you are."

I didn't know what he meant. I pressed my spine into the sofa to get away from him, but moving like that raised my hips and loosened the hug of my shorts. His fingers slithered under my panties.

"Oh yeah," he said, moving his fingers the best he could. "See now?"

I was lost. Tommy was touching a part of me that no one was supposed to. I was pushing against him, but he was so much bigger than me. And my throat, it was like someone had wrapped a band around it and cinched it so tight, I could hardly breathe. The sounds I made—because I tried, I did—they came from some other girl. They were *please* and *stop,* but so trembly that they simply shuddered up into the air.

I heard something outside, and my eyes flew to the wide front window. Christian stood on the other side, holding a stick he must have used to poke at the fire, which was still burning steadily. His hand went slack, and the stick fell, and it was so slow, the seconds drumming in my pulse, as his face registered what he saw through the grimy pane of glass. I thought, *Oh, thank you, God. Thank you for my big brother, and for bringing him here to me.*

Christian strode out of view. Any moment he would burst through the door and grab Tommy off me and beat the crap out of him.

Several minutes passed, and I started crying. Christian wasn't going to beat the crap out of Tommy. Christian wasn't going to do a thing. He'd gone back to shooting tin cans, or stirring the embers of the burning smokehouse, or sneaking more of Daddy's moonshine for all I knew.

My face was slick with tears when Aunt Tildy stepped from the kitchen into the living room, saying, "Cat, I need you in the kitchen. Ain't you heard me calling?"

"Aunt Tildy," I gasped.

By that point, Tommy had unbuttoned my shorts and yanked them down around my thighs, along with my panties. I was gripping them, trying to get them back up, but he was stronger. He no longer had his hand down my tank top, but instead had his right arm stretched along the back of the sofa, bearing his weight while his left arm rode the length of my belly, straight as a rod until the sharp flex of his wrist.

With Aunt Tildy standing frozen behind him in the doorway, he got one finger up inside me. I whimpered. He kept at it, the heel of his palm driving into my pelvic bone, until he got in two more.

Then he moaned. That sick bastard moaned, and Aunt Tildy snapped out of her trance.

"Cat," she snapped. Her face went hard like stone. "I *said* I need your help with the berries." She whipped around, went back into the kitchen, and turned the radio up way loud.

"I gotta go," I said through my tears and snot. I squirmed, but that just made it worse. It hurt. I could feel his fingernails, which I knew to be grimy with oil, and I squeezed shut my eyes, wanting to make everything disappear.

There was a bang outside, explosively loud, and Tommy jerked away. He jumped to his feet and said, *"Fuck,"* as panicked as I'd ever heard him. He straightened his jeans as best he could over the bulge of his crotch, but already he was striding for the door and out of the house.

"Shit, man," I heard Beef say.

"Fucking hell, get it outta there! Help me drag it outta there!" Tommy yelled.

"Bro, it's over," Beef said. He barked a laugh of stunned amazement. "That baby's one gone motherfucker."

Male voices washed over me: Tommy's furious; Beef's sympathetic, but not overly so; my brother's just plain flat.

Shaking, I stood and buttoned my shorts. I moved silently to the edge of the window, where I crossed my arms tight and took it in. Pieces of chrome. A fender blown several feet away when the gas tank exploded. The rubber grip of the accelerator. The smoldering remains of the smokehouse blanketing the bones of Tommy's BMW.

"Told you not to park there," Christian said.

Tommy lunged at him, and Aunt Tildy, whom I hadn't yet noticed, cried, "Boys!"

My head turned toward her voice, and there Aunt Tildy was. The boys were on one side of what was now a bonfire—thanks to the dousing of motorcycle fuel—and Aunt Tildy was on the other side. Her cheeks were flushed, and her bunned-up hair was coming down in sweaty tendrils. Her eyes were so wide I could see the whites, even as far away as I was.

But how had she gotten there so quickly? If she'd gone out the back door, which opened out of the kitchen, why hadn't I heard the screen slam?

Because of her country music, cranked up so loud. And she was sweaty because of being so close to the flames, and also because she'd exerted herself. The shed was going to collapse one way or another. Aunt Tildy just kicked a particular burning plank, maybe. The plank that would make the shed topple in the right direction.

Aunt Tildy had been incapable of coming right out and saying to her boss's son, "Tommy Lawson, you leave my niece alone," so she figured out another way to make him stop. That's what I assumed. No, that's what I *knew*.

And she didn't own up to saving me because she just . . .

couldn't. Ruining Tommy's motorcycle used up every ounce of courage she had, and there wasn't any left over for talking about it. I told myself I was selfish to want more than what she'd already given me.

As for Christian, all I knew was that he saw me and Tommy through the window and walked away. Did it kill him inside to see his friend going after his baby sister? Probably. After all, he was a kid, too. Older than me, but still a kid, and he must have felt almost as helpless as I did.

In the months to come, in moments of loneliness so deep it hurt to breathe, I tried to put aside my fury and betrayal and humiliation and forgive him. That's how much I missed him.

But Christian was my hero, and he let me down when it mattered most. I couldn't forgive him. I *couldn't*, no more than Aunt Tildy could untie the knots inside of herself so that we could talk about what happened. So that I could heal.

Daddy, for the record, didn't even come out of the garage. A motorcycle blew up in his yard, and he downed his liquor and thought, *Lookit that. Them boys got a real good fire going. Ooh boy, sure do like a good fire.*

Two weeks later, Tommy got himself a new motorcycle, a bright yellow one, and he bragged about it more than his first.

As for Christian and Aunt Tildy and me, we suffered his boasting and shoved the ugly under the rug. If we didn't see it, it wasn't there, right?

Except the ugly *was* there. It was inside me. I tried running from it, but that didn't make it go away. I dropped Patrick and

261

Bailee-Ann and the rest of my friends. That didn't make it go away, either. I looked back on those wasted years and here's what I saw: a spook retreating from the world step by silent step, until I was a ghost instead of a girl.

I came back to the present, here in my room with a dead cow tongue flung yards away in the dark . . . and I *wasn't* a ghost. My body was real and strong and capable, just as my brother was real and strong and capable. As for what happened three years ago . . .

Of course, Aunt Tildy was outside by the fire. She dashed out as soon as she heard the explosion. That she was already there before I thought to look for her meant nothing, just that my eyes had gone first to the flaming motorcycle. So had everyone else's.

As for how flushed and sweaty she was, that was from standing by the hot stove, stirring blackberries as they boiled and broke down into pulp. She'd been making jam, not kicking over a burning shed.

I felt dizzy.

"Talk to me, Cat," Christian said. "Tell me who done it."

"It was you," I said, my words as new and uncertain as a baby's. I was sixteen, and in my bedroom, and I shook my head in an attempt to unscramble my thoughts. "Not the tongue. The fire."

I shut my eyes, then opened them to make sure I hadn't made this thing up.

Aunt Tildy had found something to mess with on my dresser, and it was my brush. She lined it up straight alongside some loose hair bands, and then she tidied the hair bands, too. Her expression was as blank as meringue, smooth and bland with no place for anything to latch hold.

But Christian hadn't taken his eyes off me, and in his expression I saw a slew of emotions: shame, defiance, fury. Fear, but not for himself. For me. I saw my big brother, who carried me off the ledge at Suicide Rock when I froze up. Who came after me when I skipped off to visit Wally with his rotted-out leer. Who thought I was a fool and had no problem telling me so, but who stuck up for me anyway.

Christian stepped toward me. "Who wants you quiet? Is it Tommy? Is he after you again? If so, then *say* it, goddammit."

Aunt Tildy tutted, this close to hysteria. "You children stop picking at each other. Pick, pick, pick, when some of us got to get up early in the morning."

I blinked at her. Her image wavered.

I looked at Christian, and he was solid. I found my voice and told him, *Yes. Tommy.*

"I'll fucking kill him," Christian said, heading for the door.

Aunt Tildy got in front of him, a flapping moth. "I don't know what you two are up to, but I won't have none of it."

"Move, Aunt Tildy," Christian said.

"Getting yourselves into a tizzy over a joke!" she exclaimed wildly. "Nossir! You don't even know what it means, that business with the . . . with the . . ." She was practically hyperventilating. "Boys will be boys. They tease a girl when they like her. That's what they do!"

"My pillow has blood on it," I said.

Christian moved Aunt Tildy aside. He wasn't rough about it. I watched him stride out of my room, and I noticed how broad his shoulders had grown.

"I'll tell your daddy!" Aunt Tildy called after him shrilly. "I'll tell him to spank you! I will! You ain't never too big to be put over your daddy's knee!"

Please, I told her. *Just leave.*

When I first saw the tongue on my pillow, and I screamed, it felt like Tommy had won. Now I felt calm, almost frighteningly so, although I wished Christian would get on back. But Christian knew how to take care of himself. Anyway, it was ten o'clock on a Monday night, which meant Tommy's parents would be there. Tommy wouldn't try anything with his parents there.

I also felt a strange, floaty sense of amazement. I knew things someone didn't want me to know. I'd *figured out* things someone didn't want me to know. The tongue on my pillow was proof of that. It was also proof that knowledge was power, not being a bully or rich or thinking you were better than everyone.

Knowledge wasn't all I had. I had Jason, who was an ally and possibly a friend, and who thought I had pretty eyes. I had Christian, my brother, who loved me. Knowledge was more powerful than fear. Love was stronger than hate.

So guess what, Tommy? I said silently. *Step closer. Feel my lips against your ear. You don't scare me anymore.*

tuesday

24

CHRISTIAN CAME BACK SAFE AND SOUND. WHEN he woke me, it was past midnight. He rapped once on my door, stuck his head in, and said, "Done."

That's all, just *done*.

I tried to get my bearings. "Huh?"

"I knocked him around. Now I'm going to bed."

I nodded, and then I slept some more, and the next thing I knew, it was morning. I tiptoed past Christian's room and into the kitchen. Aunt Tildy wasn't there. She'd left a note saying she'd gone to a prayer shawl gathering, which was where ladies got together and made shawls for people who were grieving. Whatever.

Quietly, I got a Coke, took it outside, and popped the top.

I chugged it down despite my queasy stomach, knowing I'd need the buzz of energy when I confronted Tommy. For him to leave that note meant he was running scared. I was an expert in that, so I knew. I also knew that running did no good. It was time I faced my fear square on.

The articles I'd read taught me that the manner in which Patrick was attacked was called ethnic intimidation, and when a case involved ethnic intimidation, the stakes went way up. Just using words like *fag* or *homo* could get a person up to three years in prison. Add in assault, and add to that an attempted break-in at the hospital, and Tommy was in doo-doo so deep that even his daddy's money wouldn't be able wash him clean.

Tommy was nineteen, half a year older than my brother. If the case went to court, he'd be tried as an adult. So I'd tell him he had two choices: Either turn himself in to Sheriff Doyle, or I'd do it for him. And yes, it had to be me. Not Christian, not Sheriff Doyle or Deputy Doyle.

When Daddy was no more than Robert's age, rats used to come sniffing into his cramped bedroom. Daddy told me and Christian how he would wait in the night with a flashlight in his left hand and a gun in his right, a Spanish pistol bought cheap at a military surplus store. When he heard the scribbling of claws, he'd quick turn on the flashlight, blinding the buggers, so he could pick off as many as he could before they scurried back to their hidey-holes.

They didn't always flee. Not all of them. Sometimes they'd face Daddy and hiss. They'd lash their tales and show their needle teeth, and once Daddy was so startled, he dropped the flashlight, casting the room into darkness. One rat—big as a man's arm, Daddy said—came right at him, and Daddy shot it point-blank.

"It was the King Rat, see," Daddy said. "Crazy and dangerous as heck. And listen up to your daddy, kids. The *only* way to stop a King Rat is to get it before it gets you."

Daddy's mama, my dead granny Mae, cooked up that King Rat and served it as stew, because as Daddy said, "Why waste good meat?"

The rat I was after wasn't worth eating. I'd gag if I tried. Yet I kept Daddy's advice in mind, and before I biked over to Tommy's house, I hunted through the garage until I found Daddy's Spanish pistol. I stuck it in the back of my shorts for easy access.

I hoped I wouldn't need it, especially knowing that I'd be catching Tommy when he'd already been worked over. *Done,* Christian had said. I reckoned I'd find him sniveling and licking his wounds.

But like Daddy said, a trapped rat was gonna fight. This time, if it came to it, I was going to fight back.

25

I WAS SWEATY WHEN I ARRIVED AT TOMMY'S HOUSE.
I didn't care. I saw his yellow Beemer parked out front. I didn't
care. I was so hot with fear and fury that I strode right to his
fancy front door and lifted my finger to jab the bell.

He answered before I got the chance. He was holding an ice
pack to his left eye. Behind him, in the living room, Bailee-Ann
sat on the sofa. She had no makeup on, and she was wearing
shorts and a T-shirt, an outfit as simple as mine. Had Tommy
called her after my brother's late night visit? Had she rushed
right over to comfort him, throwing on any old thing?

"I didn't do it," Tommy said. He looked exhausted. "Dammit,
Cat, I already told your brother. I didn't leave no note on your
bed, all right?"

"It's true, he didn't," Bailee-Ann piped up. She pressed her legs together, each of her hands cupping a knee. "Was there really a *tongue* on top of it? *Eww,* Cat. That's so nasty."

"It was a cow tongue," I said, looking from Bailee-Ann to Tommy and back again. "Like from a dead cow? One that's been to the butcher and back? You know all about that, right?"

Bailee-Ann shuddered. "I hate dead meat. I just hate it."

Tommy gestured for me to come on in, so I did. I slipped off my backpack and perched on an overstuffed armchair across from the sofa. Daddy's pistol, tucked into the back of my cut-offs, pressed against my spine.

Tommy sat down beside Bailee-Ann, who let go of her own knee and patted his. He found her hand and squeezed it. With his other hand, he lowered the ice pack, revealing a puffy eye with a rising bruise.

"Christian do that?" I said.

"No, it was Bailee-Ann," he said sourly.

"Was not!" Bailee-Ann protested, and he shot her a wry smile, which then made him wince.

"Ow," he said.

This was *not* how I'd expected things to play out. I narrowed my eyes, determined not to be disarmed by their helpless, lovey-dovey act.

"Yesterday, when I was at your house, I was there to see your brother," Tommy told me.

"Oh, is that so? Then why'd you call out for me to come back instead of bike over to see Ridings, huh?" I looked at him hard.

"Seems to me that when I didn't jump at your command, you decided to leave your message another way."

"You went to see . . . ?" He broke off. "Cat, I didn't put that tongue on your pillow. You gotta believe me."

"I don't *gotta* do anything," I said. I heard the words come out of my mouth, and I was amazed. I was talking to Tommy—I was *confronting* him—and I had yet to go up in smoke.

"You were at my house. You knew I was learning stuff you'd rather I didn't, and then surprise, surprise, I came home to find a nice little present just waiting for me."

He looked worn down. "It wasn't me."

"Then who was it?"

"If I knew, don't you think I'd tell you?"

"Well, no, I don't, 'cause from what I hear, you're awfully good at keeping secrets." I eyed Bailee-Ann. "And that goes for you, too, Bailee-Ann."

She blushed.

But back to Tommy. "Beef told the cops you were home by one thirty the night Patrick was beat up, but you weren't, were you?"

"Actually, I was."

"No, and that's how I know you're lying, 'cause Robert told me—"

"I *was* home by one thirty," he interrupted. "But Dupree crashed, so I went back out."

"To Bailee-Ann's house," I said. "Who just happens to be *Beef*'s girlfriend."

271

Tommy sighed. He looked at Bailee-Ann, who said, "It's okay. It's already out anyway."

Tommy opened his mouth, then closed it. He focused on the floor. I stared at him, growing more and more impatient, until I had the dizzying realization that *he* was afraid to look at *me*. I myself wasn't afraid. I'd expected to have to fake it, but I truly wasn't scared to stand up to him anymore.

"Words," I said. "Use *words,* Tommy, 'cause I don't have all day. How long you think I'm planning on being here?"

He lifted his head. His eyes met mine, and I held his gaze. I could feel the heat of my blood.

"I went to Bailee-Ann's house," he said. "I picked her up, and we . . . spent some time together. Then I took her back before her daddy woke up, so she wouldn't get in trouble."

I turned to Bailee-Ann. "That true?"

"Yeah," she confessed. "When you asked, I didn't tell you, because . . ."

"Because we need to tell Beef ourselves," Tommy said. "We don't want him hearing it from someone else."

"We feel real bad," Bailee-Ann said.

Listening to the two of them was like eavesdropping on a couple of newlyweds, the way they finished each other's thoughts and played off each other. Bailee-Ann patted Tommy's leg, and he reached up and tucked a piece of hair behind her ear. He was tender about it. It filled me with rage.

"You *should* feel bad," I told Bailee-Ann. "You're cheating on your boyfriend."

To Tommy, I said, "And you're breaking the bro code or whatever. But that's what you like, isn't it? Going after what's not allowed? Doing whatever you dang please, and who cares how the other person feels about it?"

He glanced toward the entrance hall, which connected to the staircase. "Cat, my mama's upstairs. Could you maybe be a little quieter?"

I raised my voice. "Why? You don't want your mama to know what you're really made of?" I sounded shrill, like Aunt Tildy when she tried to call Christian back last night. Hearing myself made me tremble all the more. "Does Bailee-Ann know? Does she know how you went after me all those years ago, when I was just thirteen?!"

My words hit the air, and hung there, and then slowly faded away, like a church bell that's been rung way up high in the bell tower. It was silent except for my breathing, which was quick and shallow and made it sound like I was panting, which I guess I was. Tears pricked my eyes. I lifted my chin and blinked them back in.

"Um . . ." Bailee-Ann said. She bit her bottom lip and glanced at Tommy.

Tommy nodded wearily.

"I do know," Bailee-Ann said. Her words were round with compassion, but I didn't want her compassion. I stared straight ahead of me. I thought about rats and staying alert.

"Tommy and me talk about everything," Bailee-Ann went on. "And we *both* are sinners. We know that." She got up off the sofa and crossed the room to me, kneeling at my feet. "We pray about it, and we lift our sins up to Jesus. We try to do better."

"You're not trying very hard if you're sneaking out and spending nights together," I said. "Knitting hats for little babies isn't going to erase that."

"Well, you're right," she said heavily. "You're right about that."

"Get up off the floor, Bailee-Ann," I said. "For heaven's sake."

She did, only to scrunch onto the armchair beside me. Her skin was warm. "Tommy?" she prompted. "Don't you have something you want to say to Cat?"

Good Lord, the last thing I wanted was an apology from Tommy. At least I didn't think I did. Did I?

My eyes darted toward his, and I saw that he was just as uncomfortable as I was. *Good,* I thought.

"I, um . . . yeah," Tommy said. He ducked his head. "I'm sorry for treating you like that, and I shoulda told you before. And your brother was right to blow up my motorcycle. I deserved it."

I couldn't absorb this, Tommy's regret. Daddy's pistol was digging into my spine, so I pulled it out and held it in my lap.

"You got a *gun?*" Bailee-Ann said. "What you got a gun for?"

"Aw, hell," Tommy said. "You ain't gonna *shoot* me, are you?"

"You shot Ridings's cow," I said numbly.

Tommy stared at me as if I was a mad dog that might bite at any moment. "I didn't mean to. It was an accident."

"You shot his cow and somehow persuaded him it was lightning," I said stubbornly. "That is *low,* Tommy Lawson, shooting a man's cow and not even owning up to it."

"I *did* own up to it!" he said, agitated. He glanced at the gun and lowered his voice. "Maybe not to the whole world, but me and Ridings, we worked things out."

"That's not how Ridings sees it. Why didn't you give him money for a new cow?"

"He *did,*" Bailee-Ann said. "He paid to have Rosie butchered—it was heartbreaking, I know—and he gave Ridings money for a new cow. But Ridings spent all the money without even knowing it. It went to Wally, that's my guess."

I frowned, because as guesses went, hers was a decent one. I didn't like that version of the story, however. I lifted my chin, waiting for more.

"They were out in the woods, Tommy and Beef and Dupree," Bailee-Ann said. "They were high." Her tone grew disapproving. "Dupree had scored some crystal, and they were lit out of their minds."

"Shut up," Tommy grumbled. "And I wasn't aiming for Ridings's cow. I was *aiming* for the bell around her damn neck."

"Of course you were," I said.

"He was showing off is what he was doing," Bailee-Ann scolded. "Bragged about how he could hit any dang thing, any dang thing at all, so Dupree said, 'Prove it. Ring old Rosie's bell.'"

"But you missed," I said to Tommy.

"Yes. I missed." He stared at his hands, which were splayed on his thighs. "I got her in the lungs."

I grimaced, knowing how bad it would have been. I'd been around cows and horses in pain, and I could see it in my mind: Rosie on her side, bellowing and rolling her white-walled eyes, blood foaming out of her mouth.

"Tommy put her out of her misery," Bailee-Ann said. "He did it even though he was high, and something like that can mess with you big-time."

"I had to climb through a barbed wire fence to get to her. My shirt got caught, so I left it behind," Tommy said. "Smart, huh?"

"It was his football training jersey," Bailee-Ann said, as if I kept track of Tommy's wardrobe. "It was real nice, with his name on it and everything."

"How tragic," I said.

"I would have fessed up, regardless," Tommy said.

"Uh-huh."

"And I gave Ridings seven hundred dollars. I had to borrow part from Roy—"

"*You* had to borrow from *Roy*?" I said.

"But I paid him back." His Adam's apple jerked. "I suggested to Ridings that it would be better if he didn't mention it. I'd, uh, appreciate it if you did the same."

I said neither yes nor no to that request. I felt off balance. I'd waited a long time to have it out with Tommy, and now, when I finally was, the conversation kept going down paths I never saw coming. They all led to Tommy being sorry, and his regret threatened everything I'd built the last three years of my life on.

Bailee-Ann put her hand on my upper back, and when I didn't resist, she rubbed small circles between my shoulder blades.

"There is nothing okay about what he did to you," she said. She didn't glance at Tommy or use his name. This was between the two of us as girls, and also because we used to be best friends. "But a long time's passed since then."

"Yeah," Tommy said. "I'm not that guy."

"Like hell, you aren't!" I cried, my anger flaming up again.

"No. You're misunderstanding. I *was* that guy, but . . ." His hands didn't know what to do. They fluttered up and then down, an almost feminine gesture. "I don't want to be that guy. I didn't want to even when I was. And I'm not anymore. That's what I'm saying." His hands fell to his lap. "I sure do wish you'd believe me."

I scowled. I could resist it all I wanted, but I did understand what he trying to explain. How sometimes the pieces of who you thought you were didn't add up to who you really were, like with me not standing up for Patrick when he wore those pants. Like Jason calling me such a hateful name at the library, when in reality he was as sweet as sunshine.

It hurt to realize that Tommy was human and not a *total* monster after all. It hurt so much that my hands clenched, and I realized, with shock, that I was squeezing the trigger of

Daddy's pistol. It didn't budge. It was rusted in place. It was useless.

Bailee-Ann was still rubbing my back, like the way I rubbed ointment into my daddy's cracked feet. I twitched my shoulder to shake her off me. I studied Tommy's face, noticing that the bruise around his eye had darkened since I'd arrived.

"You are nothing but an egg-sucking dog," I told him. "You tormented Patrick all through high school. You stole *his pants*, for God's sake, and left him practically naked in the bathroom. Why?"

Tommy didn't have the guts to answer.

"That was a long time ago, too," Bailee-Ann said.

"Not long enough," I said.

Candypants is having his coming-out party, so step on up and take a look, Tommy had said. *He don't mind. Fags like being looked at, don't they, Patrick? And I'll be damned—here's his girlfriend, right here in the flesh! Get on over here, Cat."*

I'd frozen in the hall. Tommy said, *Whassat? No? Awww, she's shy.* Then the final nail in the coffin: *Hey. Cat. Catch. You ain't gonna get in his pants any other way.*

In Tommy's living room, I breathed hard. Tears pressed to get out, but no and no and no.

I faced Tommy dead on and finally just came out with it. "Did you attack Patrick at the Come 'n' Go? Are you the one who did it?"

"No," he said. His face was red, but he answered my question as straightforwardly as I'd asked it.

"Do you know who did?"

His eyes flicked to Bailee-Ann. I tried to catch what passed between them, but too quickly, he brought his focus back to me.

"I don't," he said.

"We care, too, you know," Bailee-Ann said. She gestured at the coffee table, and I glanced down to see today's newspaper open to an article on page three titled, "NCBI Explores Leads in Local Hate Crime Investigation."

Patrick wasn't even front page material anymore.

Disgusted, I stood up, dislodging Bailee-Ann.

She righted herself and asked, "Are you leaving?"

"Yep," I said. I tossed Daddy's Spanish pistol on the Lawsons' coffee table, and it made a fairly satisfying *thunk* that I hoped woke up his mama.

"You're not taking that?" Tommy said.

"Nope."

"But . . . why?" Bailee-Ann said.

"Because it's good for nothing," I said, keeping my eyes on Tommy. "Because one worthless piece of shit deserves another."

I strode out of the house, ignoring Bailee-Ann's cries of "But where are you *going*? What are you going to do?"

I biked for a half mile or so and pulled off the road, just to think a little.

My encounter with Tommy had sucked me dry.

Maybe a person—like me—could tell myself I was fine on my own. Maybe I could even believe it, for a while. But it was like building a wall of ice around myself. I looked out at the world through all that frozen water, and everything appeared pretty much the same, with only a few wavy spots here and there. *Air bubbles*, I told myself. *No big deal.*

Only, it was cold. I was cold. I said to myself, *So? You're tough. You can take it.*

But the cold didn't go away. It just got colder. And eventually, one of two things happened: Either the cold settled inside you and turned your heart to ice, or something happened to make you start to thaw.

Only the thawing hurt, too.

I heard a rush and a rumble, and I came out of my thoughts to see Bailee-Ann zoom past me in her truck. Then she slowed down. Then she stopped. Why? Did she see me?

Her taillights turned from red to white. She was coming back.

26

SHE DROVE IN REVERSE TO REACH ME, HER RIGHT arm stretched over the passenger seat and her neck craned so she could see behind her. She killed the engine and hopped out, wiping her palms down the front of her shorts.

"Hi," she said.

"Um . . . hi," I said.

"Why are you just sitting here?"

"I don't know. I just am," I said.

But she wasn't listening. She glanced down the road toward Tommy's house and bit her lip. She pulled her gaze to me and said, "Listen, about Patrick . . ."

She let the sentence hang, waiting for me to fill in the blank.

But Patrick was in the hospital, and Tommy said he didn't do it. What did she want me to say?

She checked the road again. Then she reached into her front pocket and pulled out a pack of matches. "I found these in Beef's jacket." She tossed them to me. "Here."

They were from a restaurant, or maybe a bar, called Billy the Kid's. The front flap boasted a line drawing of a shirtless cowboy twirling a lasso, and beneath the picture was the address. *Asheville, North Carolina,* it said. I looked at Bailee-Ann.

"I wanted to show you," she said.

"But not in front of Tommy? How come?"

"It's . . . complicated."

I snorted, because what wasn't?

She shoved her hands in her pockets. "He's not in a good place, you know?"

"Tommy?"

"No, Beef. Tommy wants me to break up with him . . . and I *will* . . . but it feels wrong to do it now."

She rehashed how strange Beef had been acting since losing his scholarship, hot one day and cold the next.

"He doesn't sleep for days. And then when he does, he's out so hard, I can't even wake him up," she said. "One time, Robert *stepped* on him, and he didn't wake up. I mean, that's *weird,* right?"

"Yeah," I said. "And?"

She pulled her eyebrows together like she didn't understand my impatience.

"Is he still doing meth, Bailee-Ann? Is that what you want me to know?"

She protested feebly, and I fluttered my fingers. "Just forget it. Don't bother."

"Don't *bother*?" she huffed. "I thought you liked Beef. I thought you cared, even though you work so hard to pretend you don't."

"Thanks for the guilt trip," I said. "But I'm pretty sure cheating on him's a worse offense, Bailee-Ann."

Pain filled her eyes. She spun on her heel and headed for her truck.

"Ah, crap," I muttered. I rose awkwardly to my feet and went after her. "So what do you want to tell me? Why'd you give me the matches?"

Her hand stilled on the door handle. Her lower lip quivered in a way I remembered.

"I *do* care about Beef," I said. "I just said that to pay you back."

"Pay me back? For *what*?"

"I don't know, because I feel bad for him," I said, exasperated. "I mean, when you're in the dark, and then you *find* out you've been in the dark . . ."

I came to the end of that line of reasoning. Sighing, I said, "Or maybe I'm just a crappy friend and wanted to make you feel bad."

She twisted her bowed head so that she was gazing at me sideways. "Are we even friends?"

I felt strange in my own skin. A breeze lifted my hair, whispering against my neck. "We used to be."

One tear, shiny as a dewdrop, rolled down her cheek and plopped onto her foot, washing the dust of the day from that one spot. Her flip-flops were pink with white polka dots, and now one of the polka dots was brighter than the others.

She turned around, resting her weight against her truck. Sounding worn-out, she said, "You should know that your brother was never a user. Tommy and I were, but we quit. We wanted Beef to quit, too." She hugged her ribs. "That's why Beef got so mad that night at Suicide Rock."

"Oh," I said. Finally, the missing piece. It clicked into place, and it fit. "That's what the guys 'discussed' with him? His meth use?"

"It was an intervention," she said heavily. "He didn't take it so well."

"You think?" He'd called Patrick a fucking pansy, and he'd told Tommy and my brother to go play with their vaginas, though as Bailee-Ann said, he didn't use that word.

"Was it Patrick's idea, the intervention?" I asked. That would explain why Patrick didn't want Robert along. Maybe he knew it would get ugly.

"Patrick was all for it, but no. It was Tommy's idea."

My eyebrows shot up. *"Tommy* set up an intervention for Beef? No way. No frickin' way."

She looked at me from under a swoop of hair as if she were so, so tired. "Tommy knew firsthand how messed up meth made you. Like with the cow?"

"Wait," I said, remembering what she'd said at her house about how running meth was easy money, and how certain folks found themselves new jobs when the local meth cookers sprang up. "Did Tommy get Beef into all that in the first place?"

She didn't answer. Well, that's not true. She did, by saying stiffly, "That's why he wanted to get him *out*. He wanted to make up for his sins."

"Fine," I said. "So Tommy, Patrick, and Christian talked to Beef. Beef got pissed. Where was Dupree during all this?"

"Dupree is Dupree," she said.

I nodded. True enough.

"Back to these," I said, lifting the pack of matches. "Do you think Beef knows something about Patrick getting hurt? Do you think this place is somehow connected?"

"What I think is that Patrick has a boyfriend," Bailee-Ann said.

I straightened my spine. "He does! Yes!"

My reaction startled her. I tried to tone it down. "Do you know who he is?"

"No, Patrick never would tell me."

I wiggled the matches. "And Billy the Kid's?"

"I think he works there. The boyfriend." She cleared her throat. "I think it's, um, a gay place."

Wow, really? I thought.

285

"They were in Beef's jacket," I said. "So has Beef been there? Does he know Patrick's boyfriend?" I said.

"I'm pretty sure," Bailee-Ann said. "I'm pretty sure he doesn't like him, either."

"What makes you say that?"

"That's just kind of the impression I get." She twined her foot around her opposite leg, hooking it behind her calf. "Like, I heard Beef and Patrick arguing one time. Beef was saying how Patrick was an idiot if he thought people could change, and that a rotten egg is a rotten egg. That kind of thing."

She wrapped her arms around herself. "Then I came into the room, and they shut up. I asked what they were talking about, and . . ."

"And?"

She shivered. "Beef can be . . . mean sometimes. Like, he has this thing where he makes fun of homos, even though Patrick is one. You know?"

"Usually he stands up for Patrick," I argued.

"But not always. Anyway, when they saw me, Beef went into this spiel about how Patrick was mad at his *boyfwiend* and wasn't that *just so tewwible*. He said it in a baby voice, like that, and he swished around and stuff."

She cocked a hip and flipped her wrist, searching my expression. When I scowled, she dropped the position. "That's all I know, but it made me think maybe Patrick's boyfriend is like that. Swishy."

I absorbed what she'd said. I tried out a scenario in which

Patrick's boyfriend drew attention to himself in a dangerous way—by acting swishy—and Patrick defended him, because Patrick would. Or what if Patrick met up with his boyfriend at the Come 'n' Go after hours? What if they had plans to meet that Saturday night, and that's why Patrick insisted on going back to the store after everything went sour at Suicide Rock? And then, later, what if someone saw Patrick and his boyfriend together?

"So I need to go to Billy the Kid's," I said. That's what it came to.

Bailee-Ann looked worried, but she didn't tell me not to. Her truck was right behind us, but she also didn't offer to give me a ride.

"Do you think a person would go to hell just for stepping into a place like that?" Bailee-Ann asked.

"No way," I said, though I had no idea. I trusted my gut, though. "I don't think people go to hell for being gay, either, because if they did, that would mean Patrick would, too. And I just don't believe God would do that."

"What if there's different kinds of gay?" she said. "Like, good gay and nasty gay?"

"Um . . . I'm not sure."

Bailee-Ann fiddled with the keys to her truck.

"Did Beef tell the police about Patrick's boyfriend?" I asked.

"He, um, didn't want to get involved. Because of other reasons."

"Such as?"

She shook her head, and I thought, *meth*. Beef and this gay bar in Asheville were connected, and not just because of Patrick's boyfriend working there. And if Beef thought Patrick's boyfriend was a "rotten egg," as Bailee-Ann put it . . .

Was it possible that Patrick's boyfriend used meth? God, was Beef his supplier or whatever?

"What are you going to do?" Bailee-Ann asked.

"Well, I have to go to Asheville, like I said. To Billy the Kid's, to find Patrick's boyfriend."

"How will you get there?"

She hadn't volunteered to drive me there the first time I threw the idea out, and she sure wasn't volunteering now. Perhaps she'd maxed out her bravery simply by telling me all this.

"I guess I'll get a friend to drive me," I said.

"A friend?" she said dubiously.

I told her about Jason. Not a lot, but enough.

"Oh, okay," she said, sounding relieved. "Good." She stood there, and the sun beat down on us, until at last she said, "So, are you going to?"

"What?"

She gave me a funny look. "Call him. Jason."

"Well, not right this second," I said. She waited for an explanation, so I added, "I don't have a phone." Plus, maybe it was a dumb idea. He said he wanted to help, but now I felt nervous about asking.

She reached into the truck and grabbed hers from the

dashboard. It was a cheapie, but she handed it to me and said not to worry about how many minutes I used.

Well, here goes nothing, I thought. I angled my body for privacy and dialed his number.

Afterward, when I gave Bailee-Ann her phone back, she gave me a tentative half-smile. I didn't know why, and then I realized that *I* was smiling. Because of Jason.

"You like him, don't you?" she said.

"Patrick?" I said, deliberately misunderstanding. "Of course. Why would I go to so much trouble for someone I didn't like?"

She shook her head and climbed into her truck. From out the window, she gave me a parting piece of advice. "Hey, Cat. Watch yourself, okay?"

"I will," I said, knowing what she was getting at. Patrick's boyfriend might have brought danger to Patrick in any number of ways, or the danger could be one step less removed. The danger could be the boyfriend himself.

27

I WAS POSSIBLY IN LOVE WITH JASON, JUST A LITTLE. Not *in love* in love. It was too soon for that. But ready to be in love with *everything* again, or everything good, anyway. That's what I thought about as I gazed out the window of Jason's car, watching the many shades of green dance and cast shadows as we drove along the twisty mountain road. Also I loved my brother, and Bailee-Ann, and even squirmy Robert, just for being a kid and liking ice cream.

I loved everyone who said *yes* to the world and tried to make it better instead of worse, because so much in the world was ugly—and just about all the ugly parts were due to humans. I counted myself among those pitiful ranks. I didn't slam meth or get stinking drunk or go off and molest anyone, but that didn't let me off the hook. I hid in the shadows, but hiding had the power to hurt, too.

I hurt Patrick and Bailee-Ann by not being there for them. I hurt Christian by thinking *coward* in my mind and scowling at him like he wasn't worthy of respect. I hurt everyone I came into contact with, because what I was sending out wasn't a *yes* to the world but a *no.*

So I was going to stop that.

Jason and I were silent as we reached the outskirts of Asheville, but it was a comfortable silence. We'd talked for much of the hour-long drive, and now we were taking a break. Gearing up for whatever lay ahead.

We started to see fewer trees and more houses, and Jason watched for street signs, occasionally glancing at the map he printed out before coming to get me.

Jason was going to go inside with me when we got to Billy the Kid's, assuming the place was open at noon. "It's either that, or no ride," he'd said after learning of my early morning visit to Tommy. He hadn't been pleased when I told him I'd gone there, and all he knew about was the tongue, not the other stuff. Maybe one day I'd tell him all of it—the fire, the motorcycle, my brother's burning courage—but not now.

Jason's concern was sweet, but unnecessary. I was almost 100 percent convinced that Tommy hadn't put the tongue on my pillow, and anyway, nothing had happened at Tommy's house. Here I was, safe and sound.

"Yeah, but we're no longer talking about Tommy," Jason said.

He glanced at me. "This boyfriend of Patrick's, we don't know anything about him. We may not even find him, you know."

"Eyes on the road, buddy," I told him, and not for the first time.

He grumbled, but the highway to Asheville was steep and twisty, and it didn't help that Jason's car was a twenty-five-year-old Chevy Malibu that used to belong to his grammy. The tires were cracked with dry rot. The shocks were shot, so we rebounded hard whenever we hit a pothole. The passenger side floorboard had been eaten out by rust, and if I looked down, I could see the asphalt moving beneath us.

On top of that, the Malibu's engine was so gunked up that it could barely pull the car up the mountain. On steep stretches, Jason has to shift all the way into first gear, and our speed dropped to fifteen miles an hour, tops. Every so often, a local got right on top of us, laying on his horn as if Jason was going slower than honey on purpose. As soon as there was a hint of an open stretch, the driver behind us would roar past, honking some more and making unfriendly gestures out the window.

It was actually kind of funny. "I'm going as fast as I can!" Jason would say. "Just pass me, dammit!"

"You're supposed to pull off and *let* them pass you," I told him. I pointed to a stretch of dirt on the side of the road. "See that? That's called a pull-off spot. It's called that 'cause that's where the slowpokes *pull off.*"

"Thank you, yes, I know what a pull-off is. But if we pull off, we'll never get going again."

"Ah," I said.

He flicked my shoulder for being a smarty-pants, and I said, "Hey, hands on the wheel."

He looked at me in disbelief.

"Hands on the wheel *and* eyes on the road. Two very important principles of safety."

"You do remember I'm the one giving you a ride, right?" he said.

I laughed, and it pleased him. I could tell by his lopsided smile, which pleased *me*. We grinned goofily at each other.

Later, our conversation shifted to more serious things. I told him about my theory about Beef dealing meth to Patrick's boyfriend. That got Jason going. He talked about addiction and how it ruined everything. He said his father gave him his first drink when he was four years old. It was whiskey, and Jason's daddy thought it would be funny to give it to his little boy.

"I remember how warm I felt after it went down," Jason said. "I can call back that feeling exactly, all these years later."

He told me about his slow realization that when one person in a family was sick, the whole family was sick. In Jason's case, the sick person was his father, who was nice enough when he was sober, but mean as a snake when he was drunk.

He'd hit Jason and then act all self-righteous, as if the hitting had been Jason's fault. He'd throw his hand out at Jason's little sister, Christy, and say, "How you feel knowing she had to see that, boy?"

Other times, if Jason didn't jump fast enough or high

293

enough or whatever, Jason's daddy would shake his head and say, "Going after *you* don't seem to make no difference, so what am I to do? Do you *want* me to hit Christy? Is that what it's gonna take to bring you in line? 'Cause sure seems like that's the only thing that'll stop you."

Christy, his sister, was eleven, the same age as Robert. Jason's plan was to get his degree, get a job, and find a place to live somewhere far away from Hangtree. "Me and Mama and Christy, we'll all go and live there," he said. "And my daddy can just sit in his own shit."

Hearing Jason talk about Christy reminded me of Beef and Gwennie. Roy used to hit Beef an awful lot. He stopped when Beef got big enough to punch him back, but Beef would always have scars to remind him of his daddy's love.

"Why didn't you tell anyone what was going on?" I asked Jason. "Like a teacher, or someone at church?"

His jaw twitched, and I felt like I'd let him down. After all, I was no stranger to sad-sack sob stories. Heck, I had one of my own, and did I tell anyone? When your life was messed up, you didn't want anyone to know.

"Never mind," I said. "Sorry."

He was quiet for a bit, and then he said, "Sometimes he'd break stuff around the house. One time, he punched the microwave, and glass shattered everywhere. You'd think they'd make the doors out of safety glass, wouldn't you?"

"Or that people wouldn't go punching them," I said.

"Or that. Right." He shook his head. "Another time, he

294

punched a hole in the wall. Christy'd be crying and Mama'd be crying, and you know what I'd do?"

"What?"

"I'd wait till my dad stormed out, and then I'd get out the Spackle and fix the wall. I'd sand it down. Repaint it if it needed it." He made a disgusted sound. "Nothing I could do about the microwave."

"We don't even have a microwave," I told him.

He glanced at me. "Neither do we."

He told me how his mama slept with her wallet under her pillow and the keys to her car in her underwear, so his dad couldn't take what little she had. He told me she'd beg his dad to get help, and he'd deny up and down that he had a problem.

I wanted to say, again, how sorry I was. Instead, I reached out and rubbed the top of his shoulder. I felt him relax into it, and my hand crept up to his neck and worked away at the knots I felt there.

"That feels good," he said, like he'd been holding a great big sack of groceries and I'd taken it from him. Like my fingers rubbing out his sore spots gave him that much relief.

"Might as well tell you, he's not *just* a drunk," he said with a sideways glance.

"I kinda figured," I said.

"Remember how I said my sister-in-law's a tweaker? And my cousin? Well, so is my dad."

"*Why?*" I said. "I just don't get why would anyone use a drug like that, knowing it would ruin your life? Why would you even *try* a drug like that?"

"Because it wipes you clean and fills you up again," Jason said. "Whatever you don't have in here"—he thumped his chest—"meth gives it to you. You're fucking Superman. You can do anything."

"That's messed up," I said softly.

"You're telling me," he said.

Eventually, our conversation circled back around to Beef's mysterious trips and Patrick's mysterious boyfriend.

"When Patrick mentioned his boyfriend, did he say anything about drugs?" I asked Jason.

Jason drummed his fingers on the steering wheel. "Yeah. I don't know if it was meth, but they fought about it."

"What exactly did Patrick tell you about him?"

"Not much," Jason said. "That he had a hard family life." He shot me a glance to say *Don't we all?*

"Do you think he's the one who hurt Patrick?" I said. How could Patrick care for a person, maybe even love him, if he had the potential for such violence?

Jason shook his head. Neither one of us could get our heads around it. That's when we stopped talking. But I didn't stay in that ugly place, and as I said, our silence wasn't the bad kind. We were here, together in Jason's crappy Malibu, because we chose to be. We weren't high. We weren't hitting each other. The forest surrounded us, but sometimes sunlight snuck through the overlapping branches and bathed us in liquid gold. We were doing our best to help a friend.

"We're getting close," Jason said, after we'd left the shelter of the woods. He glanced at the map and turned left onto New Plateau Drive. It didn't look new to me. It looked like we were heading into the seedy part of town.

Jason made a right and then another left, pulling into a cramped parking lot. He killed the engine. He turned and gazed at me for a long moment.

He said, "We're here."

28

BILLY THE KID'S WAS NOTHING FANCY, JUST A DOOR
opening out onto an alley. When I saw it, I thought, *No way
anyone's going to be here, not in the middle of the day.* But I
knocked anyway. When I gave up, Jason took over, his knuckles
pounding the wood.

From inside, a man growled, "Go 'way. Not open."

Jason and I looked at each other.

"Please?" I called. "I have a friend, and he's in trouble, and I
just want to ask a few questions?"

Nothing.

Jason tried. "We don't mean in trouble with the law. We're
not cops or anything."

"Yeah, we're just kids," I said.

"*Go. A. Way,*" the man said, but with a weariness that suggested he'd give in if we pushed a little harder.

"Just five minutes," I said. "It'll take five minutes, I swear, and then we'll leave you alone."

Silence. But when I pressed my ear to the door, I heard a heavy sigh.

"Um, otherwise we'll just stay here," I said. I held Jason's gaze so it was as if I was talking to him instead of the guy inside. "We'll just stay here, talking to you, and it'll probably be hard to get any work done, because I know we're being kind of annoying."

"Who's being annoying?" Jason said, lifting his eyebrows.

"Good point," I told him. I raised my voice. "Well, *I'm* not annoying, but the guy I'm with kind of is. And sometimes he just starts singing, just randomly, and he's not very good."

Jason's expression didn't change, but amusement flickered in his eyes, and I knew him well enough to recognize it. Already I knew him that well, even though we'd only just come into each other's lives, and it made me so happy I *wanted* to sing. I hadn't wanted to sing in forever.

I picked a song Mama Sweetie used to sing to me and Patrick when we were littlies. I'd spend the night at his house, and the crickets would chirp outside the open windows, and Mama Sweetie would rock back and forth in her rocking chair, singing softly till we fell asleep.

I, however, did not use my soft voice. "Keep on the sunny

side, always on the sunny side," I belted out. "Keep on the sunny side of life!"

Jason regarded me incredulously.

"Sing with me," I whispered

"Not happening," he whispered back.

I didn't know what to do but plunge on, so plunge on I did, and when my voice cracked on the high note, I ignored it. "It will help us every day, it will brighten all the way, if we keep on the sunny side of life!"

The door opened. A huge black man stared down at me.

"Well, if it ain't a li'l white gal singing her heart out," he said, shaking his head. "Wha'choo want, li'l white gal?"

"Oh," I said. "Um. Is this your place?"

"Yeah. So?" the black guy said. He weighed three hundred pounds at least, and he wore a football jersey over enormous jean shorts. His sneakers were white and puffy and spotless. But his eyes, though exasperated, had no cruelty in them. It made me breathe easier.

"Can we come in?" I asked.

"Hell no, I got payroll to do," he said. But he didn't shut the door, and when he lumbered to a table with papers spread out on it, Jason and I followed.

"Are you Billy?" I asked. I sat down next to him, perching on the edge of my chair.

He eyeballed me. He eyeballed Jason. "I go by the Kid," he said, pronouncing it *kee-ud*. "Now what you want? You got *two* minutes, not five. *Talk.*"

I drew in a breath of air, then blew it out. This wasn't a game. This was real, and I had two minutes to find out what I needed to know.

"Not to be rude," I said, "but is this a bar for, um . . . ?"

I looked at Jason. *Help,* I said with my eyes.

"Is this a gay bar?" Jason asked.

"Yeah," the Kid said, like what else in the world would it be? His fingers, spread out on the table, were nearly the size of corn dogs.

"Well, I have a friend in Black Creek—that's where I'm from—and he got beat up for being gay," I said. "His name's Patrick. Do you know him?"

The Kid's expression was inscrutable. After a second, he said, "Mebbe."

"Well . . . I think he had a boyfriend, and I think he might have worked here."

This time, his answer came easily. "Nope."

My gut sank. "You're sure?"

"What do you mean, am I sure?" he huffed. "Are you asking do I know my employees? Yes, I do, 'cause this here a class joint. I got *standards,* see. I go hiring a dude like that, and wha'choo think's gonna happen? Dude like that's gonna bring the law down on me, that's what."

Jason and I looked at each other. My heart beat faster. "You know him? Omigosh, you know Patrick's boyfriend?"

Billy the Kid made a sound like *chhhhh.* "I tole Patrick to drop that strung-out piece a shit. Me and my partner, we both tole him so."

"Your business partner?" I said.

Jason opened his mouth, then closed it. Embarrassment made me sink low in my seat as I caught on.

"My *partner* a decent man," Billy the Kid said, eyeballing me. "The kinda man Patrick needs to find. Me and Leroy, we both tole Patrick how his boy's a lost cause. He goin' nowhere, we tole him, that's how lost he is. And he prolly diseased on top of that.'"

"Okay," I said, nodding a little desperately. "Can you tell us his name? Or where to find him?"

The Kid leaned forward. "I said, 'Let the Kid take care of you. I'll find you someone nice. Someone *clean.*' And you know what Patrick said? He told me, 'Thank you very much, Mr. Kid, but you don't understand. I'm in *loooove* with this boy, and when you in love with someone, you don't give up on 'em, no matter what.'"

"That's Patrick, all right," I said.

"Mebbe so. But his boyfriend was a damn bag fag, and it got so I couldn't let neither of 'em in."

Bag fag? What was a bag fag?

"Now I tole Patrick *he* was welcome anytime, as long as he didn't bring his friend," the Kid said. "But he wouldn't have nothing of it."

"Mr. Kid? Sir?" Jason said. "We need to find him, Patrick's boyfriend. Can you tell us his name?"

"Other 'n cocksucker?" the Kid said.

"Other than that."

The Kid pulled a napkin from the dispenser and gave his nose a great honking blow. He examined the contents, crumpled the napkin, and said, "Nope. Would if I could, but I *tole* you. He a bag fag. Dudes like that hold their names close."

"What's a bag fag?" I asked.

The Kid swiveled his big eyes at me again. "Oh, sugar booger. You just a baby, ain't you?"

Jason educated me in an embarrassed voice. "Someone who, ah, trades sex for drugs."

"Yeah. *That,*" the Kid said. "Sometimes he be selling, other times he be looking for a hookup." He shook his massive head. "He was here more than Patrick knew, I can tell you that. Till I gave him the boot."

A thought flitted into my brain, and then back out again, too quick for me to latch hold of it. I frowned. "Did Patrick ever come here with anyone other than his boyfriend? Before you gave him the boot?"

"Gave *his boyfriend* the boot," the Kid clarified. "And *no.* I already tole you. When Patrick came, it was always with his damn lover boy, and only with his damn lover boy. That's why I had to make it all or nothin', see?"

I was confused. If it was always *Patrick and his lover boy,* where did that leave Beef—and how did Beef end up with the matches?

Maybe Beef knew about Billy the Kid's, but was too homophobic to step inside, so he waited out in the alley. Or maybe I was overthinking things, and it was as simple as Beef saying, "Hey, buddy, got a light?" and Patrick tossing him the pack from his own pocket.

Unless Beef came here on his own, without Patrick. What if Beef and Patrick's boyfriend were in business together? What if Beef, like the Kid, realized that the guy was bad news?

"Lay down with a dog, you gonna wake up with fleas," the Kid said. "And that boyfriend, he had the scary eyes. Thought he might go after me when I tole him he was disallowed, but Patrick calmed him down. Still, I keep a rifle under the bar just in case."

I chewed my lip. "Did any straight guys ever come here? To buy drugs or sell drugs or whatever?"

The Kid narrowed his eyes. "Why you want to know that?"

"I just do. I need to know."

"No you don't, so get outta here," he said. "Your two minutes done up and flown away a long time ago."

I pushed back from the table and stood up. Jason did the same.

"It's just . . . there's this guy, okay?" I said. "A white guy, about this tall"—I put my hand above me—"with dark hair and dark eyes. He used to have a crew cut, but he's been letting it grow out, so his hair's kinda scraggly."

The Kid raised his eyebrows. "And I care because?"

"He's skinny, but strong," I said, trying to describe Beef so that the Kid could see him like I did. "Used to be a wrestler. Has a nice smile. Oh, and he's got a scar under his eye, right about here." I drew a line under my left eye to show the place on Beef where Roy sliced him with his class ring.

304

The Kid folded his huge arms over his chest. "Why you playing me, gal? I *tole* you, I gave his sorry ass the boot."

I felt a tingling between my shoulder blades. "I know, but I'm not talking about Patrick's boyfriend. I'm talking about another guy."

"*Ohhhh,* I see. You talking about *another* scrawny white dude with hair that needs cutting, a pretty smile, and a moon under his eye?"

My mind put the pieces together, but my body couldn't grasp it. I swayed. Jason reached out to steady me.

"There ain't two of 'em unless they's twins," the Kid said.

"But Beef has a girlfriend," I said dumbly.

"*Beef.* Yeah, that's it," the Kid said.

"You're saying Beef is Patrick's boyfriend," Jason said.

"For the hundredth time, yeah," the Kid said. "Now get outta here."

We did, though the actual leaving part was foggy because of how my mind was spinning: Beef pushing Bailee-Ann away and blaming it on her being drunk. Bailee-Ann stepping out on Beef with Tommy. The fight between Beef and Patrick, which Bailee-Ann overheard, where Beef swished around and berated Patrick for trying to change his faggy boyfriend, who was Beef himself.

"I have to call him," I told Jason once we were in the car. "Can I use your phone?"

Jason looked at me like I was crazy. "No way."

"But . . ." I floundered. If Beef was Patrick's boyfriend . . .

if Beef was *gay,* if all along he was gay and he didn't tell anyone . . . what else was he hiding? I beat my thigh with my fist. "He knows who attacked Patrick. I just know it."

"And what are you planning on saying to get him to tell you?" Jason said.

I hadn't gotten that far, but I was beginning to see that it was going to be harder than just popping out with it all. According to the Kid, Beef had traded sex for drugs. That was one ugly, steaming pile of cow shit.

"He's kept quiet for a reason, Cat. And he wants *you* quiet, too, or have you forgotten?"

My breaths were shallow. I didn't want to think like that.

"He put a cow tongue on your pillow," Jason said.

Oh my God. From Huskers, that's where he must have gotten it. That flaccid sawed-off slab.

Jason glanced at me, and his eyes were deep pools. "You don't need to be calling Beef, Cat. You need to call the police."

I shook my head, because that wasn't the answer. At this point, all we knew was that Beef was mixed up in something bad, and not just mixed up in it but *part* of it, in so deep that he may have led that badness straight to Patrick, his best friend. His *boyfriend,* Lord have mercy.

Beef knew more about Patrick's attack than he was saying, that much was clear. But going to Sheriff Doyle wasn't the answer. It might come to that, but not yet.

I rubbed my hand over my face. I couldn't shake the feeling that I could figure everything out if I just put my mind to it.

"Do you think Bailee-Ann knows Beef is gay?" I said. "Is that why she gave me the pack of matches, so I'd find out?"

Jason's jaw was tense. "You know her better than I do. What do *you* think?"

I bit my lower lip. Maybe she knew, but didn't want to. Maybe she had a streak of Aunt Tildy running through her.

I thought about Beef and Robert's trips to Asheville. Robert on Beef's motorcycle, holding tight to Beef's waist. Beef teaching Robert "to be a man," and to never go down that faggot path, not ever, because homos always got what they deserved.

Beef had been talking about himself, hadn't he? That bad things happened if you were gay, because look what he'd gotten his very own boyfriend mixed up in. So Beef had been hating *himself*, that's what it looked like now. And maybe he didn't want Robert to face the same fate, but probably it was just more that he needed to talk his feelings out, and who better for an audience than a hero-worshipping kid?

Only Beef, with his rash of dark moods, had stopped talking to Robert . . . and he'd threatened me . . . and then there was the redneck posse, with their secretive looks and their wall of silence . . .

My blood stopped moving. For one sickening pulse, my heart quit beating, and then it started up fast and heavy.

"Jesus," I whispered. Jason met my gaze, his expression grim. He'd gotten there, too, just a flick of a second ahead of me.

I'd been so suspicious of Tommy that I'd blinded myself to

something huge: Tommy wasn't the only one with a sketchy alibi during the time Patrick was hurt. Beef's alibi was even sketchier. He'd driven back and forth along the highway deep into the night, and not just once but multiple times. Ridings told me that, and I looked right through it, choosing to see what I wanted to see and nothing else.

My mind reeled. I could hardly take it in. *Beef?*

I put together the chronology of the night as best I could, hoping it would give me the answers.

First Beef had partied with the others at the Frostee Top. At eleven thirty or so, Tommy suggested a beer run, though his real motivation was to collect Patrick. The redneck posse had decided to confront one of their own, and they planned to do so as a group. Beef argued against the trip to the Come 'n' Go—Patrick had already been riding him for screwing up his life, and Beef had no desire to face more of the same—but he was overruled.

At eleven forty-five, they pulled up at the Come 'n' Go, where Patrick was finishing up his shift. Patrick wasn't quite ready to close up, but he put off his closing duties, knowing he could return and finish them later. Everyone piled into Bailee-Ann's pickup, they dropped off Robert at Patrick's insistence, and then they drove into the forest. By foot, they made their way to Suicide Rock, where Dupree and Bailee-Ann got loopy on some old-timer's herbal remedy while the others had a talk with Beef.

He must have felt cornered. He must have been furious.

At around one, the party wound down, and Beef drove everyone back down the mountain in Bailee-Ann's pickup truck. Beef dropped the others off. Then he took Patrick back to the gas station so that Patrick could finish stocking the napkins or whatever. But Beef himself didn't turn in for the night.

Maybe he cruised by Wally's. If he scored a fix, he'd have been amped within minutes. He'd have felt like Superman. Or if Wally didn't give him a hookup, then his rage would have escalated to a new level.

I might not ever know that part. What I did know was that instead of going home, he drove back to the Come 'n' Go.

Maybe he and Patrick talked. I was purely speculating, but maybe Beef just wanted Patrick to hear his side of the story, while Patrick just wanted Beef to stop lying to himself and get clean.

Somehow things turned ugly. Patrick might have given Beef an ultimatum, like stop using or I'll tell Roy, or I'll break up with you, or I'll turn you in, or whatever. And then, because Bailee-Ann's truck was there . . .

I refused to believe that Beef set off that night planning to hurt Patrick. No and no. But people in the country always had stuff in the backs of their trucks. Tarps for spreading on wet ground, rope for lashing stuff down when there was hauling to be done, a container of gas for refueling on isolated mountain roads. In Bailee-Ann's case, apparently one of Robert's baseball bats.

So Beef, most likely high on meth, had gone with what

the opportunity gave him. He bashed in Patrick's skull with Robert's baseball bat and strung him to a gas pump. Afterward, realizing what he'd done, he'd hosed down Bailee-Ann's truck from top to bottom.

Beef made sure my truck was back in my driveway by the time I woke up, Bailee-Ann had said. *He even washed it for me. Wasn't that sweet?"*

"We have to go to the police," Jason said. "What if he does something else crazy? Goes after someone else?

"I know." I was twitching my foot like a scared rabbit. "But no one's in danger this very second, right?"

"They have a cop outside Patrick's hospital room, so Patrick should be safe," Jason said, as if he was thinking out loud. "Beef's a loose cannon, but unless something sets him off, I don't guess I see him lashing out at someone for no good reason." He glanced at me. "Do you?"

"All I know is that he pretty much hates me right now." The gift he left on my pillow made that abundantly clear. He'd hitched himself over my window while Christian was with Tommy, or possibly earlier, since I was out and about most of the day. *Stop flapping your tongue, or I'll cut yours out, too.*

"Yeah, and that's why you need to stay away from him," Jason said. "When we get into town, we go straight to the police. Deal?"

I flopped back against the seat, knowing he was right. Was that enough, or did I need to do something now? What if I didn't, and someone else got hurt?

"What about Bailee-Ann?" I said. "If Beef finds out she's cheating on him with Tommy . . . and he could, because Robert knows all about it, and he could say anything at anytime. For that matter, what about *Robert*?"

I thought about the bus trip together, and how he smelled my hair. How he waggled his eyebrows at the ice-cream shop, when I told him he was a big boy and could wipe his own mouth.

"He acted strange that day in Toomsboro," I told Jason. "Like . . . *sexual,* in a weird way."

"How old is he?"

"Eleven, same as your sister."

"Well, not to be crude, but . . ." He broke off, his neck turning red. "Guys are interested in girls by then. Even at eleven."

"This was different," I insisted. Robert had been . . . courting me, almost, as if he'd learned that acting like that got him attention. Then, after I bought him ice cream and actually *gave* him attention—in a normal way, a talking-and-listening way— he went back to being a kid. He was still Robert, don't get me wrong. He was still squirmy and annoying and yet somehow slightly adorable. But he'd stopped pretending to be something he wasn't.

"What if . . ." I stopped, not wanting to put it in words.

"Go on and say it," Jason said. The car swerved out of the lane as we rounded a curve, and he overcorrected to pull us back. The engine protested with a high-pitched whine. "Might as well lay it all out."

"In school, Beef always stood up for Patrick. Beef was a jock. Patrick was nerdy and got picked on." I quickly added, "I didn't know anything else was going on between them."

"Okay. And?"

"So . . . Patrick really looked up to him. And more than that, obviously. But then things changed, and Patrick was constantly on Beef's case, and then finally Beef just . . ."

My stomach turned over as I substituted Robert for Patrick. Being gay didn't make a person dangerous. Being lonely and depressed enough to groom a little kid into worshipping him was a different story. Add meth to the picture, and Beef's mood swings and Robert's absolute inability to tone himself down when toning down was called for . . .

Jason dug his phone out of his pocket. "Call her. Call Bailee-Ann."

"I could be wrong," I said.

"Or you could be right," Jason said. With only one hand on the wheel, he took another curve too fast, this time coming perilously close to flying off the side of the road. Five feet to my right, the mountain dropped sharply off.

"Oh God," I whimpered. "I'm really bad with heights."

"Sorry," Jason said. He tried to be less lurchy. "Tell her about Beef. If you're wrong, no harm done. But if you *are* right . . ."

I accepted the phone and felt its slimness in my hand. Bailee-Ann's cell phone number was in Jason's call history from when I'd borrowed her phone to ask him to come get me. I called it, but it went to voicemail.

"Bailee-Ann, this is Cat," I said. "Um, we need to talk, okay? It's about—"

I was cut off by a high-pitched electronic whine, followed by a nonexistent woman saying, "If you're satisfied with your message, hit one. If you are finished with your call, hit zero, or simply hang up."

Aaag. Cheap throwaway cell phone.

Her home number still lived in memory and probably would forever, since in middle school we called each other ten times a day. I punched the buttons and put the phone to my ear.

"Pick up, pick up, pick up," I chanted under my breath.

"Tell her to keep Robert away from Beef, no matter what," Jason coached.

I got their answering machine. I groaned. I didn't want to leave a message, but as I listened to Bailee-Ann's mother's prerecorded voice, I decided I better, just in case. If Bailee-Ann wasn't the first to hear it, well, the news would be out soon anyway.

At the beep, "Bailee-Ann, it's Cat. So, listen. Those matches you gave me? You were right about where they were from. And the thing is, I think Beef is that same way. As Patrick."

I gripped the phone, knowing I had to do better. "I think Beef and Patrick were . . . more than friends . . . and I think he's the one who attacked Patrick at the Come 'n' Go. I hope I'm wrong. I *really* hope I'm wrong, but keep clear of him, okay? He's not himself. And keep Robert away from him, too. Don't let Robert go off with him. Don't let—"

Beep. My time was up. I lowered Jason's phone, feeling sure I had totally screwed up. And yet, I was glad I had done it.

"Was that okay?" I asked Jason. "Do you think she'll understand? Do you think she'll listen?" I hit my knee. "*Aghh.* I should have left your number. I didn't leave your number."

"Caller ID," Jason said.

I shook my head.

"Oh yeah," Jason said, because we weren't talking about the newish landlines at Toomsboro Community College. Bailee-Ann lived in Black Creek, and unlike most of the the rest of the country, people in Black Creek didn't have caller ID.

"She'll have it on her cell," he said.

"If she thinks to check," I said. "I'm going to leave it anyway."

I redialed her home number. Again, the answering machine picked up, and I said, "Me again. I'm on a friend's phone if you want to call me. His number is—"

Jason started to supply it for me, but I said it without his help, making his eyebrows rise. I blushed and pretended not to notice and said to Bailee-Ann, "So call me *as soon as you get this,* okay? And *don't* let Robert go off with Beef. Don't tell him why, just—"

I was interrupted by scratchiness and a squeal of feedback. Someone had picked up.

"Hey, Cat," Robert said.

"Robert!" I said, relief making me feel weightless. "Is Bailee-Ann there? Or your mother?"

"The phone's never for me, so that's why I didn't pick up the first time," he said. "No one ever calls me. It's always some boring person selling something, or some boring person wanting Mama to trade shifts with her, and when I forget to write it down, Mama gets mad, so that's why."

"That's all right," I said. "Just put me on with Bailee-Ann."

"She ain't here, but I'm sure glad I am. *Your* message was real interesting, for once."

I was no longer weightless. In fact, my limbs felt like dead wood dragging me down.

Robert laughed gleefully, the laugh of knowing he had something juicy to hold over someone's head. "Is that true that Beef's a faggot, just the same as those fags he's always railing on?"

"No, Robert. And I don't want you saying that."

"Does that mean he did those thing fags do? Love on other guys and stuff? 'Cause that's *nasty.* "

I checked my watch. We were forty minutes from Black Creek. We could be at Bailee-Ann's house in thirty-five, but I wanted someone there *now.* Because Beef had called Robert *special,* and then Beef had dropped him cold. Because Robert was a master eavesdropper, and I'd just told him the best, most powerful secret ever. It wouldn't be long before he realized it.

"Robert, tell me where your sister is," I commanded.

"Was Patrick really his boyfriend? Is that what you meant by

315

more than normal friends? Did he *kiss* him, like how boys kiss girls?" His hilarity dropped a notch. "Aw, you're just messing with me, ain't you?"

"Yes," I said. "I was messing around, and it was a bad idea, and I'm sorry."

"I was right, wasn't I?" he said. "I *said* Beef beat up Patrick, and he said no he didn't."

"Okay, but we don't know that he did. Not for sure."

"He lied to me," Robert marveled.

Tilting the phone, I said, "Go faster, Jason. Oh God, I don't care if we fly off the mountain. Go as fast as you fucking can."

Jason looked at me, perhaps shocked by my language, and flexed his thigh muscle to press down on the accelerator.

"He's a liar and a faggot, and he hurt his friend, too," Robert said. "Why would he hurt his friend?"

"Robert . . ."

His voice changed. "I can't wait to see his face when I tell him. I'm gonna ride my bike to Huskers right now. *Ooo,* he's going to be in so much trouble!"

"Robert, *no,*" I begged.

"What's he saying?" Jason said.

"Do *not* go to Huskers, Robert. Do you hear me?"

There was a whole lot of nothing.

"Robert!"

It was no good. The line was dead.

"No!" I cried.

"Call Huskers and see if Bailee-Ann is there, or even Dupree," Jason instructed. "Use 411 to get the number."

So I did. Beef answered lazily, saying, "Huskers, best sammies around. What can I do you for?"

I hung up. I felt cold even in the no-air-conditioning Malibu.

"All right, then call Tommy," Jason said.

"Tommy?"

"He's the one who got his friends together to talk to him, right? So he'll understand." He banged the steering wheel, not understanding my reluctance. "*Call* him, Cat."

His insistence pulled me out of my stupor. I punched in 411 again because I sure as heck didn't have Tommy's number memorized. I asked for Ronald Lawson, and computer lady said to hold on. As the call went through, sweat popped out under my arms. My heart hammered crazily in my chest.

"Yo, wassup?" Tommy said. I would recognize that voice anywhere.

"Hello?" he said.

I couldn't form words.

"Hello? If you're there, say something. Otherwise I'm outta here."

I hated Tommy more than anyone in the world, and for three years I'd grasped onto that as my whole identity. For three years, I'd stopped talking because of him, and now, if I *didn't* talk, he was going to hang up.

"Tommy, it's Cat," I managed. "I need your help."

29

I JUMPED OUT OF THE CAR AS SOON AS WE GOT to Huskers, with Jason close on my heels. Tommy was inside, along with an anxious Bailee-Ann. Dupree, hovering near the counter, pulled a dishcloth back and forth through his hands.

"Robert's with Beef," Bailee-Ann said.

"What? *No.*" I shook my head, trying to corral my thoughts. "How do you know?"

Tommy jerked his head at Dupree. "Says Robert showed up here, and then he went off with Beef on his motorcycle. Says there didn't seem to be anything bad going on."

"Nothing at all, man," Dupree said. "Robert came in, and he and Beef took off, leaving me to take care of the store all by myself." He gestured at the sandwich shop, empty except for us. "But that's what buddies do. They cover for each other, right?"

"I don't know. Do they?" I snapped.

"Whoa," he said. "Don't jump on me, man. You're getting worked up over nothing." His Bob Marley shirt had ketchup on it, and he looked stoned as always. And yet he kept dragging that dishcloth through his hands.

"Did you know that your *buddy* left a cow tongue on Cat's pillow yesterday night?" Jason asked.

Dupree noticed Jason and blinked. "Bro. Who are you?"

"He's with me," I said, stepping closer to him. It felt better being near him. "*Did* you know that, Dupree? Did Beef get it from the walk-in or something?"

"Hey, Cat, chill," Dupree said. "I saw him wrap it up in newspaper, but he told me it was a joke. He didn't mean nothing by it."

"He left it on top a note," I informed him. "It said, 'Stop flapping your tongue, or I'll cut yours out, too.'"

Bailee-Ann made a small sound. Tommy pulled her close.

"Uh . . . he didn't mention a note," Dupree said, looking less sure. "But it was supposed to be funny, for real."

Beef had Robert. We didn't have time for this.

"Dupree, did Robert say anything when he came in?" I asked. "Did either of them say where they were going?"

"Uh, jeez, lemme think," Dupree said. "Well, Robert rode up on his bike, and goddamn does he have skinny legs. Little

319

cricket legs inside those fluffy shorts he's always wearing. We laughed at that, me and Beef."

"Not that part," Bailee-Ann said impatiently. "Tell them the rest." Without giving him a chance, she told us herself. "Dupree said Robert *was* hyper—"

"Per usual," Dupree interrupted.

"And that he was dancing around saying, 'See? I called it, didn't I? I *so* burned you, dude.' And more, like how Beef couldn't lie to him anymore because of how he was onto him." Bailee-Ann's eyes were huge. "I'm scared, Cat."

So was I, and if Robert was here, I'd have shaken him for being so dumb. What was he thinking, that taunting Beef would make Beef pay attention to him again?

My throat tightened.

"How did Beef respond?" Jason asked him.

"He was fine with it, bro," Dupree said, holding up both hands like he was swearing in front of a judge. The gray dishcloth, dangling limp and soiled, made me think of dead things. "He shot me a look like, *Get a load of this nut job, huh?* But he wasn't mean to him or nothin'."

His gaze went to each of us in turn, and it seemed to me he was trying a little too hard to convince us. "Beef's *never* mean to him, although there've been times I've wanted to jerk a knot in his tail." He focused on Bailee-Ann. "Uh, no offense. He was squirmier than a dog with two dicks, that's all."

Bailee-Ann looked like she couldn't decide whether to cry or spit. I tried to get him back on track.

"Was Beef high?" I asked.

Dupree's heavy-lidded eyes opened wider than they probably had in years. Then he went back to fooling with that dang dishcloth. "Well, uh, that's maybe none of y'all's business."

"Maybe it is," Tommy said, stepping closer. Tommy could be menacing when he chose to be, as I well knew. He chose to be now.

Dupree stepped back and bumped into the counter. "What the hell? We *all* party. Nothing wrong with that."

"Was Beef high, today, when Robert came in?" Tommy demanded.

"Listen," Dupree said. His eyes got slippery. "Just listen. He mighta been, but it was a good high. He was singing and attacking the dishes like there was no tomorrow. We were having fun."

"Meth?" Tommy said.

Dupree gave Tommy a wounded look. "What, is it my turn now to be *intervened* with?"

Bailee-Ann gave up on Dupree. She clutched my arm and said, "Cat, we have to find him." Her brown eyes shone. "He's so little, and he's always showing off, and . . ." Her desperation made it hard for her to talk. *"Please?"*

I searched my brain for where Beef would have taken him. Asheville? Unlikely, unless he planned on bashing in Robert's skull with one of those stone woodland creatures the rich folks put in the gardens of their mountain homes.

God, why would I think that? I put my hand to my stomach,

feeling queasy again. Like when Jason was driving too fast down the mountain, and I saw the ground dropping off steeply just feet from the car.

Okay, *focus.* Where else might Beef have taken Robert? The woods? His house? Somewhere completely unexpected, like the dump? Beef loved the dump, and I was sure Robert did, too. I had yet to meet a boy, young or old, who didn't.

When it came down to it, we had no idea where Beef and Robert were. I had a gut suspicion, but I didn't want to say it in front of Bailee-Ann. At any rate, we weren't going to solve anything by standing around with thumbs in our mouths.

"Jason and I'll head up into the forest," I said. "Tommy, you and Bailee-Ann go to Beef's house. Look everywhere. Call out Robert's name, call it real loud."

Tommy nodded tersely. They headed out.

I turned to Jason and said, "Let's go."

"Wait!" Dupree called. "What about me? What should I do?"

I looked over my shoulder, unwilling to waste more time when so much could happen in the blink of an eye. "Um, try calling Beef on his cell, and keep trying. Call anyone you can think of who might have seen him. Other than that, just stay at the store, in case they come back."

I fired out Jason's cell phone number. Dupree hustled to find a napkin and scrawled it down.

"If you learn *anything,* call us," I told him.

"Where to?" Jason said once we were in the car. He revved the Malibu's engine. It died, and he twisted the key again. This time, when it caught, he roared out of the parking lot and took a right, which was the way I was pointing.

I directed him up into Pisgah Forest, past the fish hatchery and past the picnic spots enjoyed by families with young kids. We drove deeper into the forest, the heavy foliage dappling the road with green shadows and pockets of shade.

Jason left me to my thoughts as we continued up the winding road, and he said nothing about my tap-tapping fingers, which I couldn't hold still. Maybe he had his own suspicions about where we were heading, or maybe he was using all his mind-power to try and keep the Malibu from stalling out. It wasn't looking good.

I stared intently out the open window, pushing my hair back when the wind tossed it about. There were no other cars on the road.

"Come on, baby," he said to the Malibu as the speedometer dropped from thirty miles an hour to twenty, to five. The engine chugged. "Come on. Come *on.*" The motor coughed, burped up steam through the hood, and went dead.

"You're kidding," I said.

He turned the car off, then on. The engine went *rrrr-rrrrr-rrrrr*. He revved the motor, and the *rrrrrr*-ing grew louder, but refused to catch.

"Fuck," he said.

"This is not happening," I said. "This is *not* happening." Only it was, so I got out of the car.

"Are we walking?" Jason said.

"Have any better ideas?" I replied, starting up the road. My thoughts went to bad places, like how Beef didn't want Patrick telling him what to do, so he bashed his skull in with a baseball bat. When he didn't want me talking, he left a warning held down by a slab of bloody tongue. What would he do to silence Robert, who couldn't keep his mouth shut to save his life?

The forest was home to all sorts of dangers. Water. Rocks. Places to fall involving both water *and* rocks.

Beef's teaching me how to be a man, Robert had said.

I'm his best friend.

We go to Suicide Rock sometimes 'cause of how peaceful it is. I ain't jumped yet, but I'm gonna. If Beef can do it, so can I.

I started to jog.

"Cat, hold up," Jason called.

Behind us, I heard the rumble of a motorcycle. It was coming up fast, and us the only ones for miles around. I stopped and held real still. We'd abandoned the Malibu, so we didn't even have that for cover.

Jason caught up to me. "You hear that?"

Of course, I heard it. But the rider was down below us. If Beef and Robert had come up this way, they'd have passed this spot long ago.

"We need to get off the road," Jason said.

"Wait." I turned around in the road and peered back, shielding my eyes with my hand.

"Screw this, I'm calling the cops," Jason said. Then, "Ah, shit. No service. *Shit.*"

The motorcycle was almost upon us. Maybe two curves away.

Jason tugged at me. "Come on. Will you get out of the road before that asshole runs you down?"

"It's okay," I said, because I knew the asshole roaring over the hill. I recognized the sound of his Yamaha. "It's my brother."

When Christian came into view, he was crouched over the handlebars and leaning into the curve. He righted himself as he approached. He skidded to a halt and flipped the visor of his helmet.

"Jesus, Cat. What the hell? You call the whole world, and you couldn't call me?" He looked at Jason, who tentatively lifted one hand. Christian turned back, too pissed-off to even ask.

"You're my sister, and you're off on some fool mission, and I had to hear it from *Dupree,*" he said. "What the fuck?"

Oh, I thought. And I *did* feel bad. I'd forbidden myself from seeing Christian as my hero for so long now that I was simply out of practice.

But he was here now.

I jogged over, nudging him to let him know I was climbing on. "We'll be back," I called to Jason. I wrapped my arms around my brother's ribs and said, "Get me to Suicide Rock."

It wasn't but four or five miles farther, which was nothing on Christian's Yamaha. We pulled into the broad area of packed dirt where people parked their cars. There was a lone picnic table where a family might eat their pimiento cheese sandwiches. Next to it was Beef's black motorcycle.

"Well, I'll be dipped," Christian said.

I hopped off the bike and started for the swimming hole. Christian loped to catch up with me. He'd taken off his helmet, and his hair was slick with sweat.

"So what's the story?" he demanded.

I gave it to him in shorthand: *Beef's high. He's got Robert. He's dangerous.*

"Holy goddamn," Christian said. He raked his hand through his hair, but he didn't seem terribly surprised. "And just what do you think you're gonna do about it?"

I scowled, because maybe I didn't know that part.

The ground was wet and matted with rotted leaves. I stumbled over a root, and he caught me. He held on to my arm and made me stop.

"You stay here," he said in a low voice. We were getting close enough that if Beef and Robert *were* up ahead, they'd be able to hear us. "I'll check on up ahead, and if I see them, I'll let you know. Then you go back to that new friend of yours and find a way to get the sheriff, all right?"

I glared, because no, that was *not* all right. I twisted out of his grasp.

The path was slippery with mulch and decay. A couple of empty beer cans littered the pebbled beach. I stopped right at the outskirts of the clearing, but I didn't spot Beef or Robert. I scanned the murky surface of the swimming hole. Nothing. I glanced at the giant water-soaked log we liked to sit on when we were kids. Nothing.

I stepped forward in order to get a good look at the cliff face on the other side of the swimming hole. At its base was a thick undergrowth of mountain laurel and rhododendron, which after a couple of yards gave way to ferns and slick green moss. Above that rose sheer gray rock. I grew light-headed as I took in the narrow footholds and crannies used for climbing. Everything was too bright. Too high.

"Well, hey, there, Cat," Beef called down, making my heart stop. I craned my neck, and there, at the very top, was Beef. He had Robert in a choke hold, his hand over Robert's mouth. Robert looked very small and very frightened. And—his skinny legs did look ridiculous jutting out of his too-puffy shorts.

"Beef," I said. They were above the jumping rock, standing at the edge of the higher, more tucked-back rock the swimming hole was named for. Robert's eyes were round. Beef's eyes . . . well, I was too far away to really see. But they didn't look right.

"Don't," I managed.

"Don't what?" Beef said. He grinned and fake pushed Robert over the edge, thrusting him forward and jerking him back. Robert made a noise behind Beef's hand and struggled to get away.

"Robert, be still," I commanded. Struggling could lead to slipping. "Just . . . stay put. I'm coming up."

"Hey, fan*tas*tic," Beef said. "The more, the merrier. Get on up here, Cat."

327

His words came fast. He sounded manic and not like himself. I moved fully into the clearing.

"Cat," Christian said under his breath, but I kept going, and he was smart enough not to try to stop me. Beef thought I was by myself—at least as far as we knew—and that was good. I didn't know *how* it was good, because what was Christian going to do? Ride back down the mountain and fetch the sheriff himself? Nonetheless, the knowledge of Christian's presence was one thing we had that Beef didn't.

I had to cross the swimming hole to get to the climbing side of the mountain, so I kicked off my flip-flops and dog-paddled through the cool green water.

"Why, look at you," Beef said when I climbed, dripping, onto the opposite bank. "I can see your titties! Look, Robert! Cat has titties!"

"Yep, it's a flippin' wet T-shirt contest," I said, my face flaming. I wanted not to care. I knew better than to care, because that's what Beef was after: power.

Playing on that, I pouted and said, "Would you let go of Robert's mouth so he can breathe, please?"

Beef wasn't broad-shouldered and imposing like Tommy, but he was strong and quick. He had a wrestler's ability to twist people into all sorts of positions, and I wanted his hands off Robert. "Seriously, Beef. What's he going to do, scream?"

"You gonna scream?" Beef asked Robert. Violently, Robert shook his head. Beef shrugged and removed his hand. "There. You happy now?"

Robert didn't reply. He probably thought that Beef was talking to me. But Beef kneed him in the back of his legs, making him cry out and crumple a little.

"I *said,* you happy now?" Beef repeated.

"Beef, quit it," I said sharply.

"Cat, I ain't having fun," Robert whined. "I want to go home."

"'I wanna go home,'" Beef mocked. "Dude, you sound like a little girl."

I started up the face of the rock. The angle made it so that I couldn't see Beef and Robert anymore, but I could hear them.

"So, little girl," Beef said. "Now that Cat's here, want to tell me again how I'm not a man 'cause of my . . . now, how'd you call it? My faggot ways?"

The rock was slick, and I lost my footing. The moss coating the surface was spongy in places, almost gelatinous, and when my bare toes squelched into it, I thought of cow tongue. I shuddered, and it gave me just enough adrenaline to shout, "Of course, you're a man, Beef. Nobody's ever said you aren't."

"Yeah, and I'm not a little girl," Robert piped up. Apparently, my phony bravado had kicked his into gear. "*You're* the one who kisses boys. That makes *you* the girl."

"Robert?" I said. "Shut. Up."

"But he did! You told me so! You told me he kissed Patrick!" I couldn't see what happened next, but I heard, *"Ow!"*

"Beef, please," I said. "Nobody cares that you and Patrick . . . you know." I made it to the jumping rock. I hauled myself up and took a breath, leaning forward and resting my hands on my quads. "I mean, God. Patrick's awesome."

"'Cept when he was harping on me," Beef said, his voice coming from above. "I told him to leave it, but he wouldn't."

I straightened my body. To get to Suicide Rock, I had to climb five or six more yards. *You can do it,* I told myself. I knew better than to look down, but like an idiot I did anyway. The far away water swayed.

"He was worse than his own granny, the way he got into my business," Beef kept going. "Don't do this. Don't do that. You're ruining your future, you worthless sack of shit."

"Patrick would never say that," I said. I found a crevice for my right foot while my fingers fought for a grip. My skin was clammy from sweat and creek water, and there was a good chance I might throw up. Or pass out.

No, I told myself. *Not allowed.*

I steeled myself, and with a grunt, I hiked my forearms over the ledge. My face was within kicking distance of Beef's feet.

"Move so I can come up," I panted.

"Why? So we can chat some more? I don't think so."

"My muscles are giving out," I pleaded. "Please?"

He snorted scornfully, but he stepped back, dragging Robert with him.

Was it a trap? I had no way of knowing. I couldn't stay where I was, however, so I heaved my midsection up onto the rock, then one leg, then the other. I scooched on my butt as far back as I could, all the way to where the rock met the damp black soil. It smelled like worms and decay.

I swallowed and tried to get a hold of myself.

"You always were afraid of heights," Beef remarked, as if that made me weak and pitiful. It did, I suppose. When I didn't respond, he said, "Look at me. Look at me, you stupid bitch!"

I raised my head. He *did* have scary eyes.

"Okay," he said. "*Okay,* then. Now that we're all one happy family, my buddy Patrick's gonna prove he *is* a man." Beef gave Robert a shake. "Ain't that right?"

"I'm not Patrick," Robert cried. "Why'd you call me *Patrick*?"

Beef look confused.

"It's Robert," I said. "And I know you don't want to hurt Robert any more than you wanted to hurt Patrick." I watched Beef's face, because I still didn't know for sure—not 100 percent, absolutely for sure—that he did hurt Patrick.

His features contorted, and I felt unbearably sad.

"You didn't mean to, did you?" I said.

"It was . . . it was . . ." Agony rippled over his features. "It's just that he wouldn't let up and he wouldn't let up . . ."

"I know," I said.

"And the baseball bat, it was just *there.*" He looked confused. "I don't know where it came from, I swear."

I kept quiet.

"I don't even know how it ended up in my hand," Beef said. "I think . . . did someone *put* it there?"

"No, Beef," I said.

"No," he repeated. He shook his head. "No."

I got to my feet, moving slowly.

"And after, with the gas nozzle . . ."

"You didn't want people to know it was you," I guessed. "You thought making it look like a hate crime would cover it up, since you weren't like that." He wasn't a gay basher was what I meant, but as I thought it through, I realized he was, in a backward sort of way. Maybe he hated the gayness inside of him, and *that's* what he was lashing out at. Except also in doing so, he was also lashing out at Patrick, who loved him. And Beef bashed in his skull and strung him up to a gasoline pump.

"You wished you hadn't hurt him, so you made it look like it wasn't you." I eased closer, sliding my feet along the cold stone. "It was just a big mistake."

"Yeah," Beef said. He gazed at me, and also through me. "A mistake."

"You know, I sure wish you'd let Robert go," I said. "You're scaring him."

"Nuh-uh, I ain't scared of no homo," Robert said, confirming that he was indeed the stupidest dang kid on the planet. He twisted in Beef's grip. "No way, you big, stupid pussy."

"Robert . . ." I said, straining to sound casual. "Take it down a notch, okay, sweetie?"

"And I ain't your sweetie," he retorted. He stomped on Beef's toe. "Now take back what you said about me being a dumb girl. I'm more of a man than you any day."

"Can you believe this runt?" Beef said, his melancholy turning back into anger. He muscled Robert forward. "Well, let's see it, big man. Show me what you got."

"He can't jump from there," I said. "He'll never clear the jumping rock." I couldn't breathe, knowing that failing to clear the ledge beneath us meant smashing into it instead. He'd end up with a bashed-up skull, just like Patrick.

Beef shrugged. "Oh, I don't know. It could go either way." He *thwomped* Robert on the back, making him step forward to catch his balance. Loose rocks skittered over the edge. "To find out, you gotta go for it. Right, buddy?"

Beef let go of Robert, who immediately twisted so that he and Beef were belly to belly. He tried to squirm past, but Beef scolded him, saying, "Nuh-uh. Time to man up, buddy."

"He doesn't have room!" I cried. "He'd have to *run* and leap, and even so, only a fool would try it!"

"I'll give you to three," Beef told Robert. He looked over his shoulder and winked at me. "And then it's your turn, sweetheart."

Dread washed over me. This wasn't Beef. This was Beef running scared, amped to a place where he was unhinged. Monstrous.

"One," Beef said.

"Never mind, I don't wanna," Robert said, trying to worm past Beef again.

My limbs weren't working, but I had to *make* them work. I stepped backward, since what was true for Robert was just as true for me. Without a running start, I'd have no chance.

"Two," Beef said, drawing it out.

Robert, his back to the water, started to cry.

"Oh, the little baby's crying," Beef said. "You're just a poor little baby, ain't you?"

"And you're a"—Robert was struggling to get the words out, he was gasping and sniveling so much—"just a fucking fraidy-cat faggot!"

Oh shit, I said to myself. I saw Beef's triceps flex as he gripped Robert's scrawny shoulders, and I ran.

"Cat, no!" I heard my brother call as I charged across the overhang. He must have come around the swimming hole and hiked to where we were from the other side. He was close, from the sound of it, but not close enough.

Beef released Robert with the slightest push—a baby bird thrust from the nest—and time spun away. Robert grabbed for Beef, but Beef stepped nimbly to the side. And then . . . and then I was in the air, launching myself at Robert's torso before I knew I was doing it. I flung myself around him, propelling us as hard and as far as I could.

Limbs flailed. My shin scraped stone, and the pain was like fire. Eons later, we smacked the cold water, and it slapped the breath out of me. We went down. Down and down, and scrawny Robert grasped and twined around me like the laurel tree branches on the bank, the twisted lovers. I shoved at his warm flesh. It made him cling harder. His face in the murky water was the face of a river fairy. The bad kind of fairy, not the fairies I made gardens for once upon a time. Robert had bulging eyes, and he wanted to pull me down and keep me down, forever.

My vision blurred, and I felt my lungs bursting.

My feet touched bottom. They sank into cool, wet river mud. I bent my legs, and with my strong thighs, I shoved us up. The water grew lighter. Sun glinted on the surface, and we burst through, gasping and coughing. Snot dribbled from Robert's nose. He was a baby clinging to my chest, but I fought the weight of him and got us to the log.

"Let go now," I told him. He wouldn't. "Let go, Robert." I pried his arms off me. "You're okay. You're safe."

He threw himself over the log, arms stretched long and cheek pressed to the bark, and he let himself sob.

I sobbed, too. I couldn't believe we'd done it. *I'd* done it. I'd propelled us over the death ledge below.

Six inches away, the water jumped. I jerked my head reflexively. *What the . . . ?* There was another spray of water, and almost simultaneously, the sound of the first shot registered. Still, my brain couldn't process it. Was Beef . . . was Beef shooting at us?

I looked up and saw Beef standing at the edge of Suicide Rock. His feet were planted wide, his arms rigidly extended. His face wasn't his own.

He aimed his Colt, and my senses shot into overdrive.

"Robert, get down," I cried, tugging to get him off the log. He blinked, not making sense of what was happening. I threw myself at him and pulled us both underwater, fishtailing my legs to get us deeper. Robert struggled. His face was green, with seaweed hair—my hair—twining around him.

He fought free, bursting back above the surface and coughing out water. "What the hell's wrong with you?"

I could see Beef. Robert couldn't. Behind Beef, I saw Christian wrestling to get the gun. He was arguing with him, and his voice seemed to alternate from loud to not loud as it bounced off the rock. Beef shrugged Christian off, his eyes fixed on me and Robert. His mind was no doubt racing overtime with meth and rage and a single-minded compulsion to shut us up for good. He probably thought he could deal with Christian later, if he thought about it at all.

A bullet kicked up the water right behind Robert's shoulder. He turned at the splash, and once again I shoved him under, which was why I, and only I, saw Christian grab Beef by the shoulder and spin him around, so that Beef's back was toward the water. Christian was after the gun, that's all he wanted, and as he reached for it, Beef jerked it high over his head. The movement was violent, throwing Beef off his center of balance.

If I'd looked up two seconds later, I wouldn't have seen. If I'd ducked back under, if I'd let the dark water hide me . . .

It didn't matter, did it?

Beef was shooting at us, and then he wasn't. He struggled with Christian. His hand flew up, and the momentum made him take several steps backward, to the lip of the cliff. His spine arched. His arms pinwheeled. He cried out, a stunned and terrible howl.

Patrick once took a nasty fall on the steps outside our high school. Someone tripped him, maybe Tommy. The smack of his head against concrete made my insides curl.

The sound of Beef hitting the rocky ledge was a thousand times worse. It was as awful as the crack of a bat against the skull of someone you loved, I imagined. Maybe more so.

There was a great, long stillness. The world was suspended. Then Robert was yanking my arm, wanting to know why I'd screamed. I stared at him, unaware that I had.

"And why do you keep pushing me under the water?" he demanded. "I don't like that. I don't like being dunked."

"I know," I told him. "I won't anymore." I locked my eyes on his so he wouldn't glance over his shoulder and see my brother retrieving Beef's pistol. It had flown from Beef's outstretched fingers, but not far enough. Christian wiped it off with his shirt, then flung it into the middle of the swimming hole, where the water was the deepest. He knelt to gather the bullet casings. He threw them down, too.

Robert turned at the sound of the splashes, but the water had already swallowed everything up.

"I'm sorry I dunked you," I told Robert. "I guess I was just scared."

He considered staying mad, but he must have decided it was too much work. He wiped the snot from his nose and said, "Well . . . I guess I was, too." A more fragile expression furrowed his brow. "But you saved me."

"Yeah, and you know what that means?" I said. "It means you owe me."

He laughed.

Bluebirds called from the trees. Water bugs sploshed. Christian climbed carefully from Suicide Rock to the ledge below, stepping around the thing that was there. He sprang off the jumping rock and landed cleanly in the river.

He swam to us, and when he reached the log, he shook his hair out of his eyes that way boys do.

"Where's Beef?" Robert asked him. His bony shoulders tensed. "That wasn't nice, what he did. He was playing mean."

Christian looked at me, and in his eyes I saw what saving us had cost him. Beef was Christian's friend, just as Patrick was Beef's friend, and more. We lived in a small town. Almost everybody was a friend, if you let them be.

Robert shook Christian's shoulder. "Where is he? Is he up there still?"

Christian swallowed. "He . . . he . . ."

"He slipped, honey," I told Robert.

The last time I was sweet with him, he threw a fit. This time, he said, "On the rock?"

I nodded. "You and I made it. We were lucky." My voice grew thick. "Beef wasn't."

Robert looked up at Suicide Rock. Then he dropped his gaze to the deadly ledge below. From where we were, there was nothing to see, which was a blessing.

"Was that the sound I heard?" he said.

"Yeah."

His eyes brimmed with tears. Mine did, too.

From the highway, we heard sirens. Jason must have gotten the Malibu turned around. I could just imagine him pushing it down the road, one hand on the steering wheel and the other on the open door, then jumping in and popping the clutch to the engine. He must have called for help as soon as his phone got service.

We swam to the pebbled beach of the swimming hole. Sheriff Doyle and his brother, Deputy Doyle, tramped down to us, and we told them what happened.

"Beef fell," Robert said. "He was being all crazy, and then he fell."

"Being crazy?" Deputy Doyle said. "Meaning what?"

"You know Beef," I said. "Always being a goofball, always taking risks." My throat tightened. "Always having to be the life of the party."

A shadow crossed Sheriff Doyle's face. He and Roy were drinking buddies. "What'd he do? Try to jump from that damn rock?"

I nodded. My tears ran down my face, a waterfall of sorrow.

"And now he's dead," Robert said. "He's up there on those rocks, 'cause he wasn't lucky." His expression changed, and he looked very young. "But I was real brave, and so was Cat." His hand found mine. "She took real good care of me."

I looked over Robert's head at my brother. I didn't have to say anything for him to know what I was thinking, which was that he'd taken real good care of me as well.

tuesday

ONE WEEK LATER

30

BEEF'S FUNERAL WAS LAST SUNDAY. EVERYONE showed up for it, even my daddy. Beef's mama was there, too, looking older than I remembered. Her eyes were sunk deep in her uncomprehending face, and I wondered what she could possibly be thinking. She'd missed out on her son's entire life, practically, and now he was gone.

It was a closed-casket service, but a framed picture of Beef sat on top of the coffin, showing Beef after a wrestling meet, his arms thrust up triumphantly and a grin splitting his face. Tommy's grandmother made sure there were flowers: a vase on either side of his photo.

People said nice things about the boy Beef once was, and no one said a word about his gun, which was buried in the muck and decay at the bottom of the swimming hole. Nobody was sniffing around for it, because no one but me and Christian knew about it.

"Beef fell, and that's that," Christian had said to me the day it happened, making sure we were out of Sheriff Doyle's earshot. "No reason to complicate things." He was protecting himself, yes, but more than that, I think he was protecting Beef's reputation. Taking a fall, though awful, wasn't as awful as the truth.

As for Robert, he seemed muddled about the whole incident, and he didn't talk about it, except occasionally to me. He wanted to erase it from his mind, I suppose. Maybe, rarely, that was the best thing to do.

During the service, Pastor Paul talked about how sometimes bad things happened and we couldn't see the bigger picture, because only God saw the bigger picture. He said that grief had the power to transform us, because when our hearts were hurting, we often let God in. We were imperfect, every one of us, but through God's love, we could be healed.

Aunt Tildy was sitting next to me in the church pew, and at that part of the sermon, her hand found mine. She focused on Pastor Paul, but she gave me a squeeze. After a moment, I squeezed back.

Later, at the burial, I stood by Gwennie, who'd stepped away from Roy and her shell-shocked mama. I knew there were certain sadnesses a person had no choice but to live through, but I put my arm around her anyway. I decided a hug did make a difference, and even if it was the tiniest difference ever, it was better than nothing.

When Beef's coffin was lowered into the earth, I bawled like a baby. I hoped that wherever Beef was, he was himself again, free of pain and pure of spirit. I squeezed shut my eyes and silently uttered my favorite benediction, sending it to Beef with all my heart: *The Lord bless you and keep you. May He lift His face to shine upon you.*

Since then, I'd been spending my days going back and forth between Patrick's house and the hospital. At Patrick's house, I pulled out their old push mower and mowed the lawn. I cut back the trumpet vines with their huge orange flowers, and I used a broom to sweep the cobwebs from the eaves of the porch. I also climbed on top of the porch railing and carefully lifted Mama Sweetie's wind chimes from the screwed-in metal hook. The nurses, who decided I was as close as Patrick had to a relative, said it was fine to hang them in his room, so now they dangled near his open window. The hospital had air-conditioning, but fresh air was good for a person's health. That sweet nurse, Kelly, agreed.

Often when I visited Patrick, Jason accompanied me. Christian came once, standing over Patrick's thin frame and looking at him for a long time.

"Get better, buddy," he said in a husky voice, and he lightly punched Patrick's shoulder.

Today Christian was off with Tommy, probably riding their motorcycles or shooting at traffic signs. I'd asked Christian why he'd kept being friends with Tommy all these years, and he'd quoted one of our old teachers who always wrote famous sayings on the blackboard: "Keep your friends close and your enemies closer."

I looked at him like *oh please,* and he added, "We can't all be like you, Cat, needing no one but yourself. I don't know if you've noticed, but there aren't all that many people to choose from when it comes to having friends in this town."

I thought about that now as Jason sat beside me in one of the plastic hospital chairs Kelly had let me haul into Patrick's room. Jason was reading, and just his presence made me feel warm inside, and I thought how untrue it was, the idea that I needed no one but myself. When I looked back at who I was two and a half weeks ago, I hardly recognized myself. I'd been a ghost girl who cared about nothing. I existed, but just barely.

When I almost died trying to save Robert, I realized I *did* care, about everything. And I didn't die. I was still here. I still existed.

Now I saw the world through new eyes. I saw people through new eyes, especially. People like me, and people who were completely different from me. Maybe they lived in Black Creek, or maybe they lived in Atlanta, or maybe as far away as New Mexico. As far away as India, even.

I once read that in India, cows roamed freely in the streets and did whatever they wanted. I thought that was downright strange. But then, an Indian girl would probably find catching crawdads in empty Pringles cans strange.

I guess what I'd decided was that looking only at people's outsides—what they wore, what they did, how they regarded cows—wasn't good enough. I needed to think about their insides, too. I needed to remember there was a difference. For a while there, I think I forgot there was one, and so I spent a lot of time comparing my insides to other people's outsides, which made me feel broken and didn't get me anywhere.

Had Beef done that, too? In his mind, had he come up lacking?

My sadness about him sat dark and heavy in my heart, but I think it would have been worse if it didn't. It was right to be sad when sad things happened.

I swiveled my head and looked at Jason. He must have felt my gaze, because he looked up from his book, which was *To Kill a Mockingbird.* He'd never read it, and which blew my mind, so I'd given him my copy. Judging by how quickly he was moving through it, I figured he liked it.

I smiled at him. He smiled back. He must have seen that I was feeling melancholy, because he put down his book, leaned toward me, and cupped my face with his hands. He kissed me, and his lips were soft against mine. Our souls mixed. Something passed between us, an invisible but glowing light.

He drew back, his expression a question. Had his kiss helped? Had he made me feel better?

I pushed my fingers through his soft hair. "Go back to your book. I'm fine."

"We can talk if you want," he said.

"It's okay. Really."

I was lost in my thoughts, anyway. Thinking about Beef. Thinking about my brother and my aunt and Robert. Thinking about just all of it.

"Cat," Jason said in a hushed voice. I blinked and was back in my plastic hospital chair.

"What?" I said.

He nodded at Patrick's bed.

I followed his gaze, my skin tingling. Patrick's eyes were open. When he saw me, he smiled.

"Hi, Cat," he said, his voice hoarse from lack of use.

I was too stunned to talk. I was too stunned to breathe, so I just soaked him in. His lips were so chapped they'd split open in places. He'd grown a scraggly beard, with unruly hairs sprouting above his jaw line. He'd shave it off, I was sure, because Patrick was *so* not a beard guy. I liked it, though. He looked handsome. He looked like a man instead of a boy.

He quirked up one eyebrow in that way of his that drove me bonkers. "What's the matter?" he said. "Cat got your tongue?"

My mouth fell open. Patrick loved throwing those dumb sayings at me: *Cat got your tongue?* Or *When the Cat is away, the mice will play.* Or his favorite—and the one I detested the most—*Curiosity killed the Cat.*

Not this time.

I ran and just about threw myself at him before remembering his still-healing body. I hugged him, carefully at first, and then tighter. I hugged him like there was no tomorrow. Except there *was.* Tomorrows and tomorrows and tomorrows, and who knew what was in store for any of us? What I did know—maybe all I knew—is that we got to play a role in deciding.

I pulled away. A smile shone on his face, and I smiled back.

Then my gut clenched as I thought about the flip side of endless tomorrows. The nurses would come running in soon, and they would call Sheriff Doyle. Sheriff Doyle would drive to the hospital. Maybe not right away, but soon, and he'd ask Patrick the hard questions.

Gently, I hip-bumped Patrick to make room for myself on the narrow bed. It was so familiar being with him, and so easy, that I couldn't believe I'd punished myself by staying away from him for so long.

I took his hands. His monitors were singing a glad song, which told me the nurses and probably Dr. Granville would be bustling in any minute. We didn't have much time.

"Beef's dead," I told him, because there was no other way.

Patrick's smile fell away. "What?"

"He's dead. Beef's dead." I'd have the chance to go deeper later, but right now my job was to lay out the bare bones of the story, because Patrick had a decision to make, even if he didn't yet know it.

I stumbled over the words: Robert, Suicide Rock, my brother. The gun. Patrick's confusion turned to shock, then anguish, and then to a bottomless sorrow. I went there with him, and I willed his grief to flow into me, so that I could bear it on his behalf.

From the hall came the sound of footsteps and excited voices. I glanced anxiously at Jason, who rose and went to the door. Hopefully, he could buy us some time.

"They're going to ask you what happened at the Come 'n' Go," I said to Patrick in a low voice. "They're going to ask you to tell them who hurt you."

Patrick furrowed his brow. "They don't know?"

I bit my lip, feeling horrible about telling Patrick that Sheriff Doyle and Deputy Doyle hadn't gotten anywhere with their investigation. I felt as if Black Creek had let him down.

"Well, they've been looking into leads and everything," I said. "They've been trying real hard. They just . . ."

Ah, screw it, I thought. Anyway, only some people in Black Creek had let him down. Not everyone.

"They're saying it was a truckful of out-of-towners," I told him. "They're probably ready to close the case, unless you tell them otherwise."

I bit my lip. I wasn't out to sway him one way or another, and I hoped he knew that. I hoped, too, that he knew that Beef *had* loved him, just as he had loved Beef. I was sure this was true of the Beef I knew and loved, the Beef before everything went bad.

"A truckful of out-of-towners," Patrick repeated. He stared at his hospital sheet. When he looked back up at me, his eyes were a full shade darker. "That sounds about right. Too bad I can't remember a dang thing."

The nurses broke past Jason and descended on Patrick like

349

cooing doves. Kelly, the nice one, pulled at me and said, "I need you to move back now, sweetie. This boy of ours has gone through a lot."

I squeezed Patrick's hands, unable to let go. Kelly had to pluck at me to get me off him.

"Hey," she said when she saw that I was crying. Patrick was crying, too, and from behind me came a loud sniffle that Jason tried unconvincingly to turn into a cough.

"*Hey,*" Kelly said again. "This is a *happy* day. My goodness. And Patrick's going to be just fine." She placed her hand lightly on his head. "We're just glad he's back with the living, aren't we, kids?"

The barest breeze moved through the half-cracked window, making Mama Sweetie's wind chimes sing their silvery tune. It felt like a miracle, and maybe it was—or maybe it was just a breezy summer day.

"Yeah," I said, only my throat was so clogged with tears that I sounded like a frog. I laughed in a sobbing sort of way. "Welcome back, Patrick."

EPICALLY LONG ACKNOWLEDGMENTS

Where the heck to start? I wake up every morning saying, "Thank you, God," for all the amazing people in my life, and I go to bed saying the same thing. So, first of all, thank you, God/ the universe/spirit-and-soul/love-and-life-in-all-its-beautiful-forms! Really, that about covers it, but to be more specific:

My Abrams people! Y'all are so cool. Thank you thank you thank you for making my books exist. Michael J., I've not always made your professional life easy, but you just keep on supporting me anyway—and always with a smile. Maria, you are an artist, lady, and dang, am I lucky you were in charge of *Shine*'s cover art. It is stunning, as all of your work is. (And yes, manly Chad, I know she learned it all—well, almost all—from you.) Brett? You chat with me when Susan makes the slice-her-hand-across-her-neck silent gesture to you that means, "Tell her I'm not here!" As you are delightful to chat with, I do not mind at all—so thank you. To everyone in sales and marketing and publicity: My books would be invisible if not for y'all. I am so grateful not to be invisible. Mr. Scott Auerbach, you're just plain funny, even when you don't know you are. I love grammar, and I love the fact that you do, too. Tamar, I know you don't work directly with me—you've got your own fab authors upon whom you lavish your attention—but you are very much part of my Abrams support group. Thank you for introducing me to great music, and thank you for helping me overcome my fear of skinny jeans. Maz, you are an artistic soul who is nonetheless able to handle the very scary details of, like, schedules and dates and events. I don't know how you do it, but you do, and I am full of appreciation and awe.

Howard, Maggie, and Laura . . . hi! *waves enthusiastically* I sure do like y'all!

As for Jason and Susan, just hold yer horses, you two. I'll be getting to y'all later . . .

Seth Viney, thanks for the exploding shoes. They were in the book, but my editor—ahem—made me take them out. ☺ Seth's lovely wife, Terace? Omigosh. Thank you for sharing your stories so openly and courageously, and with such level-headedness. Also, good golly, thanks for helping me type in my revisions at the end of the *Shine* marathon!

Sara Hayden? Thank you for being my girl Friday. Along with Terace, you also helped me insert last-minute changes to the manuscript, and you did so brilliantly. Of course, you do everything brilliantly.

I need a lot of help getting through each day, and to that end, thanks to multiple sweetie-pie "assistants": Chelsea Alles, Lauren Karbula, Amy Hayden, and Stephanie Swanson. You enrich my life while at the same time keeping my kids safe . . . and making my house look a whole lot better . . . and folding my laundry (omigod, thank you, LK!) . . . and giving me the inside scoop on all things "young adult" I ask you about. You are the youth of America! And with America in y'all's hands, we'll do just fine.

Yo, Ian Mahan. You kept me straight when it came to "guy" talk. Thanks. And yo yo yo to all my Starbucks pals. Y'all work at the best Starbucks in the whole world, and the reason it's so great is because of y'all.

Jim Shuler, as always, thank you for telling how to hurt people—or rather, for telling me what would happen, medically, once a (fictional!) person gets hurt. And as always, anything I got wrong is on me.

Jim, thanks also for talking to me about guns, and I extend that thanks to my uncle, Jack Mitchell, and my neighbor, Dave Taylor. Dave, you used a straw to show me how one might pistol-whip someone . . . and you demonstrated on your wife, Pretty Jenny! So, Pretty Jenny (who is much more than simply pretty), thank you for letting your husband straw-whip you. Pretty Jenny, thank you even more for reading an early early-embarrassingly-early draft of the novel, and for lying and saying nice things about it. You gave me encouragement when I desperately needed it—and you gave me great advice on how to make the novel better.

Early readers are invaluable, and along with Pretty Jenny, I thank Nina Romantio and Holly Warren for their insights. Y'all were awfully nice and supportive, too. Jackie, babe, I know you would have gladly read an early draft for me, but I screwed up and didn't get your copy to you. Bad me! Rain check?

B-O-B spells Bob, and it also spells Best Official Buddy-System, if you pretend that Buddy-System is one word. Love ya, Bob. You look very stylish in your leopard print thong, by the way.

To my agent, Barry Goldblatt: I think it is often the case that we authors don't have a CLUE how much you agent-types do for us. I know that's true in my case. For all the things I've thanked you for, thank you again. For all the things I haven't thought to thank you for, or haven't known to thank you for, please accept my heartfelt thanks now. You da real deal, Care Bear.

Jason Wells, aka the Energizer Bunny. Oh, sweet Jason, this book would not exist if not for you. It simply wouldn't, and you and I both know it. Thank you for our road trip talk that day when we could not and could not find the book warehouse. Ideas spring from marvelous sources, and you, yourself, are a marvel.

Sarah Mlynowski and Ermengarde Lockhart (oh dear, did I out you?): I have told you this before, but I must tell you again. You two do not lie when it comes to giving me feedback on my novels. Instead you are quite straightforward in telling me what sucks . . . but then you tell me how to fix it! And the angels sing from on high, and y'all are the angels, and yes, SM, you can be a Jewish angel, 'kay? 'Kay. Without y'all, I would be a sad, shriveled version of myself, so thank you for not making me need Botox. Your friendship—and your generously shared writing expertise—make me a very happy Lauren.

To my big ol' sprawling family, which is a glorious mishmash of conservatives, evangelical Christians, Jewish wine enthusiasts, veggie-chewy enforcers, computer geeks, bleeding heart ~~Susans~~ liberals, dog people, cat people, baseball players, and food-and-book lovers: Y'all are mine, and I am y'all's. I hug you all.

To my parents, all four of you: holy creamed corn, I am blessed beyond measure to have y'all in my life:

Sarah Lee, you taught me about making jam and how long to soak green beans, two skills I'll never use in real life as there is plenty of delicioso jam out there already, and because green beans are nasty (as are big hunks of fatback, even if they supposedly make the beans more flavorful). The knowledge you shared helped me flesh out Cat's day-by-day reality. Thank you.

Dad? As in, my North Carolina I-sprang-from-your-loins Dad? Omigosh. You are so . . . I am just . . . ai-yai-yai. Can't even find the words to express how much I appreciate your help with this book. Black Creek is not the North Carolina town you live in, nor is the town I grew up in. Nonetheless, you answered every single one of my questions in your characteristically meticulous way. You told me about Spanish rifles. You told me about rusty cars and antique dirt bikes rebuilt from the frame up. You told me about moonshine (!!!) and backwoods potions and mongrel dogs that guard the trailers hidden deep in the woods. You also told me about beautiful things: breaking ivy, the way moss looks on a water-soaked log, the way the air smells when a storm is coming on. Thank you for my "hill girl" childhood. I love you.

To my Atlanta Dad: You taught me that family isn't defined by blood. It's defined by love. You embrace me as your daughter as wholeheartedly as Mama Sweetie welcomes Cat into her warm and open arms. The fact that you're proud of me—and that you tell me so—makes my heart swell. Children never stop needing their parents; I wish Cat had been as lucky as I am.

Mom, you told me when I was little that I had a light inside of me. Do you remember? You told all of us kids that, I'm sure, but as a seven-year-old, I listened, and I believed, and the faith in myself that you inspired helped that light burn bright. You are the best mom in the world, and I want to be just like you when I grow up. And—as if that wasn't enough—thanks for reading this novel again and again and again, helping me make it better each time.

Jack, Al, Jamie, and Mirabelle—oh, I love y'all so much. I tell y'all that every day, so I won't go crazy here, except to say that y'all are the light of my world.

To everyone who shared stories of addiction, abuse, and intolerance: Thanks for helping me understand, and please know that I'm rooting for you. SN, remember your five life goals? Mix 'em up, dude. Kick the meth and then get yourself a spankin' new grill. You can do it, I swear to God.

And finally, Susan Van Metre, my beloved editor. I know you get embarrassed when I gush over you, but too bad. I love you for your guidance, your vision, and your relentless drive to ~~make me burn the midnight oil, get zero sleep, and never get to watch tacky TV~~ help me be the best writer I can be. More than that, I love you because you are my friend, and—though it does not fall within the job description—you inspire me to be the best me I can be.

ABOUT THE AUTHOR

LAUREN MYRACLE is the *New York Times* best-selling author of many books for young adults, including the Internet Girls trilogy—*ttyl, ttfn,* and *l8r, g8r*—as well as the supernatural thrillers *Rhymes with Witches* and *Bliss*. She was born in the Blue Ridge Mountain town of Brevard, North Carolina, and she grew up dividing her time between North Carolina and Georgia. She now lives in Colorado, but her love for the South blooms forever in her heart. Visit her online at www.laurenmyracle.com.

This book was designed by Maria T. Middleton. The text is set in 10-point ITC Century Light, a typeface originally designed in 1894 by T. L. DeVinne and Linn Boyd Benton for *Century* magazine. The Century font replaced older, less legible faces previously used by the magazine. In 1975, designer Tony Stan was commissioned by the International Typeface Corporation (ITC) to revise and expand the Century family. The display font is Gor Light.